Unexpected Visitors

Book One of the "Unexpected" Series

Jodie Lemmert

ISBN - 979-8-9853490-1-6
ISBN-979-8-9853490-0-9

Cover design by: Jodie Lemmert
Printed in the United States of America

ii

Chapter 1

I pulled up and put my pickup in park in front of the door at the hangar building of the Flight School that Ty and I had taken up a partnership in some years back. Ty Anders was a great friend, all the way back to our toddler days—as if either of us could remember that far back. I sat here looking into the overhead door of the hangar; I knew Ty was still working in the office. I could see the light shining out into the hangar bay. I knew sitting here looking into the building that I was about to rock the boat, so to speak.

I finally got out of my pickup and walked into the hangar. Just as I'd thought, Ty was sitting at the desk in the office. I sat down in the chair next to the desk where Ty was working on the computer.

"Hey, Owe, what's going on?" Ty said, looking up from the computer. "I thought for a while that you'd abandoned everything. Haven't seen you around lately. I even stopped over and talked to your dad."

"Yea, he said you'd been around. I did want to talk to you about some things. I've done a lot of thinking lately and you know I went out of town."

"Owe, what are you telling me?" Ty asked, looking at me, concerned. I guess I had given him reason for concern. We had a short break between classes, but usually Ty and I worked here at the hangar doing maintenance and paperwork. Except this time around, I left after classes were finished a couple weeks ago and hadn't come back to help Ty. Now, I was leaving almost entirely.

"I think we should talk about the business, Ty."

"What about the business, Owe? Business is great. Does this have anything to do with Lindsey? I know that whole thing's been bothering you."

"Lindsey? I haven't been in contact with her for months. She said I hurt her, and she moved out of town. I still haven't figured out how I'd hurt her, but that's what she told me."

"Oh please," Ty said, shaking his head and brushing his hand away. "You wouldn't hurt a fly. Well, if it's not Lindsey, what's eating you?"

"You remember me telling you about the rescue organization up north, the article I was reading about?"

"Yea, you'd said they do some really great work; but what's this got to do with our business?"

"I did some other research and then I went up there last week. I found out they have an opening for a pilot."

"Nope, nope. Hold it right there, Owe, you're not thinking about applying for the position, are you?" Ty asked, running his hands through his hair and sighing.

"I did more than apply." *OK, here goes nothing, time to rip the band-aid off.* "I applied for the job, went and visited the facility and talked to the lead."

"Well, I'm glad you had a nice visit, Ty said. "But just to remind you, we have a class starting on Monday."

"It's more than that, Ty. I got the job."

"Owe, what are you doing? What are you doing to me? I can't run this joint alone; you know that. I suppose now you want me to buy you out."

"No, I hadn't thought of that, I don't intend for us to dissolve our partnership. I'm just stepping back from the day-to-day."

"Owe, you didn't make any sense before and you make less now. How do you think you're going to be a part of the business— you got a job five hours away? What's all this about? Have you talked to your folks about this?"

Ty kept throwing questions out; I couldn't even answer them for myself, let alone, clue Ty into all this. "I don't know, I can't explain it. It's just something I feel I need to do; like I'm being pushed into it or something. And no, I haven't talked to my folks."

"I didn't figure you had. When I stopped to talk to your dad all he said was we should pray for you. I feel like there's something more that needs to be done. Is there anything I can say to make you change your mind?"

"No, Ty," I said, shaking my head. "I sold my house here in town and I bought a house up in Silver City."

"You bought a house already; this is just nuts. You don't just wake up one day and decide to upset your entire life. What have we got—a few weeks, before you're expected up there? Maybe we can talk some sense into you," Ty said, chuckling. "This isn't happening."

"Ah, yea it is," I told Ty. "I'm leaving Friday morning and I start at the center on Monday."

"Oh, wow," Ty said, the smile that had creeped in disappearing completely. "You can't be serious; how am I going to start this class on Monday?"

"You'll be OK," I said, standing up. "I've gotta go and talk to Max before I head out to the folks."

"What about Max and Elaine and the kids? Those kids will be lost without their Uncle Owe. I'm telling you, you better reconsider."

"No, I've got it all figured out. I'll still see everyone, just not as often. Well talk before I leave."

"Your darn right, we'll be talking," Ty said as I stood up and started to leave the office. *I left the office; I was glad that talk was over with. I doubt this will be the last I hear about it from Ty. I feel bad about leaving, but I'm drawn to this place I can't really put my finger on it.*

I stopped by Max and Elaine's. They weren't home. Figures, Max was probably still at school for track practice. I never understood the sport of running in circles, but my brother loved it so much, he became the coach.

"Hi, Dad," I said as I stepped into the barn. I'd missed Max and Elaine, so I made it out to the farm earlier than I'd expected. I wasn't surprised to find Dad in the barn.

"Hey, Owen, nice to see you. How's your day been?"

"It's fine, Dad," I said, sitting on the stool next to the bench where Dad was working. "Can we talk?

"Of course, what's your mind?"

"Well, you know I went up north for a few days. I went and visited that rescue center I'd told you about. I've been interested in it since I read an article about their work. I also learned they have an opening for a pilot."

3

"And you're here to tell your mom and me that you got the job?"

I just sat there looking at my dad. He looked about as bad as Ty.

"Yea, Dad, I did get the job and I bought a house up there in Silver City."

"Does your mother know about this?" Dad asked.

"No, I just pulled in and figured you were working on something out here and thought I'd come check it out."

"Oh, not much doing today," Dad said in his nonchalant manner.

"Come on, Dad, you're always tinkering with something in this old barn; you've spent half your life out here. It's your home away from home."

"Yeah, this old barn's a part of my bones, and yours too, Owen," Dad said, looking up into the rafters. "We've worked on a lot of planes out here together."

"Yeah and a few cows have come through here too, Dad."

"Well, maybe not so many come fall. I've been thinking about reducing the herd, and maybe eventually selling them all off.

You're moving off to the big city and Max and Elaine have the kids to worry about; your brother doesn't want a herd of cows. It might be time to downsize."

"I can't say that I blame you, Dad, and I'm kind of happy for you. What's Mom say about all this?"

"What do I say about what?" Mom asked, stepping into the barn.

"Hey, Ma," I said, turning to her.

"I thought that was your pickup out here. What brings you around here?"

"I came to talk to you and Dad. I found Dad out here and we got to talking about the herd."

"Owen's moving to the big city," Dad told Mom, sounding almost unconcerned with what I was planning to do. But that's Dad: he was always there for Max and me but never told us what to do.

"The big city?" Ma asked. "When and what are you going to do?"

"Guys, I'm not moving to the big city," I said, chuckling. "Silver City is a ridiculously small-town north of Boulder. I hardly ever go into the city—you know I'm not a city guy. You guys should come visit when I get settled and see for yourself, it's a nice area. The guys at the rescue center said there's some great fishing spots we could check out, Dad. I'm leaving on Friday, and I start work on Monday."

"So soon? And what work, Owen?" Ma asked.

"I took a pilot job at the Colorado Mountain Rescue Center."

"Have you met anyone yet?"

"Ah, yea, there's a few guys at work I visited with when I visited the center."

"Your mother wants to know if you found yourself a girlfriend, Owen."

"No, no girlfriend." *I had screwed up too many relationships in the past; I'm pretty sure I've hit some sort of quota. The gods that line these things up have probably deemed me helpless in that department.* "I need to leave, guys; I have a lot to do," I told Ma and Dad, hugging them both before I left the farm.

Chapter 2

"Are you ever going to get the door unlocked, Kar? Your bed's kind of heavy and Levi's not holding his end up."

Standing here on the porch, I'm staring at these two gold inanimate objects, the keys to the house I'd just bought. I bought this huge, two-story brick home on the north edge of town. This house had immaculate colonial pillars on the front porch that I found had an air of nostalgia. And I loved the shutters adorning the windows on the front of the house. I could hear my brother Lane hollering about the heavy bed as I stood here thinking over this move back to town. I was moving back to my hometown of Silver City, since my boss Craig had recently closed our downtown Denver offices and sent us out into the world to be his little marketing specialists. I still worked for Denver Marketing; most of us now just won't have the privilege of having an office. It's not like I used my office there much, anyways, I was usually at a client's office. There were plenty of things I was excited and grateful about because of these new turns of events in my life. For one, all the Grainer clan was back in the same zip code again; I suppose if I asked my dad, he'd say this was all his idea. And another very compelling reason: I was no longer down the hall from Curt Townsend, one of the agency's purchasing specialists. Let's just say he's better off purchasing elsewhere. But as I stood here on the porch looking at these keys, I still felt something was off, something wasn't right.

"What is going on, Karla? You having trouble getting in?" Eide asked, sidling up alongside me on the porch.

"Hi, Eide," I sighed. "No trouble getting in," I said to my best friend of, well, a lifetime. "I guess I'm just thinking."

"Well, you going to be alright. Cause we might want to get a move on it. We don't want to give the Grainer twins back there any permanent damage and hey, let's face it, I'd like to see this house sometime soon. You've been talking about it for weeks."

"Alright, Eide. Let's go."

"That a girl!" Eide said. "And moving day continues," she hollered back to everyone else. "I still think you're crazy for buying this big of a house, Karla," Eide told me as we walked into the foyer. "But I'm not complaining, it's just great you're moving back."

"I know," I groaned. "I've been wondering the same thing, but oh well, the deed is done, so to speak." I mentioned my concerns to Eide again as we walked out of the foyer and through the living room to get out of the way when the guys started bringing my furniture in. Eide must have brushed off my concerns, she was far more interested in looking this house over, so I guess if Eide isn't concerned maybe I shouldn't be, either. Eide has a deep-seated sense about these things.

"Look at all these windows," Eide said as she passed the living room windows on our way to the kitchen. "Great natural light in here. Just don't invite me to help you clean these suckers." Eide, Mom and I were all carrying boxes labeled "kitchen." Did I really have this much kitchen junk, I thought as Eide started exclaiming about the kitchen.

"Holy moly, what a kitchen," Eide said, startling Mom and me. "You could film the next great episode of The Food Network in here!"

"I know, right? I don't think my condo's kitchen was half this size."

"We're having all the family dinners over here from now on," Mom announced.

"Yea, I kind of figured you'd say that." I said, laughing. "But I don't think there'll be much time for that, I have a lot of traveling coming up."

"Well, you better find some time," Eide said, looking out the window after she set the box she'd carried in from the trailer on the counter. "Would you look at that patio."

"You sure you don't want to move in here?" I asked Eide, looking at the ashen trim around the kitchen window that looked out into the backyard. The grey backsplash between the cupboards was trendy and suited my style. I set my box on the counter next to Eide's and put my long curly brown hair into a ponytail, getting set to start unpacking.

"You should think about putting in an outdoor kitchen," Eide said thoughtfully.

"A kitchen? No way! I don't think so. I don't have time for entertaining, unless it's pizza and beer for the moving crew, lugging all the heavy furniture around."

"Did we just hear something about pizza and beer?" Lane asked.

Leave it to my brothers Lane and Levi, Boulder's Premier Landscapers by day and champion beer pong players by night— well, at least back in their U of C Boulder days. And not to mention their sidekick, Garratt Klein works as an assistant for our dad's real-estate development firm and over the years has become like another brother.

"I was just telling Karla, the fun-hater, that she should someday get an outdoor kitchen for the patio," Eide announced, sticking her thumb in my direction. Levi cozied up behind her, kissing the side of her neck. These two were a great couple.

"I'd vote for that," Lane chimed in.

"Of course, you'd love the idea, that's because you, dear brother, are borderline barbaric," I joked with him as I patted him on the back. "I appreciate the advice and especially the moving help, but I'm not putting in an outdoor kitchen, I'm too busy."

"Karla's right, everyone, let's get busy. Chop! Chop!" Eide said, clapping her hands together. "Everyone back at it. We have to get this done today, so we can get to church tomorrow. Laurel, would you make a pizza run, please?" Eide asked Mom.

"Of course, coming right up," Mom said, heading out of the kitchen.

Mom soon returned with pizza, and we all found a somewhat relaxing place in the living room to sit. This was completely, against Eide's ideals. She thought we could grab a piece and get back at it. Gotta love her—I think she'd make General Patton soft.

"Lane?" Eide barked.

"Hmm, yes, Eide," Lane said, nearly choking on his pizza.

"What time's Molly get off work today?"

"Uh uh," Lane said, still recovering from his near choking. "She isn't coming anywhere near your war zone, Eide."

"Oh please. Don't worry about it, I'll text her myself. Alright, everybody, break's over, back to work. We've got to get done today—you know, church tomorrow, come on," Eide said, standing in my living room in full-on preacher mode.

"Eide, why are you so concerned about making sure we get to church in the morning?" Lane asked. "We'll go."

"Well, at least Karla," Eide said.

"Why Kar?" Lane asked, chuckling. "Is she being dedicated, or something?"

"Eide, what are you up to?" I asked, eyeing her.

"Nothing, well nothing bad."

"Eide, seriously what's up? I know your bad, and you're coming up on its rear end."

"There's someone I'd like to introduce you to. I saw him there last week, so I asked about him."

"What? No, I think that door's closed—like permanently closed, bolted shut. You remember Curt Townsend?"

"Oh, yes, I remember, little fink," Eide muttered. "This is different, just say you'll come. He's a pilot."

"Oh, well that explains it all right there, his ego probably precedes him everywhere he goes."

"Don't judge, just say you'll meet him."

"I don't know; I'm very busy, remember? Oh, that reminds me, I forgot, can someone give me a ride to the airport next week?"

"The airport?" Dad asked. "Whatever for."

"I have a work trip to Baltimore."

"Baltimore," Mom said, sounding distressed. "You're traveling already? I didn't realize your schedule was changing so drastically, so quick."

"Yea, I can take you, just let me know what time," Dad offered.

"I know, tell me about it. I go from having a few local accounts to an account in Baltimore. In a couple weeks I'll go to San Francisco, Austin and who knows after that. Craig's building his marketing firm and I rack up the frequent flyer miles. Not really the way I'd have done things."

9

"Alright everyone, Karla's stuff isn't going to magically unpack itself," Eide announced as she started picking up pizza boxes. I stood there thinking about what Eide said and all this traveling I was scheduled for; none of it set well with me. It was almost like I was making a mistake. I really hope it's just buyer's guilt, I thought, brushing it all off and getting back to unpacking.

That night after my family and friends left, I looked through my big new home, reflecting on the day. The guys had followed Eide's specifications; in true drill-sergeant fashion she had them shifting and relocating furniture nearly all afternoon. Bless her heart, Eide was so good at the whole feng shui thing.

It was a nice evening for so early in the spring. I had the kitchen patio doors open while listening to music on my iPod. It was nice; I had my own space, and I didn't have to worry about interrupting the neighbors anymore.

I was pondering the decorating tips Eide had left me with. Maybe Eide, Molly and I could find time for a girl's weekend, go to a few antique stores, and maybe find a few new unique pieces. It would be good to have a girl's weekend; in different ways we're long overdue for one. I stood there thinking it all over, I should also have a proper thank-you meal for everyone that helped today. I could get something put together when I get back from Baltimore.

As I stood in the kitchen immersed in my thoughts, I realized the music must have been too loud to hear the doorbell because when I happened to glance out the patio door, there was a lady out there looking in. *This is odd,* I thought as I stepped out onto the patio. "Hello, can I help you?" I asked the somewhat older lady with the short, displaced grey hair. She looked like a reasonable woman; yet why was she standing on my very empty patio?

The lady just looked at me. Finally, rather salty, she said, "Hi, are you my new neighbor?" The lady looked around unsettlingly.

"Yes, I just moved in today. I'm Karla Grainer," I said, smiling and extending my hand.

"I know. I'm Marsha Turner," she said rather curtly and unfriendly. What exactly did she know—that I'd just moved in or my name or both? *Weird,* I thought. "I live across the way," Marsha said, pointing off in the distance. "I saw all the activity going on here today."

"Nice to meet you, Marsha," I said, extending my hand again. "I hope we didn't bother you today?"

"No, you were fine. I was friends for many years with the Cartwrights, who used to live here, and I just loved their house. Do you mind if I look around?" she said, walking into the kitchen.

"Well, I'm not really ready for guests," I said as Marsha crossed the kitchen and into the living room, looking out the windows. I decided she wasn't really hurting anything as we stood there looking out the window, at what I didn't know. She was probably just remembering times spent with her friends.

Chapter 3

I got an early start today to head back to Silver City. I packed up my house all day yesterday. I never did get a chance to stop back by Max's and visit with him and Elaine. I figured I could call them on the trip sometime this morning, but since I hadn't slept well last night, I decided to get a start on the trip, so it was still too early to call. Max and Elaine prayed every Saturday morning that Luke and Caity would sleep in, so I didn't think I'd take the chance and call this early.

Ty had been by the house several times yesterday; I think he thought he was going to talk me out of my plans. After the second time he'd showed up I told him he had to start helping. He helped me load a few items and then left again only to return about an hour later.

I pulled into Silver City late that morning, I drove past the church I attended when I came to visit. This seemed like a nice little church, and I planned to come back on Sunday. It made me think I should have stopped at my church back home and talked to Pastor Charles to tell him what I was up to. I made a note to stop in and visit with him when I returned home.

I drove down the street to the house I'd bought; this was a small town and seemed quiet, maybe not as sleepy as West Creek. *It will be great,* I thought, parking in front of my house and sitting there looking at the glass front door. This little A-frame, three-bedroom house was nice. *I didn't need anything glamorous*, I thought, still looking across the yard at the house. "Come on, Arnold," I said looking in the backseat at my dog." Let's go check it out," I told the feisty hound when I opened the door to let him out.

Arnold made a mad dash into the yard as soon as I opened the back door for him.

I took a few things in the house and looked around. Arnold did his looking and sniffing too, probably wondering what I'd done to him. I had the trailer to unload but most of it was bigger furniture items that Ty and I loaded yesterday.

I left it alone for now; maybe I could find some help Monday after work. I changed into shorts and a t-shirt and decided to take a short jog around the area.

I was just coming up the sidewalk when I noticed a pickup pull up in my driveway. I hadn't even been in town two hours—who even knew I was here? The guy must be lost. The guy stepped out of his pickup and waved as I met him on the sidewalk in front of my house.

"Hi, are you Owen?"

"Yes, can I help you?"

"I'm Todd Samson. I work for Colorado Mountain Rescue; sorry I missed meeting you last week when you were in town."

"Oh, that's alright," I said, shaking Todd's hand. "Nice to meet you."

"Nice to meet you, too," Todd said. "Aaron, the facility lead, told me you were coming to town today and I thought I'd come over and see if you needed a hand with anything."

"Well, nice of you to stop by, I was going to see if someone would be able to help unload some furniture out of the trailer on Monday after work."

"Let's just knock it out this afternoon," Todd said, motioning to the trailer.

I went over and opened the fold-down trailer door. I looked back at Todd. "You sure you want to lug this furniture around?"

"Oh sure, man," Todd said, grabbing an end to the mattress Ty and I had slid in between things in the middle of the trailer. I took the other end and headed into the house. We set the mattress in the back bedroom and went back to the trailer for the box spring.

"Where you from, Owen?" Todd asked as we continued taking furniture into the house.

"West Creek."

"Never heard of it, where's that at?" Todd asked, chuckling.

"Nobody's heard of West Creek. It's about halfway between Colorado Springs and Durango."

13

Todd and I had the trailer unloaded apart from the couch; that was our last trip. We set the couch down in the living room and sat down on it.

"Ah, thanks, man, I appreciate the help," I told Todd sitting on the couch. Todd sat down beside me.

"No problem. Didn't mean to interrupt your jog but thought you could use some help."

"I was finished with the jog; I was thinking about making a run to the store but grateful for your help. You want a glass of water? That's all I can offer right now," I said, laughing.

I filled us each a glass of water and sat back down on the couch.

"You like this neighborhood? Todd asked as I handed him his glass.

"Uh, yea, it seems nice, quiet. I haven't seen much of it. I took that jog earlier and saw some of the neighborhood. A couple streets up, by the creek, there was a family moving into a house. Some woman hollered out, 'and moving day continues,' so I don't know, maybe it's gonna get a little rowdy."

Chapter 4

Thoughts of my conversation with Eide yesterday quickly took over as I stirred in bed, waking up. I decided to get up and get busy, I still had plenty to unpack. I figured a cup of coffee would be a good start. My thoughts rolled back to Eide telling me she wanted me to meet someone at church as the coffee pot started to brew. I stared at the dark liquid streaming into the pot. *Why did Eide think I needed to meet someone anyways? I'm sure that ship has sailed. Am I so pathetic I can't even find my own dates anymore? Besides that, I don't have time for a relationship.*

Oh man, my mind was on overdrive and the strong cup of coffee I was pumping into myself had yet to quell my thoughts. One would certainly think it was time for me to get into the dating scene again, but after the last guy I dated it was good we'd both moved on. Curt Townsend still gave me the shivers.

As past relationships paraded in front of me like an antique-car show, my cell phone rang. *Who would be calling, and especially so early in the morning?* I had one guess, looking at the screen. *I know how this is going to go!*

"Hello, Eide, is everything all right?"

"Good morning, Karla, yes everything's fine. I think, why?"

"What do I owe the pleasure of this early morning phone call? Are you sick, maimed?"

"Ha ha, of course not," Eide said, sarcastically. "So, church this morning?"

"How do you know I was even awake."

"Cause, I know you; you were up, thinking this over. So, are you going to church?"

"Of course, I'm going to church. I'm just not sure that's the right venue for arranging blind dates, especially one whose ego precedes him."

"Now just wait a minute, you haven't even met him yet, so stop judging. Can you at least wait and meet him before you start labeling him? How about I come over and we go for a run, clear our heads? I'll be there in a half hour; be ready."

"But Eide—" Before I could say anything, I was listening to a dial tone.

"Isn't this refreshing?" Eide asked as we were making our way down the street.

"I hardly call it refreshing, you drug me away from my coffee," I whined to Eide.

"Oh, you're such a delight this morning."

"Well, I didn't sleep well last night. My thoughts have been all over the place, and now I think you're going to kill me before we even get to church; you know I don't exercise."

"Yes, you do—you've always jogged, even when we were in college."

"Yeah, when I was young and dumb."

"Stop whining," Eide told me. "You're going to be fine; you're going to go home, take a shower, put on a cute little dress, and get your ever-loving butt to church. I'm tired of taking care of you."

"Well so-rrrry, I didn't know I was such trouble for you," I said, chuckling.

I got home in time to shower and change for church. *Was I really going to do this? Meet somebody Eide knew, somehow. Does she even know him? Eide just said he was someone at church. This was so not a good idea.*

Against my better judgment, I headed off to church.

I arrived at church and slid into the pew beside Eide and Levi.

"Eide, how do you even know this guy?"

"I've seen him here at church, I think he just moved here."

"So, you don't know anything about him?"

"Well, I know he just became a member of our church," Eide said, nodding her head.

"This is outlandish, Eide. I'm not meeting him."

16

"Ladies, keep it quiet; this is church," Levi told us. "I should not have to be the one to tell you that."

"Look Karla, that's him," Eide said, nodding her head at guy walking up the aisle, heading to a pew towards the front.

Well, he didn't look like he'd just walked out of a *GQ* magazine article, but he was very handsome. I noticed as he greeted the couple he was sitting down beside, he had a charming smile that would set the summer sun on fire. I had to give him that. He was tall, and he had some serious dark hair.

It's funny, when Eide started trying to convince me to meet this guy, I hadn't really considered his looks; I was more concerned about his ego. Good grief, God's going to strike me down on this one for sure.

Pastor Tim's message this morning spoke on family and communication, specifically, a classic passage from the New Testament of Ephesians 5:21-32, which spoke in depths of marriage and singleness. Pastor Tim said these are just an open door to our hearts with a walkway to learn guidance in our marital status. Well, thank you, Pastor Tim, are you also trying to marry me off this morning, too? It felt like Pastor Tim's message was being spoken directly to my heart. Which didn't help my thoughts of the man sitting a few pews ahead of me. All these thoughts swirled in my head, making me wonder if I should really oblige Eide and meet this guy.

As Pastor Tim continued his message, I thought he'd written this message for my benefit alone. I sat there consumed with Pastor Tim's message and Eide's plan. What was Eide's plan? Before I knew it Pastor Tim was reciting the Benediction and then dismissed his congregation.

As we stood to make our way out to the fellowship hall. Eide hurried out of the pew, almost tripping over Levi.

"Eide, what are you doing? You almost knocked us over," Levi questioned her.

"Just hold on, I'll be right back," Eide hollered back as she hurried away from our pew.

I stood there questioning Levi what Eide was doing when she returned, practically dragging the guy she'd pointed out earlier.

"Karla, this is Owen."

"Owen, this is my life-long single friend Karla."

"Eide???" As if she couldn't make this the most awkward situation ever, Way to go, Eide, make the guy think I was forever pathetic. If this wasn't church and we'd just heard Pastor Tim speak from the Bible, I think I'd surely kill her now.

"Hello, life-long single friend of Eide, my friends call me 'Owe,'" Owen said, smiling and extending his hand in a gesture to shake hands.

"'Owe,' as in you tend to owe them money?" I asked Owen, jokingly.

"Huh, guess I've never been addressed that way before. It was nice meeting you," Owen smiled again, his bright smile nearly catching my breath.

"Say, Owen, my friend Karla here got shorted on her morning coffee, you think you could help her out with that? You do drink coffee, don't you?" Eide asked.

"Eide? Enough." I was completely appalled at the way she had just put Owen and me on the spot. All the while Levi was standing beside us, watching all this go down and seeming to have a hard time keeping from laughing.

Again, Owen chuckled at Eide's attempt to set us up together. "Well, yes, as a matter of fact I love coffee, drink lots of it. Gallons of it, in fact," Owen told Eide and me sarcastically, still maintaining the smirk on his face.

"So, see," Eide told us, waving her hands toward the door. "Run out and grab a cup already."

Owen agreed to meet me at a coffee shop near the church. On the drive over, I thought of Eide and her embarrassing anecdotes. I realize she's doing this out of love and friendship, but I think she needs the butt kicking of a lifetime.

Owen was standing in the order line when I arrived and had already ordered a tall black coffee for himself but held off paying to add my drink to his order. I, too, ordered a tall black coffee.

18

The barista handed us our cups, and we went to find a table; it was busy this morning.

"I'm sorry about my friend wrangling you into this. If you'd rather not do this, I'll understand."

"Ah, don't be, she seems like a good friend. Besides, it's good to get out in the community and meet people. I probably would have just gone home to my dog, anyways. We can have a nice chat and you can tell Eide she did her friendly duties of 'offering you up!'"

"Oh wow! That's kind of a low blow," I said, surprisingly settling into conversation with Owen.

"Well, she did kind of throw us together."

"Yes, she did and embarrassingly so."

"Oh, it's alright," Owen assured me. "Maybe she needs a little payback," Owen joked.

"I like how you think, I was thinking the same thing on the way over."

"So, tell me about yourself. You and Eide? Lifelong friends, I hear."

"Well yes, at least until an hour ago, maybe. Although, I have to say if we hadn't been in church this morning, the thoughts of killing her would have been much more prevalent."

"Ha ha, I bet," Owen said, chuckling.

"Yes, Eide and I go way back. She's actually dating one of my brothers."

"Nice, one of your brothers?" Owen asked with a questioning look on his face. "How many brothers do you have?"

"Just two—well, sort of three if you count Garratt, but with those three it's like having ten brothers. They're the best!

"Levi dates Eide, Lane's been seeing Molly for, well, quite a while. And then there's Garratt, their brother from another mother,' as they have dubbed him. All one big happy family.

"Levi and Lane run a landscaping business; they claim they could grow palm trees in the mountains in the dead of winter!"

Owen sat across from me looking very engaged as I rattled on about Lane and Levi. He had some serious dark eyes to match his hair. It was stirring things in me that I'd thought were closed, for good.

"Garratt, Levi and Lane are like The Three Musketeers and have practically been joined at the hip since college."

19

"So, I take it you all are pretty tight?"

"That's one way to describe us. What's your story, Owen?"

"Well, we're definitely a story: one brother, a sister-in-law, a niece and nephew, several aunts, uncles and a platoon of cousins."

"A platoon?" I asked, chuckling.

"Yeah, well, I've never actually counted them."

"Oh gosh. Eide thought you just moved here?"

"I did, from southwest Colorado, to join the Mountain Rescue Team."

"That sounds like an interesting line of work. Interesting rescues?" I asked Owen.

"I understand they can get intense. It's a blessing when it's a boring day at work. If they have an intense and exciting rescue it means someone, or someone's family is not having a particularly good day, or their vacation is likely not going to have a happy ending. What do you do for work?"

"I work for a marketing analysis firm in Denver. I rebrand existing products to make them more profitable."

I noticed Owen abruptly switched the conversation away from his career.

"Oh, that sounds...interesting."

"Uh, yea, 'interesting.' It has its days," I said, chuckling. Even though I wasn't particularly excited with the path ol' Craig had chosen. "Do you like living up here? Are you glad you made the move?" I asked Owen.

"I do," Owen reaffirmed after he finished a drink of his coffee. *Man, this guy had a smile and smirk all combined into one, it sure was tempting.*

"This is a great area. I'm excited about being near the hiking and fishing spots in this area of the state. We have hiking and fishing spots down south, but not like it is up here; it's quiet and not as touristy."

"I know, it seems as though Denver to Colorado Springs has gotten to be just one big metro area. I was so ready to get out of the city when I moved back up here."

"So, do you commute every day?" Owen asked with a questioning look.

"No—well, I guess you could put it that way. I have a whole new schedule now; sometimes I work from home or the client's office, but now I'll be traveling to other states. Oh, goodness, do

20

you realize it's almost three o'clock?" I was surprised we'd been here this long; I really enjoyed visiting with Owen, and I didn't even detect a hint of the ego I figured would precede him.

"No way. We've been here that long?" Owen said, looking at his watch.

"Actually, we have, have I kept you too long?" I asked.

"No, of course not. I've had a nice time chatting with you. But I really should get home and let my dog out. Uh, say, are you available later this week? Maybe for dinner?" Owen asked. "I'd like to see you again."

"Yes, maybe later in the week, can I check my schedule and let you know?"

We exchanged phone numbers and I told Owen I would text him later this evening and we could make plans to have dinner this week. It was nice chatting with Owen, and I was already looking forward to seeing him again, I thought as we walked out of the coffee shop.

My phone rang on the way home; no doubt it was Eide again. She'd already texted me three times. Honestly, I was surprised she hadn't called sooner. *I'll wait and call her when I get home*, I thought. *I suppose she's just sitting there brooding over this.*

"How was it?" Eide said when she answered the phone. I had dialed her back after I'd parked in the garage.

"How was what? Hello to you, too, by the way."

"Yea, yea, hello. Now how was coffee with Owen?"

"Hot! Coffee is usually served hot; I added a splash of creamer to mine."

"Not what I'm talking about—how was the company?"

"Oh, right. It was nice."

"Nice, *nice* is all I get. Are you going out again?"

"Ya know, Eide, you shouldn't put people on the spot like that. It's embarrassing, for him and me. I think he was humiliated."

"Oh please, you both survived. Somebody had to kick you in the pants and I'm glad it was me. So, when's the next date?"

"I was thinking you and I and Molly need a girl's weekend." I was doing everything I could to avoid Eide's question.

"Absolutely, that's a great idea." Eide said. "I'll call Molly and maybe we can get some details out of you."

21

"OK, we'll figure something out. I gotta go, Nosy Nelly."

"But Karla—" I could hear Eide trying to get my attention.

"Bye, Eide," I said as I pressed "end call." I wasn't about to tell her I liked visiting with Owen. She's too nosy for her own good. Gotta love that girl.

I was sitting at my computer, checking my emails. I reviewed my schedule and decided Friday should work for a family supper. As I sat there thinking things over, I decided to text them all. I sent out a group text. I was really excited about this first dinner in my new home.

Thank-you supper—My house—Friday night, 7 p.m. or before, looking forward to seeing you!

I got a resounding "Yes" from everyone and started thinking about the meal. Maybe Eide was right, maybe the patio would be a great entertaining spot for us. Maybe I should get a patio set; we could hang out there Friday.

Everyone arrived Friday evening, Mom and Dad arriving earlier than the rest. Although I wasn't surprised.

"Hey, kiddo." Dad's famous nickname for me as though I would forever be eight years old. "How's it going?"

"Oh, it's going great!"

"How are you guys?"

"How's the house?" Dad asked, looking around as though the place was going to fall down around us.

"It's great. Although I haven't been here much, you know, just traveling. By the way, Dad, thanks for taking me to the airport."

"Yea sure, no problem, kiddo. Whatcha got going for supper?" Dad asked as we walked into the kitchen to find Levi and Eide hanging out in the backyard. I could hear Levi making a crack to Lane, so I decided Lane and Molly must be coming up the back walk.

"This meal is incredible." Mom said.

"Yeah, Karla, I didn't know you could barbecue burgers this well," Lane piped up. "Wish I could!"

"HAHA, very funny, Dad grilled the burgers, and I made the salads."

"I'm glad you decided to at least get a patio set out here, Kar; otherwise, were you going to make us sit on the ground?"

"Actually, I contemplated having you bring your own chair today, Lane. You know, BYOC!"

"It's really nice. Thank you for inviting us," Molly remarked. "Where are you headed to next? I feel like we see you less since you moved back."

"No kidding," Eide commented humorously. "Just leave us lowlifes back in the hood!"

"Maybe you better tell at least one of us when you have flights scheduled."

"You know, Dad, that might not be a bad idea, plus I might need some more rides to the airport. Some of the flights might be super early and the Ubers don't run that early."

"Oh well, then count me out," Lane retorted. "We don't run that early, either."

"Cut it out," Molly said jokingly as she slugged him in the gut. "We are happy to help you, Karla, at any time of the day or night."

"I'll get you to the airport, Kiddo. Just let me know when."

"Thanks, Dad. Can I just add my trips to your calendar?"

"Yeah, that'll be fine." Dad said.

After we finished eating, Eide, Molly and I moved inside to clean up the dishes. As Eide was putting leftovers in the fridge she turned around to address us.

"So, ladies," Eide said, interrupting. "Are we going to have a girl's weekend?"

"Yes, definitely. I'm so ready!" Molly exclaimed.

"I know, right," Eide said. "We're long overdue!"

"Aren't we, though, this is going to be great," I said, agreeing with Eide and Molly. "I was thinking of hitting up a few antique stores and getting a few new items for the house."

Before we could continue the discussion, the guys came in. They had been discussing their own ideas.

"Hey, ladies," Levi said as he walked up behind Eide, hugging her from behind. "What's going on in here?"

"We're planning a trip to Denver for a little girl fun," Eide told Levi.

"A what?" Levi feigned innocence.

"A girl's weekend," Eide reiterated to Levi.

"Ugh, shoot me now! Well, we have been talking about a camping trip, —you gals want to go with us?" Lane wanted to know, eyeing Molly.

Molly and I both said we'd look at our schedule but once again, Eide was all for it.

Chapter 5

"Hey Justin, what're you working on?"

"Oh, hey, Mark, nothing really. I was looking for some kind of lodging."

"Planning a trip?" Mark asked. "Wait, you never take off—you alright?"

"Yea, well at least a mini vacation. I thought it might be nice to check out some fly fishing up north, like I used to do with my grandpa when I was little." That had been a lifetime ago now just thinking about it.

"Oh, that sounds great, catch one for me. Or better yet, take me with you."

"Yeah, that could be arranged, but won't the wife miss you? I thought I'd find something other than a hotel, so I was looking at vacation rental sites. Each site produces worse results than the last. Here's one listing for a horse trailer in the field, nice and rustic. I wonder if they charge extra for the horse manure for the rustic experience."

"Really, a horse trailer? Do you even get a cot, or do you have to sleep under the stars?"

"Oh, wait these listings get better, there's an old something or other. I do not even know how to classify this place—an old movie set, or maybe someone was murdered here."

"You'll find something."

"There's even an option to share a space with someone. 'We have a great private room for your stay,' no thanks," I told Mark dejectedly.

I really could use this trip, I thought after Mark left my office. *I don't think I've even taken a full day off in the last five years.*

"Hey Karla, what are you doing here?" Lane asked as I pulled up outside Molly's house and stepped out of my car.

"One could ask you the same thing, bro. We're going antiquing for the weekend, don't you remember?"

"I did, just didn't realize it was today."

"So, how's it going, Kar?" Lane asked skeptically as we stood on Molly's porch waiting for her to come out the door. "I heard through the Grainer grapevine that you had coffee with a pilot fella."

"Yea, I did have coffee, at Eide's insistence, with a Mountain Rescue pilot."

"How'd that go?"

"Pretty well," I said coyly. I didn't tell Lane or anybody else in the family that I had been to dinner with this "pilot fella" twice since the so-called coffee date in question. And things were looking up for another date.

"Well, good," Lane said. "So, antiquing, huh? I think you gals should take my pickup, better for hauling."

"Hey guys." Molly said as she came out the door, carting her luggage.

Lane grabbed Molly's luggage and put them in his pickup and then he transferred my luggage to his pickup and handed Molly his keys as he caught a kiss on the cheek from Molly.

"Thanks, hun," Molly told Lane.

"Yea, thanks, Lane," I said, getting settled in his pickup, giving Lane and Molly a moment.

Molly jumped in the driver's seat and Lane stepped up to the window and told us to be careful and he'd see us Sunday.

"What was that about?" I asked Molly. "Lane didn't exactly seem like he remembered we were leaving today."

"Oh, he did too, he just wanted to see us off and this was his way of being casual, nonchalant; besides, he mentioned the other day we should take his pickup."

"Are you telling me my brother has a romantic bone in his body? I thought Levi got all the romance!"

"Don't worry about Lane's romance, he's got plenty!" Molly said with a snicker.

"Hey, Mark, I just sent off the latest reports," I announced when I stepped into his office.

26

"So, does that mean this project is finally complete?"

"Yes, and good timing, too, I might add. I'm taking off for a few days."

"So, you found a place?"

"Yea, I looked again a couple days ago and found this great-looking spot, a little big for just me but that's OK. I'm gonna head out, I'll see you next week."

"Yea, man, have a nice trip."

Molly and I picked up Eide, and Molly hit the interstate.

"Morning, gals," Eide said, settling in the backseat.

"Morning, Eide, how are ya?"

"Great! So ready for this!" Eide said. "I was reading online this morning there's this cute antique shop on Colfax we need to check out. The pictures show some amazing items."

"Sounds great!" Molly said. "We'll stop there first."

"Hey, Karla, come look at this," Eide said, walking into French Garden Antiques. "It's a nice bureau; it would look great in the space between the two bedrooms at the far end of the upstairs hallway." Eide was right: this place had some cute things.

"Eide, thanks, you have a great eye for these kinds of things, you should have one of those fix-and-flip TV shows where you do the decorating after all the good-looking sweaty, hunky dudes do all the carpentry work." We all laughed at my joke and kept looking through the store. I found two additional pieces and was offered ten percent off for the package deal. A couple of dudes came from the back and loaded the three pieces into the back of Lane's pickup.

"We should go get some lunch," Eide said as Molly pulled out of the parking lot. "It was hard work watching someone load furniture."

"Oh, yes, I'm starved, too," Molly agreed with Eide. "There's a great little deli not far from here, want to check it out?"

"Sounds great!" I told Molly. "Work for you, Eide?"

"Yep."

"So, Karla, tell us what's going on with the 'Owe' front," Eide questioned me with an inquisitive look as we sat down at a table in the back after getting a sandwich.

"Oh, and lunch was going so great," I groaned.

"What's the 'Owe' front?" Molly asked, looking at Eide and I with a confused expression on her face.

"So, there is something on the 'Owe' front," Eide said excitedly. "Owen, or 'Owe,' as his friends call him was introduced to Karla in church a couple weeks ago," Eide said, filling Molly in.

"Excuse me, he was introduced to me, you say? Ms. Cupid over here shot her deathly arrow, striking both Owen and me, coercing Owen to take me to coffee after church that morning. It was quite embarrassing, and she needs her ever-loving butt kicked for sticking her nose where it doesn't belong."

"Oh, this sounds juicy," Molly commented. "What have I missed?"

"Nothing, I went to coffee with him, we chatted for a while and then I came home and talked to Eide, after she texted me three times and then called. You'd think she was wounded or something."

"So, what's next? Eide questioned me. I knew what she was getting at, but I planned to evade her question as long as possible.

"How about we hit up a few more antique stores, there's some more down the street."

"Give me a break, I'm not talking about shopping; I'm talking about you and Owen."

"Well, I'm talking about shopping, and I think we should, that's what we came for."

"You're incorrigible! I will get this out of you yet," Eide told me as we left our table and went outside.

"Do you want to get breakfast, or shall we grab some coffee and head home with our treasures?" Molly asked, looking at her phone. We had spent all afternoon on Saturday visiting one store after another. Quite frankly, I wasn't sure I could handle another day.

"How about grabbing coffee and heading home—God knows the pocketbook could use a break," Eide said sarcastically.

28

"I secretly think that Molly wants to get home and see Lane," I said, snickering.

We dropped Eide off at her house after we got back to town and then Molly and I headed over to switch vehicles with Lane. Molly pulled into her driveway, and Lane, Levi and Garratt were all sitting on Molly's porch.

"Molly, why are the guys sitting on your porch?"

"Lane told me before we left to let him know when we left Denver, that's why I wanted to know about breakfast. The guys are going to unload your new furniture, at your house, of course. That and Lane wants his pickup back, he said your SUV is too sissy for him."

"Oh nice, those guys are the best."

Molly quickly put Lane's pickup in reverse and backed out of the driveway after we spoke to the guys for a moment and said we'd meet them at my house. When we pulled in, Eide pulled in right behind us.

"Hey, long time no see," I told Eide as I jumped out of Lane's pickup.

"Right! Plus, I wanted to make sure they put your furniture in the right spot."

"Go easy on us," Levi told Eide as he and Lane walked by with the bureau.

The guys carried the bureau upstairs under Eide's directions, which should have been an easy feat.

"Eide, you're impossible; we've moved this dresser nearly a dozen times, I think it's in a great place." Lane chuckled as Molly, and I just stood back laughing.

"Eide, come on, let's leave the guys to do the heavy lifting, we'll put the lights up on the patio."

I grabbed the lights out of one of my bags I'd left in the foyer and met up with Eide and Molly in the kitchen. Eide was picking up a candy-bar wrapper off the kitchen floor when I came into the kitchen with the lights.

"Where did you get that?" I asked Eide.

"It was on your floor; you must have dropped it when we left Friday."

"No," I said, shaking my head. "I didn't have a candy bar on Friday, or all weekend, for that matter."

"Must be one of the guys," Molly said.

"What 'must be one of the guys?'" Levi asked as he and Lane, along with Garratt, came strolling into the kitchen.

"Eide picked this up off the floor and thought I dropped it, but I think one of you guys lost it."

"Not mine. Yours, Levi?" Lane asked, turning to Levi. "Molly and I are going to head out."

"Oh, OK, thanks for your help and for letting us use your pickup."

"Yeah, yeah," Lane said, flopping his hands. "Now maybe we can get that camping trip put together instead of concentrating on these frilly girls' trips."

We all laughed at Lane's theatrical commentary; he always has been the family comedian.

"Yes, Lane, we'll go camping but I'm going to San Francisco before then."

"Oh man. Already?" Eide asked.

"Yes, already," I groaned alongside Eide. "This is the client that pushed my boss over the edge getting him to take on other clients."

Chapter 6

I was packed and ready for my San Francisco trip. This was becoming old hat, packing and unpacking all the time. I was getting to the point that I wouldn't even need to unpack. I added the trip info to Dad's calendar. Adding my travel dates to Dad's calendar was working out well. I still texted him about a ride to the airport.

"Hi Dad, headed to the airport in the morning and need to leave around five AM; can you give me a ride?"

Dad sent me a reply almost immediately.

"Of course, kiddo, where ya headed to this time?"

"San Francisco, I put the info on your calendar."

"Oh, OK, for the week?"

"Yea"

"Ok, kiddo thanks for letting me know C U in the AM."

Karla had been on my mind all week; I'd been wanting to go out with her again; but our schedules didn't work out. We'd been to supper a couple times since her friend insisted, we go out for coffee and every time we lost track of time. I had been wanting to call or text her all week but had resisted the urge; she was busy, and I didn't want to interrupt at the wrong time, but I couldn't wait anymore.

"Hey Karla, what's up?"
"I'm getting ready for a business trip to SF tomorrow."
"Oh, OK. When you get back?"
"Friday afternoonish."
"Can we get together and have dinner, hang out after you get back?"
"Of course, I would love to! I'll let you know when I get back."
"Sounds great, safe travels."
"Thanks Owen, talk soon."

"Hey, Justin, how was the fishing?" Mark asked when I got to work Monday.

"It was incredible, Mark. Well, not in the sense of catching fish, but the time away was great. I'm going to see about going back for a week soon."

"Well, it must have been great, I haven't known you to take a long weekend, let alone a week's vacation. Are you sure you're alright?"

"Yeah, everything fine. I just haven't been out of the city in a while, but I better get to work, at least check my email."

I reviewed the backlog of email from being away and found one from the homeshare site thanking me for staying and asking for a review. I thought why not, it was a great place. At some point, today I wanted to look to see when there was availability for a week's vacation so I could get approved for the time off.

I didn't see any available times, so I marked the box to be emailed in the event of a cancelation. I could always decide at that time if something came available.

"Good morning, Kiddo!" Dad said as I opened the door. "Am I on time?"

"Good morning, Dad, yep, you're right on time. I'm almost ready, I have to run into my office and grab a bag."

"How's things been?" Dad asked, pulling out of my driveway.

"Great, Molly, Eide and I went to Denver and did some antiquing last weekend. I picked up a few nice pieces."

"I heard, sounds like you girls had a good time. I also heard something about a pilot."

"Oh, yea," I said, smiling. "I suppose Eide's been yakking to Levi, and he told you."

"Something like that. So, what about this pilot?"

"The one from church. Eide embarrassingly threw us together, and basically forced him to take me out for coffee, it was all rather embarrassing. We went out for coffee and then we've been to dinner a couple times since."

"Ah, sounds nice. Have you told your mother any of this?"

"Well, no, there's nothing to tell really."

"OK, Kiddo; you'll tell us when you're ready, in the meantime, have fun and be safe. Call if you need anything."

"Thanks, Dad."

"When's your return flight?" Dad asked as he pulled up to the terminal drop-offs.

"I'm scheduled to be back Friday afternoon, but I can get an Uber."

"OK, Kiddo, have a safe flight and if things change, let me know. Love you."

"Love you, too, Dad," I said as I stepped out of his pickup to go into the terminal.

My flight to San Francisco arrived on time. I grabbed an Uber, and the driver took off towards the client's office. Once I arrived at the client's office, Ms. Lindstedt greeted me and showed me around the office. She introduced me to the team that she had assembled. I shared my agenda for the week and what I planned to accomplish this week. I answered questions and delegated the preliminary tasks.

33

When Friday arrived, this team had blazed their way through the agenda, and I knew I wouldn't have any trouble getting out of there that afternoon. I wish all my clients were this involved and productive.

"Thank you for working with my team, Ms. Grainer, we did some great work this week," Ms. Lindstedt said, praising our work from the week during our recap meeting. I had to agree with her, it was a very productive week. Ms. Lindstedt worked right alongside her team and accomplished a great deal.

"We did do some great work. The pleasure was all mine, Ms. Lindstedt. I hope everything comes together as you planned. I will forward the financial portfolios once I complete them."

"Sounds good, thanks again for your time, and safe travels. Bye now!"

"Thanks again, Ms. Lindstedt," I said, walking out of her office.

As I stood at baggage claim, I thought of Owen. I hoped we'd still be able to have the fore-mention date this weekend. I mused as I walked away from baggage claim but was suddenly distracted and nearly dropped my luggage.

I couldn't get Karla off my mind this morning. I think she's heading home today. For some reason, I decided it was a good idea to rob Eide's phone number out of the church directory to get Karla's flight information. *What was I thinking*, I thought as I listened to the ringing after I dialed her number. I had been out on a few dates with Karla, her long, flowy, curly brown hair and charming, gracious smile had me hooked. I had made up my mind if I wanted to see her again and due to her busy travel schedule, it might very well have to be in an airport pickup/drop off situation. I was thinking this might be a mistake calling her, hmm, but too little too late. Eide answered the phone.

"Hello," Eide said. I could tell by the tone of her voice she didn't know who was calling her.

"Um. Hi, Eide, this is Owen Kaster."

"Owen, as in 'My friends call me 'Owe,' that Owen."

"Yes, that one in the same," I said, chuckling. "How are you?"

"No no no, never you mind with the pleasantries," Eide shot back. "Karla hasn't told me an ounce of details about the two of you and now you're calling me. Something doesn't smell right in Denmark."

"Could I ask you for a favor?" I asked Eide while laughing at her joke.

"Oh, this is getting good," Eide said excitedly.

"Do you know any of her flight details?"

"No, but I can do some checking and get back to you."

"Thanks, I appreciate it."

"Sorry, man, who died?" Mark jumped me as I went by his office, bright and early Monday morning.

"No one, why do you ask?"

"You've been gone a week, you didn't give me a heads-up, you just vanished."

"Oh, yea, sorry. Remember a few weeks back I went up north and did some fishing over the weekend? It was great; I decided to go back for the week."

"I kinda forgot about it, thinking you'd changed your mind."

"No, I didn't change my mind. Remember, I told you about the places available were crazy? The horse trailer?"

"Yea, you didn't buy the horse trailer and decide to make it into a summer home or something?" Mark chuckled.

"Good lord, no. The place I stayed at last time had a cancellation for the week; so, I emailed Mr. Hightower and took off."

"Oh, well, glad no one died."

Mr. Hightower appeared. "Who died?"

"No one, Mr. Hightower, I was just discussing Justin's trip with him."

"Oh yes, how was the vacation, Justin—didn't you say you were going fishing?"

"Yes, took in some fly fishing up north."

"Did you catch anything?"

"Yes, I did. There was great fishing, a little hiking, mansion of a place to stay."

"Sounds like a great time, maybe I should talk to the wife about taking the family up there. They like to go skiing and it might be a nice change of pace."

"I'll send you the info. They always seem to be booked so you should check it out now, maybe you can get something reserved."

Eide called me back in a matter of minutes after checking Karla's flight details. It turned out if I left now, I would be able to meet her just in time. Apparently, Karla hadn't told them much about the few dates we'd been on. I seemed to have raised some suspicions when I attempted to pick her up today. But that's OK, I was still going.

I arrived at the airport shortly before her plane was due to land. I went inside and waited in the terminal where I figured Karla would come around looking for an Uber or when she went to baggage claim.

I heard the announcement of the incoming flight she was scheduled to arrive on and knew she'd be coming out soon. *I just hope Karla's OK with this. I hadn't thought about her plans until now; she may want to get home after being gone all week. Good job, Owen.*

Lost in my thoughts I heard my name.

"Owen?"

I glanced up to see the most attractive woman, ever.

"Owen!"

"Yep! That's me," I said as I stood there staring at my feet, feeling a bit self-conscious about what I'd done.

"Oh gosh, what are you doing here?"

"There's this girl, coming in on a flight from San Francisco; thought I'd take her for a ride, maybe out for a nice dinner."

"Ah, what a nice surprise."

"Is this all your luggage?" I asked Karla as I started taking her luggage from her.

"Yes, got it all. I was headed out to wait for the Uber driver, so now I'll just cancel the ride."

"So how was your trip?" I asked Karla as we walked out of the terminal.

"Business as usual, I have some portfolios to finish."

"How have you been?" Karla asked me.

"Just life as usual. Truth be told, I've been anxiously waiting to take you to dinner. If you need or want to get home, I completely understand, and we can go out tomorrow night."

"No way, I'm good. I would love to go out to supper with you."

She flashed me that charming smile I'd been waiting to see. She had her hair parted down the middle and laid across her shoulders. Even though she had worked most of the day and probably like crazy all week and then traveling this afternoon, she still looked so beautiful.

I took Karla to a small, out-of-the-way Italian restaurant. The waitress brought us some water and breadsticks and then took our orders.

"Oh, these look good. I haven't eaten at all today, I'm starved," Karla said, picking up a breadstick.

"So, I might have caused some problems with your family today," I said, grabbing a breadstick.

"How's that?" Karla asked.

"Well, I wanted to surprise you and pick you up, so I called Eide and now I think that might have been a big mistake."

"Ah, did Eide give you the third degree?" I asked Owen, laughing.

"Well, somewhat, but I think I safely deflected her questioning. But she had to call your dad, so not sure how that went. I hope I didn't rock the boat for you."

"Don't worry about it. They've all been doing some serious gossiping about us—or should I say Eide's been stirring the pot. In fact, when my dad took me to the airport Monday, he brought you up."

"I didn't mean to put the spotlight on us, if you're not ready."

"No, it's all good."

We finished our meal and left the restaurant. I took the back roads toward home and stopped at a mountain lake where the moon was shining down on the water.

"What are we doing, Owen?"

"Come back here and find out." I'd stepped in the back of my pickup and laid out some blankets. "Come have a seat."

37

"This looks cozy," Karla said.

"How do you feel about a little stargazing?"

"I haven't been stargazing in ages."

We sat down, and I covered us up, then nonchalantly put my arm around her, and we sat back looking up at the sky. It was a nice, cool, clear evening, perfect for stargazing and it was nice just sitting here with Karla. We sat watching the sky, there were lots of shooting stars. We tried to find the Big Dipper; but guessing neither of us had enough astronomer in us to know. We'd point things out and laugh at our findings. So perhaps we actually did see it. We sat there wrapped in each other's arms until the night grew late and the air got chilly. We best call it a night, I told Karla as I started to sit up.

Owen dropped me off at my house a while later, he carried my luggage into the foyer. Before stepping out the door, Owen held me tight, whispering in my ear. Not quite sure I was ready for the night to end.

"I had a nice time tonight, thanks for stargazing with me," Owen murmured.

"You're thanking me, I should be thanking you, you're the one who stole the show today."

"No, this was just as much for me as it was for you. I've missed you like crazy, when can I see you again?"

"Well, I have to finish up the portfolios tomorrow. What's your schedule like?"

"We have flight training tomorrow; can I text you when I'm done?"

"Sounds good, and thanks again for today."

Owen smiled at me, and held my hand a bit longer, staring into my eyes before he said good night, and brushed a kiss across my lips. "Good night, Karla."

"Good night, Owen."

I took my luggage upstairs and decided to start unpacking. Working through the suitcases, my cell phone rang. I must have left my phone downstairs on the sofa table; I ran to get it but didn't quite make it. No doubt Eide wanted details. Before I could answer her call, the call went to voicemail.

Hey Karla. You can be proud of me only contacting you once, even though I'd have good reason to, God only knows what you and Owen are up to, and you don't even bother telling your best friend. Well, I'll set a good example for you; Levi and I are going out of town for the weekend. Levi called at lunch and said to get packing, sweet cheeks, we're leaving town! Secretly, I think it has something to do with Owen trying to track you down; but that's between you and me. Anyways, have a good weekend and talk soon."

I snickered at Eide's message and walked into the kitchen for a bottle of water. I was instantly hit with a powerful smell of cooked fish. That's odd, who would have cooked fish in here? I stood there pondering the fish smell as my phone rang again.

"Hey."

"Hey, Kiddo."

"Oh, hey, Dad."

"Not who you were expecting, I take it."

"No but good to hear from you, too."

"How was your trip, did you get picked up from the mystery man? Is this mystery man and the pilot fella the same person?"

"Uh. ya," I finally answered after a pause, when I noticed crumbs on the stove.

"Are you alright, Kiddo, you seem distracted."

"Well, not really distracted, trying to decide what happened to my kitchen."

"Why, what's wrong with your kitchen?"

"Did you guys have a fish fry here while I was gone?"

"No, not that I'm aware of, sounds like a good idea, though. What makes you think that?"

"As you were calling, I came walking into the kitchen and was instantly hit with a strong smell of fried fish. You know, heavy cooking-oil smell, and now I just noticed crumbs on the stove. Like the breading didn't get wiped up."

"Hmm, that's odd."

"Oh well, no big deal. I'm probably just tired."

"Ok, Kiddo, I don't mean to keep you, just wanted to make sure you got home OK. Have a good night."

"You too, Dad, tell Mom hi. Love you guys, bye."

I looked around the kitchen a little more; there was a strong cooked-fish smell in there. I'm probably just imagining things or

I'm tired. Things will look differently tomorrow—or in this case *smell* differently. I went upstairs, looking at my luggage; I decided to forgo unpacking until tomorrow and grab a shower and go to bed. As soon as I stepped into the shower, I was instantly sickened; I thought I cleaned this shortly before I left. How did it get this dirty?

The next morning, I woke up but didn't move too far too fast. I lay in my warm, comfy bed, not ready to get up, yet. I lay there thinking back to last night with Owen. He surprised me by picking me up at the airport. And then we went stargazing, just sitting there in the back of his pickup. We talked and joked about our infinite astronomy wisdom, but it was just nice sitting there with him. I decided I better get up and get to work on the portfolios. As I was getting dressed, I remembered the mess in the kitchen and the shower and decided to clean them up first. I gave the shower a good scrub down and decided the toilet could use a cleaning as well. I swore I cleaned this bathroom shortly before I left. I must not have done a good job. I cleaned the kitchen and the stove and sprayed some Febreze, which helped with the smell.

I got started on the portfolios later that morning. I became blurry eyed from looking at the screen all afternoon. They were time-consuming and becoming tedious. I figured jetlag must have set in and decided to take a break and go for a walk. I went outside and walked down by the stream; this was such a nice and peaceful area. It was a beautiful afternoon to be out walking; I probably shouldn't have stayed out so long and gotten back to the portfolios.

When I got back to my desk, I noticed I had a text from Owen.
"Hey what's up?"
"Had a busy day and now I'm exhausted (thinking jet lag has set in) just got back from a walk."
"Nice, same problem here, minus the jet lag. How would you feel about Arnold and I coming over with a pizza?"
"That sounds great; see you soon."
Owen replied with a starry-eyed smiley face emoji.
An hour later Owen and Arnold arrived. Owen was toting a pepperoni pizza and a cheesecake.
"You didn't have to bring dessert."

"I know, but this stuff is the bomb. And after training all day, I was in the mood."

"Oh, right, how was that?" I turned and asked Owen after I got some plates and glasses out of the cupboard.

"Same old, same old. How was your day? How was your trip? You didn't say much about it yesterday."

"It was actually pretty good; this client had a pretty good team assembled."

"That's good," Owen said serving up the pizza.

"Oh hey, Eide called last night and left me a message. She and Levi took off on some romantic getaway this weekend."

"Cool, any special occasion?"

"Not that I know of. Eide blames you."

"Me?" The question caused Owen to nearly choke on his pizza. "Why me?"

"Because you called her to track me down. Levi talked to her later and told her to get packed. She was a spitfire in her message, I think she was excited."

"Well, that's great, but Eide's always a spitfire and they probably deserve the time away."

"They do deserve the time away, but I think Levi's got something up his sleeve. I wouldn't be surprised at all if Eide came home with a rock on her finger."

"Oh, wow, you think he's going to propose?" Owen said with a questioning look and then smiled at me.

"Hmm, just a hunch," I said, shrugging my shoulders.

"Tell me about these pictures," Owen said, referencing the pictures on the sofa table behind the couch.

"This picture is Levi, Lane and me," I said, pointing to a picture of three young children dressed in snow attire.

"Oh, OK, yea, I recognize you."

"We had been skiing somewhere up the mountain that afternoon and Mom took this shot. Mom said years later she tried so hard to get a nice shot of the three of us against the white-capped mountain, but as you can see, Lane there on the right refused to have a decent picture. I don't think there's a picture of Lane anywhere before the age of sixteen that he isn't doing something weird, crazy or both in the shot."

"That's funny," Owen said, laughing.

41

"What about this one?" Owen said, pointing to the one next to it of another set of kids in their teens but a much older picture.

"That one is my parents when they were growing up."

"Your parents knew each other growing up?" Owen questioned.

"Yea, since about fourth grade or so. Mom's parents moved here when she was about nine years old, and as she tells the stories, her and Dad were a hit right off."

We chatted over the pictures some more, enjoying the evening. It was nice to just relax together and share random stories. We had done this a few other times now, but usually just out on the patio. And just like the other times Owen and I had shared together, time this evening just flew away.

"Hey Karla, earth to Karla, where ya been?" Owen asked. "You look a million miles away."

"Sorry, what were you saying?"

"Actually, I said I was thinking that Arnold and I better call it a night. Now I think we really should," Owen said, chuckling. "Especially if you're gonna zone out on me!"

"Arnold lets go, boy!" Owen told his obedient dog as he stood up from the couch. "Are you going to church in the morning?"

"Yes, I am, are you?"

"I am, can I come pick you up?"

"Sure, would love it."

"OK, see you then. Good night," Owen said, smiling back at me as we stood at the front door.

"Bye, Owen, thanks for the pizza and cheesecake. It really was the bomb," I said, laughing.

As always, Owen was right on time—this was getting annoying! I hadn't even had time to put any makeup on when the doorbell rang.

I jogged downstairs and grabbed the door.

"Hey, Owen," I said as I started back upstairs.

"Good morning, Karla," Owen said looking up the stairs at me.

I jogged back upstairs, leaving Owen hanging.

"Sorry, Owen, I'm not quite ready. I'm putting makeup on," I hollered at Owen from the bathroom.

"It's OK, we've got time."

I finished with my makeup and came down the stairs. Owen was standing at the base of the stairs where I'd left him a few moments ago; he was staring straight at me. I thought something was wrong by the look on his face.

"Owen, you, OK?" I asked him, breaking into his reverie.

"Yes. Sorry," Owen said. "I was just caught up in the moment."

"Ah, well, I'm ready now, we can go."

"Good, I thought we were going to miss church!"

"Ha ha, very funny," I told Owen and jokingly I swatted him. "Owen grabbed his arm in a feigned injury motion.

"Pastor Tim won't take too kindly to your abusing me before church."

"Pastor Tim had a very nice message this morning, don't you think?" I asked Owen as we left church.

"I agree, I think Pastor Tim does a great job; I feel like he connects with us all in his messages."

"Oh, I know, I've felt many times that his sermons were directed to me."

"Would you like to get some lunch?"

"I would love to, but I need to finish up some portfolios. Thanks for the offer, though."

"I understand, maybe we can get together later this week?" Owen said with an inquisitive look on his face.

"I'd love that, there's a concert series in the park—maybe we could check that out."

"I heard about that, sounds pretty cool," Owen said. "I'll call you later."

"OK, thanks for taking me to church." I walked up to the porch and looked back, smiling. Owen was sitting there watching me walk up the steps.

When I sat down and was reviewing the portfolios, I realized I'd left more work to do on them than I'd thought, I should have gotten more done yesterday. I had been working on the portfolios all afternoon and evening was setting in. I had made some progress but still had quite a bit to do when the doorbell rang. I saved my work and ran to catch the door.

I opened the front door and Garratt was standing on the porch.

"Hey, Garratt, what a surprise, what are you up to? Please come in."

"Hi, Karla, I was in the neighborhood and thought I'd drop by and say hey."

"Hey, yea, I'm glad you did. How ya been? Would you like a cup of coffee or tea?"

"I'd take a cup of coffee if you're offering."

"Sure, come here in the kitchen. So, what's new in your life? I haven't seen you since we went camping, over a month ago now."

"Oh, nothing new, just work. Your brothers and I don't even get to hang out as much as we used to."

"Yea, summer and fall are their busier times of year."

"Is Dad keeping you busy?"

"Yea, business is booming, so to speak," Garratt chuckled.

"New developers want in this area; they think this is the new tourist hotspot," Garratt said, looking around the kitchen.

"Oh no, Garratt, I don't like hearing that. I'd rather not see us become one of those tourist trap towns. Dad mentioned something about this the night I had dinner for everyone, but I didn't really know it was coming to this. By the way, where were you that night?"

"I don't know, had an appointment or something," Garratt said with a mysterious gleam in his eye.

"Well, you can't miss the next one."

"When is the next one?"

"I don't know, I guess they might be skipping me, too. I'm never home. I just got home from San Francisco."

"Oh nice. That's a cool place."

"Well, not really. I have some rather long days and I usually come home and finish up the portfolios for the clients. I have portfolios to FedEx to the client in the morning, so I usually never get away from it."

"I shouldn't keep you then, Karla. I just stopped by to say hey. I didn't mean for you to caffeinate me."

"Hey, I'm happy to supply the coffee, anytime. It was nice of you to stop by and catch up."

"I'm glad we got a chance to visit, Karla. We don't usually have the chance when all the others are around."

"We'll chat again soon, Garratt," I said as he stepped out onto the porch.

After Garratt left, I finished the portfolios in nearly record speed. I must have found some new motivation, either from the coffee or the visit with Garratt. Either way, the portfolios were ready for shipment. As I got ready for bed, I was surprised to hear my phone ringing. *Hmm, I wonder who's calling me now? It's nearly midnight.*

"Hello."

"Karla???" Eide screamed out excitedly.

"Eide, what are you doing?" I said, moving the phone away from my ear to tone down her screeching.

"Levi and I, we're engaged."

"Oh, wow, that's great! I wondered if he didn't have something up his sleeve. So, when's the big day, have you decided?"

"We've been discussing things and you'll hear all about it soon. We're going to have everyone over Friday night to discuss things."

"You'll do no such thing. I will have an engagement party for you guys. You're only my best friend, of course I would be the only logical choice to throw you this party."

"OK, OK," Eide said excitedly.

"I'm glad you called and told me, let's meet up for coffee in the morning. I have to send some portfolios out; we can meet at that little café in the village."

"OK, see you then, bye, Eide said.

"Bye, Eide."

Oh, wow, Levi and Eide engaged. It was about time. *How exciting for them*, I thought, lying there in bed. I smiled to myself. Eide was so excited she was screeching.

I shipped the portfolios out and then headed down to meet Eide for coffee. It was a bright, crisp, beautiful fall morning. No doubt Eide and I would have a nice chat at the outdoor café.

"Hi, Eide," I waved towards her. "Do you have a coffee?" I motioned to her from the counter as I ordered mine.

Eide held up a cup and I completed my order. I set my coffee on the table and hugged Eide. "Alright, let me see it."

Eide held up her hand.

"Not bad, my brother did a pretty good job," I said, holding Eide's hand and looking at the shimmering stone with smaller stones set and twisted around the larger setting.

"Oh, Eide, this is beautiful. How was your trip?"

"We had a very romantic weekend. We stayed at a little cottage along a creek way up in the mountains and took a drive down Million Dollar Highway."

"So, what was Levi's big proposal, your moment?"

"We agreed, no discussion of it until Friday night," Eide said very sternly.

"Ah, come on, that's not fair, I'm only your best friend and engagement-party host! Just give me a smidge of detail," I said, holding up my pinched fingers. "Besides, you owe me for that little stunt you pulled with Owen."

"Nope, Friday night. We'll all talk about it together."

"Hi honey," Mom said, answering after about one ring. She must have been waiting for a call.

"Hi, Mom. Were you waiting for a call?"

"No," Mom said. "What makes you say that?"

"You just answered so quickly, I thought you had your phone up like Quick Draw McGraw. Anyways, have you talked to Eide or Levi today?"

"Yes, we talked to Levi early this morning. Said he proposed to Eide over the weekend, I assume that's why you're calling."

"Yeah, I know. Isn't it wonderful? I'm going to throw them a little engagement party on Friday. Which is supposedly where we will get the wedding details; must be quite the story there."

"I asked Levi about things this morning and he sort of gave me the brush-off. I figured they haven't made any plans yet; these things take time."

"So, will you and Dad be available Friday?"

"Of course, well make it. It sounds nice, what can I help you with?

"Actually, if you could figure out a cake or dessert, something along those lines would be greatly appreciated."

"Consider it done, but I can do a lot more. You have a lot going on these days. Hang on, your dad just came in, let me put you on speaker. It's Karla," I could hear Mom tell Dad as she got the phone switched to speaker.

"Hey, Dad."

"Hey, Kiddo, what's going on? You leavin' town again?"

"I'm not sure about my travel schedule now. I was just telling Mom about the engagement party I'm working on for Levi and Eide."

"Oh, geez," Dad said, grumbling. "Isn't the wedding enough? When did people start having engagement parties? When is this wedding anyways?"

"We don't know yet, Darren. I don't think they've decided."

"Come on, Dad, this is exciting."

"Yea, for you, maybe." Dad groaned again.

Mom and I were just discussing her bringing a dessert Friday night.

"Oh, OK. I suppose I can do that," Dad said.

"I'm bringing the dessert, Darren. You'll have to figure out something else to bring."

"Mom, Dad," I said, breaking into their side discussion. "All I need is a dessert, I can figure out the rest."

"Let your dad bring something, he can smoke something, right, Darren?" I could hear Mom sounding sterner all the time towards him.

"Yes, I can do that. I'll smoke some ribs. Will that work for you, Kiddo?"

"Well, yea, that'd be awesome, but only if you want to."

"Oh, no. I'll bring them. Otherwise, your mother won't let me come," Dad said, chuckling.

"That's right," Mom said.

"OK, guys, I need to go." *Holy cow, those two make Ozzie and Harriet look like lightweights*, I thought, laughing to myself after we hung up.

I immediately pulled up Lane's number and dialed him.

"Hey, Kar, what's up?" Lane asked when he answered the call.

"Hey, Lane. I'm calling about Friday night."

"Yea, I heard about that, I guess."

"What do you mean 'you guess?'"

"Levi didn't tell me a darn thing. He even waited until later in the day to tell me he'd proposed; and here I thought we were closer than that."

"I saw Eide this morning and all I got was 'We'll talk about it Friday night.' So, are you and Molly available?"

"I am, I'll have to ask Molly about her schedule. I'll text her and maybe she'll answer here shortly."

"Well, it doesn't matter. I'll just count her in anyways. Is she working tonight?"

"No, she went to see her mom and take her some books. She might be on her way here now."

"How's things going with the pilot?" Lane asked.

"Let's just say things are flying. Maybe he'll be here Friday."

"Hey, that's great, Kar. I look forward to visiting with him.

"We'll he's last on my list to call so if he's going to be at the party, I better call him."

"Alright, see you Friday. Bye, Kar."

"Bye, Lane."

As I listened to the phone ring on Owen's end, I was excited to be inviting him to officially meet my family. I know he's seen them at church and the encounter with Eide. This is different; this is just our clan. The pressures on.

Eventually, Owen's voicemail picked up. I told him I had an invitation for him for Friday night and to call me when he had a chance.

That was a terrible message, I thought after hanging up. I should have just told him to call when he had a chance.

I was still having deep thoughts about Owen and the fact that I was inviting him to a family dinner, when my phone rang, breaking into my reverie.

"Hello," I said, trying to sound as casual as possible.

"Hey," Owen said, just as casually. "Sorry I missed your call; Arnold and I went out for a jog, and I hadn't gotten out of the shower. I was close to your neighborhood; I like jogging out that way."

"Oh, well you should have stopped by."

"So, what about this invitation?" Owen inquired.

48

"Remember how I was saying that Levi and Eide were taking a romantic trip this past weekend?"

"Yea, you kinda thought your brother might propose soon."

"Well turns out he did propose over the weekend."

"Oh, hey, that's great! So, are you inviting me to the wedding?"

"Probably, but I don't know when that's going to be. I called to invite you to a little engagement party I'm having on Friday, and I'd like you to be my date."

"So, does this mean you want me to meet your family?"

"Absolutely not, someone else's family," I joked with Owen.

"Phew," Owen said. "Dodged a bullet there. So, whose family will be there? Please tell me Nixon's, I have so many lingering questions."

"I'm sure my dad can answer them all," I said laughing.

"Oh, good," Owen said. "So, when is the big day?"

"Seems Levi and Eide are a bit tight-lipped about their plans; I even tried to get details from Lane, but that was a bust."

"How funny. Maybe they have a big adventure planned."

"Wouldn't that be cool; my mom thinks they don't really have any plans yet. Which would make sense—I mean, they did just get engaged."

"Well, in answer to your question, yes. I'd love to be your date. What time? Or is there something I can help with before?"

"Any time before seven, and I think I'm good. Dad's going to smoke some ribs, so I won't have much to take care of."

I could smell the potatoes cooking in the crockpot as I came downstairs from finishing my hair. I was going to go check them when the doorbell rang a little after six o'clock on Friday evening. *Wow*, I thought, *I'm ready to go for once and Owen's just getting here, that means he's late.* It was Mom and Dad standing on the front porch when I looked through the window. Dad was carrying the smoked ribs, which smelled amazing I noticed when I opened the door. Mom came in behind him carrying a cheesecake that looked almost as scrumptious as the ribs smelled. "Hey, you two, you both went to a lot of work. I made a potato casserole that will complement those ribs to a T. Thanks, Dad. You sure made my day a lot easier."

"Hey, Kiddo, how ya been?" Dad said, half-hugging me.

"I'm fine, Dad, how are you? Wore out from all the smoking?"

"Ah, no, these are pretty easy. I just like giving your mother a hard time," he told me after Mom went into the kitchen to put the cheesecake in the fridge.

"It'll be our little secret," I told Dad with a small wink to him.

"Hey, did you get everything taken care of with your kitchen the other night? That night it smelled like cooked fish in here?"

"Oh, yes. I forgot about that. I must have just been tired; it's fine," I said, heading to the patio where everyone else was gathered.

"Hey, you," Owen said, coming up behind me, whispering in my ear. "Your hair looks beautiful, and you smell like a field of daisies."

"You don't look so bad yourself there, cowboy!" I said, smiling deep into Owen's eyes.

Soon everyone was gathered, and congratulations were extended to the happy couple. And when I say happy couple, there was never a truer statement. I had been seeing it in the way Levi and Eide looked at each other. *I hope I have someone look at me that way for a long time,* I thought, turning to my side to see Owen looking back at me.

We all gathered around the table, and following a prayer for thanks and blessings to Levi and Eide, we all dug in.

"Dad, you outdid yourself on the ribs," Levi said.

"Yes, well, I am the smokin' king," Dad joked.

"All the food is very good," Molly said. "But seriously, we all know why we're here."

"Yes, because I love this girl," Levi exclaimed, holding up Eide's hand.

"And I love your boy," Eide said, turning to accept a kiss from Levi.

"Alright you two, enough already, what's the story?" Lane asked.

Everyone laughed at Lane's statement. Levi and Eide stood as if they were going to address the nation.

Levi cleared his throat, holding up his wine glass. "Well, you all know I've loved Eide for a very long time and she's agreed to marry me."

"Yes, I'm still shocked," Lane chimed in.

"I know, me too," Levi poked back at Lane's comment. "Well, I can't wait that long for Eide to be my wife, so when I proposed, I suggested we elope."

Everyone fell silent and stared at Levi and Eide. Was he joking?

"You guys eloped?" Mom nearly shouted at Eide and Levi. "You mean you're already married?"

"Hold on, Laurel, that's not what Levi meant," Eide said, shaking her head.

"Well, he said you guys eloped," Mom said, a little short towards Eide.

"Well, yes, technically that's what he said. What he should have said is that we are planning a destination wedding in January."

"What, you guys are crazy? You can't plan a wedding in three months," Mom said heatedly. The rest of us sat there a little shocked as the barbs kept flying between Mom and Eide.

"Actually, we're all a little crazy, Mom," Levi joked. "You just turned up the heat, a little."

"I called today for preliminary info."

"So, what? You're planning to exchange vows at some 'Elvis Chapel of Love' in Vegas?" Mom asked. "I am not having my son get married at some two-bit, cheap and dirty chapel in Vegas."

"Geez, Mom, lay off the dramatics. We're thinking Mexico. We just want our clan, so we thought why not make a vacation of it."

"I think it's a great idea," Dad said. "So many less details to contend with; and with a little luck I can get out of wearing one of those monkey suits!"

"Actually," Lane piped up. "A nice cobalt blue tux would just bring out the color of your eyes so well, Darren," Lane said in his true theatrical self, flopping his hands around.

"Most definitely, Darren," Garratt agreed with Lane. "We'll get you a little beach tie to match."

Lane and Garratt's joking about the tux did a pretty good job of loosening the tension between Mom and Eide. Which made a good segue into discussing dresses and details for the wedding and other events for the vacation.

"I'm planning on just getting a nice simple, floral flowing gown. You ladies can wear something similar," Eide told us. "And I was

51

just thinking about fun beach clothes for the guys, nothing formal."

"Oh, good, now I can go," Dad teased.

"And shop," Molly quipped.

"Or drink!" Lane chimed in.

"I'm sure there are plenty of fun places to shop," Eide said, ignoring Lane's comment. "I just called and got information on the wedding. We have to be in Mexico three days prior to the ceremony. So, there'll be time to shop."

"Definitely," Levi snidely whispered to Lane.

It was nearly midnight, and all the excited talk of Levi and Eide's wedding had toned down. I still wasn't sure about Mom's feelings about it all, but I thought it was a fantastic idea. Eventually Mom would warm to the idea.

Owen and my parents were the last to leave. They helped me finish the cleanup.

"This was a nice evening," Dad said as we all stood in the foyer before they left.

"I guess," Mom said reluctantly. "Thank you for everything, Karla. It was nice seeing you, Owen, although I guess all the wedding talk foreshadowed your visit."

"Oh, come on, Laurel," Dad said, taking Mom in a half-embrace. "I'm taking you on a vacation; you should be excited."

"This doesn't count as a vacation, Darren. You're being forced to go."

"Oh, would you listen to the abuse I'm subjected to—and now I'm being forced to go to Mexico. I'll be lucky if she brings me home. I think I'll change my insurance policy in the morning."

"Oh, dear, just stop," Mom said and jokingly slapped Dad. "Come on, take me home."

"I agree, let's go home," Dad said, smirking at Mom. "See you two later."

"Bye guys," I told Mom and Dad as Owen and I stood in the foyer. Owen turned to face me after Mom and Dad walked down the sidewalk to their car. "So, do you have plans next weekend?"

"I do, I have a really hot date with this pilot fella."

"Oh wow, sounds like a great guy. Do I know him?"

"What'd you have in mind?" I asked.

"You'll have to wait and see; I'll talk to you later," Owen said as he brushed a delicately placed kiss on my lips.

"Good night, Owen," I said as he went out the door a moment later.

The next morning, I checked my email and found a message that the San Francisco team wanted me back for another product series. Not exactly the plan I had but Craig, my boss, insisted that I was the one to go. I had already established a working relationship with the team.

I spent the afternoon planning; I was going to have to fly out tomorrow afternoon. Looking over the proposal. I noticed Ms. Lindstedt requested a two-week session. Shoot! *Owen and I were supposed to hang out next weekend*, I thought as I finished the agenda for the session. *I'll call him later, hopefully we can change his plans.*

"Hi Karla, how's it going? I had a good time last night."

"Hey Owen. I did too, but that's not why I was calling; actually, I'm calling to break our plans for next weekend."

"You what?" Owen said, sounding shocked. "You don't even know what my plans were."

"I know, but I have to go back to San Francisco. The team I worked with a couple weeks back has requested I come back for another project."

"Oh, well, that's good, I think. At least it wasn't anything I did."

"No, it's not you. I was hoping we could reschedule."

"Uh sure, how about we discuss it when I pick you up for the airport, when is your flight?"

"Are you sure you want to take me to the airport? I need to leave tomorrow afternoon; probably shortly after church."

"No problem, Owen's express at your service," Owen said laughing. "Do you have time for a quick lunch before we hit the airport?"

"That sounds great, Owen. Thank you."

The next evening, I landed in San Francisco and noticed I had a missed call and message from Eide. I needed to catch my Uber ride and decided I'd have to connect with her later. Eide's message indicated she was worried about me about something. *Oh goodness sakes, I do this all the time*, I thought as I listened to Eide's message. On Monday morning, I met up with the same team as I had a few weeks ago. They appeared to be eager to get started this morning.

By Thursday, the team was rolling along, and we were all surprised at the amount of progress made. On Friday morning, the team had already worked well through this week's agenda. I anticipated getting a lot done on the portfolios over the weekend. We agreed to knock off early so everyone could get to their weekend plans. I grabbed an Uber back to the hotel.

It was almost four p.m. when the Uber driver dropped me at my hotel. When he pulled up to the hotel, I was almost wishing I'd gone to get something to eat. *Oh well, I can have something delivered later.* I needed to go in and call Eide anyways; I hadn't been able to connect with her this week and she left two more messages. She was going to yell at me for sure; especially since one of her messages said she was worried about me or something. *If I don't call her and alleviate her concerns soon, she was going to send the posse after me,* I thought, walking through the hotel lobby. As I got partway through the lobby, I happened to look over. I thought for sure Owen was sitting in a chair reading a magazine. "Owen?" I mumbled. *Really,* I thought, looking again.

"Owen?" I said, smiling. "What are you doing here?"

"What's a guy gotta do to take a pretty girl on a date? We had plans for this weekend, and you canceled on me," he said, pointing at me with a stern, ornery look on his face. "Besides, tomorrow's my birthday," Owen said as he put his arms around my midsection, hugging me close.

"Oh, my goodness, you came all this way to see me. And wait, it's your birthday. Did I know about this?"

"I don't think so," Owen said, shaking his head. "I was thinking on the flight this afternoon; I don't even know when your birthday is. Why have we never talked about this?"

"I don't know. This is so awesome, Owen. Did you talk to Eide?"

"Not this time, why?"

"Oh, she left me a message a couple days ago about being worried about me or something, and I haven't been able to connect back up with her."

"Well, you better get her called if she's worried about you; you know how she is."

"Yes, I do. I was going up to call her, but a certain handsome Coloradoan detained me. I'll go call her and freshen up and then we can head out. Will that work for you?"

"Yep, I'll be waiting for you," Owen said as he sat back down.

"Your birthday," I said, shaking my head as I walked away. *Good job, Karla. How'd you let this happen*, I thought as I headed towards the elevators.

"Hi, I'm back," I said as I walked up to Owen. I couldn't believe it, was Owen really here? Nobody ever flew in to see me when I traveled for work.

"Good, is Eide alright?"

"She was relieved to know I haven't fallen in the ocean this week. I swear she has a sixth sense, which is not always a good thing."

"Apparently, you didn't tell her I was down here waiting for you?"

"No, not yet" I said sheepishly to Owen.

"Is that a good idea?"

"At the moment, yes. Where shall we go?"

"You pick," Owen said as he held out his hand in a gesture for me to go ahead of him. "You're the one that's been hanging out in this town."

"Oh, I don't know about hanging out in this town. All I know about is the route to my client's office, and I don't recommend that, all business. I've never gone out when I was here."

"Karla," Owen said, sounding goofy, putting his hands on his face looking shocked. "It's time you lived a little."

"Come on, ya goof," I said, laughing and taking his hand. "Let's check with the concierge and get a recommendation." Out of the suggestions the concierge offered, the Fisherman's Wharf sounded the most fun. We grabbed an Uber and left the hotel. Riding along in the cab, I thought, *how awesome is this to be having a date night with Owen in San Francisco.* I've never been with a guy that flew three-plus hours just to spend the weekend with me, no matter the reason. Most of the guys I've dated never really cared whether I was in town or not.

55

"It says on the website, there's a place called the Fish House—would you like to eat there?" Owen asked.

"That sounds great to me. I haven't had anything to eat since this morning."

We were seated and the waiter brought us each a lemon water and told us the special of the day was catfish and rice pilaf.

We both chose the special and the waiter took our order and left the table. Being on the ocean the fresh fish seemed like a no-brainer.

"I'm looking forward to this catfish," Owen commented after the waiter left with our orders.

"I know, right." Owen and I discussed some possible sights to see tomorrow.

The waiter arrived with our meals, and we continued our chat and made plans for the next day.

"This fish isn't as good as I thought it would be. How's yours?"

"Ah yea, they did something a little weird with it," Owen said, looking over the piece of fish he had stuck on his fork, looking like he was debating the next bite.

I decided not to finish mine and I think Owen was planning to leave the rest of his on his plate.

I think I've had a better fish at Wendy's," Owen commented as we prepared to leave.

I know, what a letdown.

After Owen paid, we walked along the pier. I noticed the view off the pier, it was just incredible. All the boats anchored around the Golden Gate Bridge were a sight to see. "Wow, Owen. Look at the Golden Gate Bridge in the setting sun; it's just beautiful."

"Oh, that is some view, stay right there," Owen said, backing up and pulling his phone out. "Say cheese."

"OK, your turn now."

"How about one together?" Owen said, positioning himself next to me. "OK, ready?" I smiled at Owen as he snapped the selfie.

When we finished with the pictures; Owen took hold of my hand as we strolled further down the pier.

56

The next morning, I woke up to the sun shining bright into my hotel room window. It was going to be a great day. I sent Owen a "Happy Birthday" text with party balloons and a cake emoji. I couldn't believe I was just learning it was Owen's birthday. This surely constitutes as bad girlfriend move #42. Owen texted back and said he wanted chocolate cake for breakfast, and I better hurry up.

Owen and I took an Uber across the Golden Gate Bridge as the morning sun reflected across the San Francisco Bay. It was beautiful and almost made me think I was dreaming. *Owen was here,* I giddily thought to myself again. I wanted to pinch myself; this was so great.

Later we had the Uber driver stop off at the Cake Gallery to pick up some chocolate cake.

We went to Golden Gate Park and walked through, enjoying the sights, the Prayer Cross, and the Oak Woodland Towers. Both were breathtaking.

"Oh, wow, Karla, have you ever seen such giant windmills?" Owen asked as he pointed them out.

The park was beautiful and not like the ones back home. We found some park benches in a quiet area and took a seat to dive into the cake we'd gotten earlier. All the reviews claimed the Cake Gallery had the best cake in all California.

"Alright, Karla, when's your birthday?" Owen asked as he stabbed into a piece of cake.

"I celebrate my birthday with fireworks," I said, smirking back at Owen.

"Nice!" Owen said. "Wait a minute, we had a date right around then."

"Hmm yea."

On Sunday, Owen and I visited a few different places in the morning and returned to the Fisherman's Wharf, forgoing the Fish House this time. We both really enjoyed the views and walking along the pier.

"I hate to ask, but do you have a flight today?"

"No," Owen said, taking a drink of his lemon water. "I have a flight tomorrow mid-morning."

"Oh good, I was almost afraid to ask if you had to hurry to the airport, yet this afternoon."

"No, I want to see you off to work and then I'll go to the airport."

We walked around the pier and looked in some of the shops that afternoon and then headed back to the hotel just as the sun was setting.

"Good morning, handsome," I said, walking up behind Owen as he stood in the breakfast area waiting for me.

"Hey beautiful, good morning," Owen said, casually taking me in his arms.

"Wow, Monday rolled around way too fast," I whined as I laid my head on Owen's shoulder.

"Yes, it certainly did, but hey, it's that much quicker until you get home."

We grabbed our breakfast and sat in a breakfast nook for a short time. Before too long, Owen and I were standing in front of the hotel waiting for our Ubers. Owen hugged me tightly, saying goodbye.

"So, when are you coming home?"

"If things go as well as they did last week, I should be able to finish up Wednesday afternoon or Thursday morning."

"That's great. I'll be waiting for you," Owen said as he moved in, pressing his lips against mine. Oh, my, Owen's kissing is almost dangerous, such passion in that man.

"That might just be able to hold me tight until you get home," Owen said, stepping out of our embrace. "Let me know when your flight is, and I'll meet you at the airport."

"I will, thanks for a great weekend; I hope you had a great birthday."

"It was one of the best, thanks to you. Bye, see you soon."

"Bye, Owen," I said as I got into my Uber.

Ms. Lindstedt and her team were deeply committed to this project, and it showed in their work, more ways than one. We completed the project on Wednesday afternoon. Riding in the Uber back to the hotel, I changed my ticket to get a flight home today, which turns out I would land around eleven-thirty tonight. Once the Uber driver was on the way to the airport, I sent Owen a text.

58

"Hey Owen, I'm headed home today. My flight lands around eleven-thirty tonight. If that doesn't work for you, that's OK, just let me know so I can get a ride."

Owen sent me a GIF message back of two people dancing, followed by another text: *"I'll be there."*

Waiting at baggage claim, I sent Owen a text. *"Headed to baggage claim, be out shortly."*

"Hey gorgeous, I'm out front."

"Hey, good-looking," I said, stepping out into the chilly night air. Fall has definitely settled in.

"You got all your things?" Owen asked as he put my bags in the back.

"Yes, thanks."

"Oh, come here, you, it's great to see you," Owen said, swinging me around.

We chatted all the way home about our time in San Francisco and how great it was. We also discussed Levi and Eide's wedding, which was rapidly approaching.

"Owen, thanks for picking me up, it's going to make a short night for you to get to work tomorrow."

"It's all good, I told you I'd pick you up. I like hanging out with you, even if it's an airport pickup/drop off."

As we stood in the driveway at my house talking, I looked up and noticed a light on in a back upstairs bedroom. Owen must have noticed me tense up, knowing something wasn't quite right.

"Everything OK, Karla?"

"That's odd, I don't even remember the last time I was in that room," I said, looking back at the lighted window.

"I'll take your luggage in and check things out."

I stared at the window for a moment. "No," I said, shaking my head. "It's fine. I was probably just careless."

Owen picked up my luggage and carried them to the front door and set them in the foyer. "Are you sure you don't want me to go upstairs and have a look around?"

"I'm good, it's nothing. Thank you, though."

"Alright, call me if you need anything. Let's get together tomorrow, OK?"

"Sounds great. Good night, Owen."

"Night, Karla," Owen said hesitantly as he looked around behind me and then reluctantly stepped out into the cool night air.

I took my bags upstairs and started to unpack, but quickly decided it could wait until tomorrow. It had been a long day and I was tired. I crawled into bed a few minutes later after washing my face and brushing my teeth.

I must have drifted off to sleep quickly. I woke up later to what sounded like the front door opening and closing. *What was that? This was crazy, I must be exhausted*, I thought sitting up in bed. I don't even know if I could hear the front door open and close from up here. *Go back to sleep, weirdo*, I thought, rolling over.

Several hours later, I woke to the same sound. *This is crazy*, I thought, looking at my watch. It was near six in the morning—why would I think the front door was opening and closing again?

I got up and went downstairs to check the front door, just to be on the safe side. The door was locked and seemed fine. I contemplated going back to bed, but then I remembered the light was on. I figured I might as well get with it, I had laundry and unpacking to do, too.

I got upstairs and opened the door to the back bedroom to flip the light off. When I opened the door, I was confused. The light was already off. *It was off*, I thought, staring into a dark room. Did the bulb burn out? I flipped the switch, testing it and instantly the room was bathed in light. *This is just weird.* Apparently, I was just very tired last night—I don't even know when I was last here. I closed the door, shaking my head.

Later, I was sitting in the living room, folding laundry, when my phone rang. I grabbed it, putting it on speaker and continued with the laundry.

"Hello, Eide."

"Hey Karla, how's it going? I won't keep you too long, I know you're at work. Where you at, anyways? I can't keep up?"

"I'm good, I'm home. I was in San Francisco, but I caught a flight home last night."

"Oh, good."

"I was supposed to hang out with Owen last weekend, but I had to cancel for this client. Well, as I was coming into the hotel Friday, who should be sitting in the hotel lobby, Owen!"

"No way, he flew to San Francisco for a Friday night date?"

"Yes, well, he stayed all weekend and left Monday. Saturday was his birthday, so we did a bunch of sightseeing, it was great."

"And here I was all worried about you, Turd! I guess you got Mr. Right following after you. Good grief, I don't think Levi's ever traipsed after me before," Eide whined a little.

"Come on, you're getting married. I'm sure Levi's done plenty of traipsing for your benefit."

"He has. Anyways, I really did call for something besides getting sucked down the Owen rabbit hole."

"The Owen rabbit hole!" I laughed. "So, what's up, Eide?"

"Wedding shopping. It's already November; the wedding's going to be here before we know it."

"Yes, ma'am, what's the plan?"

"Probably just go into Denver, if that works for you and Molly and hopefully Laurel."

"Yes, that will be great. Mom'll go," I said, laughing. "Now that she's convinced, you're not dragging her baby off to a cheap Vegas love chapel!"

"I think she will, too," Eide said. "I've talked to her a few times—she and I've been working on details since you're never home. What's your schedule like?"

", I'm kind of hoping it will be slow until January. Not a lot of clients want to beef up their marketing plans at the end of the year. And then I put in my vacation for your wedding."

"Good, we have all kinds of things to do for this wedding. What are you doing today?"

"I'm cleaning my house and doing laundry. Later I'm going to meet up with Owen, so no, I can't meet up with you."

"Ah, seriously, did you just ditch me?"

"Yea," I said, chuckling. "I think I kinda did."

"Ah, I am so hurt. Not even for a coffee? You have coffee all the time with Owen."

"Not today, I got in late last night and I need to finish cleaning the house. It's a pit. How about we tentatively plan to go shopping right after Thanksgiving?"

"What, why that long?"

"This weekend I'm going out with Owen and next week is Thanksgiving. Do you really want to shop Thanksgiving weekend?"

"Yea, you're right."

"I know I am, and now I'm going to hang up."

"Oh fine, bye Karla."

"Bye Eide, thanks for calling."

Chapter 7

Owen and I had tickets to a play at the theatre from my boss. We planned to get dinner afterward and I assumed he would be early as usual. I needed to hurry my butt up, so there was some resemblance that I could get myself ready. I hadn't even gotten in the shower at this point.

I finished up in the shower and picked out a dress that didn't make me look too frumpy. I really needed to find some new clothes. *These are so old school; it's a wonder Eide didn't throw them out when I moved here last spring. This is pathetic, I don't even have any good dating attire. Maybe when we go wedding shopping, I can pick up a few things.*

I actually managed to get myself ready before Owen rang the doorbell tonight.

"Hey, good-looking," I said, opening the door.

"Oh wow, who cares about good-looking, you look terrific, Karla. This dress looks fabulous on you."

"I literally just pulled this out of my closet. I feel like my wardrobe needs a little updating."

"Well, don't let this little number get away!" Owen said, taking my hand, twirling me around.

"That's kind of you to say, but we need to go if we're going to make it to the theatre on time."

A few hours later Owen and I walked into the restaurant following the play.

"The tickets were a nice gesture, but that play wasn't very good."

"Well, I didn't want to say anything because it was a work thing," Owen said. "I wasn't that impressed; it's two hours we're never getting back."

"Isn't that the truth," I chuckled.

"Oh, and what was up with that guy that kept trying to talk to you? Did he sit next to you that long?"

"Oh geez, yes—you also notice I didn't talk to him, either? That was Curt Townsend, one of the company's procurement specialists. Let's just say he's better off buying someplace else and I'm grateful I don't have an office down the hall from him." *I sat down the hall from him for years, even after,* I thought, trailing off.

"So, I take it you used to date this feller?"

"I did, sad as that may be. But I haven't seen him since the office closed and we hadn't been on a date since long before that."

"I see. Well, I don't think the guys over you, yet." Owen said with a questioning look.

"Oh, well that's no longer my problem. Let's not discuss this anymore. Do you have plans for Thanksgiving?" I asked Owen.

"Well, I usually just go to my parents'. See some cousins, that sort of thing, but I could be easily persuaded to change my mind this year. Do you have any plans?"

"I don't know yet; we usually try and work our plans out around Molly's work schedule. She doesn't like to ask off for holidays."

"You could always go visit my parents with me," Owen said, looking excited.

"That sounds nice. You didn't mention your brother, though. What about him?"

"Right, if you're going, I think I'll tell him to stay home this year."

"Owen."

"No," Owen said, laughing. "It's the wife's holiday. They take turns with the in-laws; they'll be at the farm for Christmas this year."

"When are you leaving?"

"That could be negotiated; you make plans with your family, and we'll work around that."

"Serious, you want to take me home to meet your family?"

"Of course, why are you so surprised?"

"I don't know, just surprised," I said, smiling at Owen. We finished our meal and left the restaurant.

"Can I pick you up for church in the morning?" Owen asked, standing in my foyer after we'd made it back. Owen was exploring my lips. He held me in a light embrace, finding his way across my lips.

"That'd be great, does it come with a side of coffee?" I asked Owen, when he stood back and just had a hold of my hand, before saying good night.

"Absolutely, it is our Sunday standby. Good night, Karla," Owen said, finding his way back to my lips and placing a delicate kiss on my lips. He moved back, let go of my hand and walked out into the snowy night air. Owen's kiss had left me speechless; there was so much passion in him waiting to erupt I couldn't speak or move. I couldn't even tell him good night. Owen turned back and looked at me for a second with those dark, bold eyes shining.

I finally went into the house, almost too weak to move after Owen drove off.

Owen took my hand as we walked into church that morning and took a seat next to Levi and Eide. Eide reached over and half-hugged me. "Good morning, guys," Eide said, looking from me to Owen.

Molly and Lane and Mom and Dad came in and sat behind us and we all exchanged a quick greeting as the service started. Pastor Tim stepped up to the pulpit; his message this morning reminded us to count our blessings for Thanksgiving and every day. We should be mindful and grateful of not only the coming holiday this week but every day. Pastor Tim recited several passages from Psalms, but I think my favorite was Psalms 66: "Shout joyfully to God, all the earth!" *I for one wanted to shout joyfully!*

Pastor Tim closed his sermon, blessing us all and wishing us all a grateful and Christ-filled Thanksgiving; he followed with the benediction. We turned around and chatted a minute with Mom and Dad and then headed out of the church.

Owen asked me on the way out of church what I had planned for the afternoon and wanted to know if I wanted to go see a movie? We could go or we could get a rental and see one at home.

As we were discussing, Lane and Molly came out and caught up with us.

"Hey guys!" Molly said. "What up? Would you like to grab some lunch with us? I think Levi and Eide are going to join us."

"That sounds great," Owen said, looking expectantly at me.

"Absolutely, sounds great."

"Meet you there shortly," Lane said.

"OK," Owen said.

We walked into the restaurant and Owen told the waitress we were meeting some people here. The waitress directed us to a table in the corner.

"Hey guys. Didn't Pastor Tim have a nice message this morning?"

"He did," Molly said. "I always like when he reads from the Psalms."

"Me too."

"How's everyone doing?" Owen asked after holding my chair as I sat down.

Eide started in, discussing wedding preparations. "Can you guys still go in two weeks?"

"Sure can, Eide," Molly said.

"Whoa, hold up, gals; I hate to interrupt," Owen said, looking at us. "I have something I want to ask first."

"Of course," Eide said. "What's up?"

"More a question for Molly. Karla said you'd have to check your work schedule to figure out holiday plans. Do you know what you're working for Thanksgiving?"

"Well, let me look," Molly said, pulling her phone out of her purse. "I'm pretty sure I work Thanksgiving Day."

"What do you two have planned?" Eide questioned us as Molly scrolled around on her phone.

"I work Wednesday, Thursday, Friday," Molly said before either of us could answer Eide.

"Perfect, we could do Thanksgiving, Saturday, at my house."

"I'm good with anything I don't have to cook. What do you two think you're up to?" Eide questioned us again.

"Let me text Mom and Dad," I said, ignoring Eide's question again.

"What exactly are you two planning?" Eide asked again, sternly.

"Owen asked me to visit his family. Mom just texted back and said they were going to Aunt Jane's for Thanksgiving and won't be back until Saturday night. You guys want to meet Sunday?"

"Yep, works here," Eide said.

"Molly?"

"Yep, we're square, just tell me what to bring."

"Well, yeah, me too," Eide said reluctantly.

"I'll bring the turkey." Levi said.

"Oh, well. there ya go, you're off the hook, Eide. Levi's got ya covered. Anybody talk to Garratt recently? I just sent him a text about Thanksgiving, and he hasn't responded."

"No," Lane said, shaking his head. "He's been MIA recently; let me know if you get a reply."

"Now, let's talk wedding," Eide said. "You two think you can pull yourselves away from your busy, fabulous lives?"

"Oh, geez, Eids. You sure got the busy part right but the fabulous is a bit off. I don't know, this Thanksgiving dinner might just kill me; I might not be recovered."

"Oh, stop it, you're not getting out of it."

We finished our lunch and Molly said she needed to go get ready for work. We all agreed it was time to go; Owen said he needed to let Arnold out.

Eide hollered back and shook her arm in the air to us as we left the restaurant. "Have fun at Thanksgiving—we'll see you Sunday. I want details."

"Eide's crazy," Owen said, shaking his head and smiling as he drove out of the parking lot.

"I know, she must make it her goal to embarrass us. Oh Eide," I sighed. "Are you sure you want to take me home to meet your family?" I asked Owen.

"Oh, heck yeah! How about we leave Wednesday, about nine a.m.?"

"I'll be ready," I told Owen as he slowly leaned in for a kiss. Owen's kisses can really knock a girl into oblivion. I barely made it across the threshold letting myself in the front door.

I heard the doorbell ring as I was working on my hair. No way, Owen, what are you doing here this early? We agreed to leave about nine, not about eight; *he must be excited*, I thought as I rushed downstairs.

"Good morning, Owen!" I said to him as I pulled the door open. "Listen here, pal, we're going to have to synchronize our times. You're early, I'm late; you'd think we'd meet somewhere in the middle."

"Hi," Owen said as I attempted to run back upstairs. "I'll meet you in the middle anytime," Owen said as he grabbed my arm, stopping me mid-flight.

"Are you a little anxious to get going?"

"Yea, a little," Owen said, chuckling. "A road trip with you. What's not to look forward to?" Owen asked as he flashed his crooked smile at me.

"I might embarrass your family."

"Not a chance, you forget about who their son is. They've had practice. Just don't ask Ma and Dad to tell you about the practice runs; I don't need them to give you any ideas."

"Bahahaha! I gotta finish getting ready," I said, backing out of Owen's embrace and ran back up the stairs.

Owen hit the interstate as the sun was peeking out on an otherwise cloudy day. "Would you like music or podcast?" Owen asked.

"What's on the podcast list?"

"Here check it out for yourself." Owen said handing me his phone.

"Well, we got Serial Killer, Crime Junkie, Motive for Murder."

"Geez, Karla, a little dark, wouldn't you say?"

"Well, I don't think we want one that talks about finances; we'll fall asleep."

"Good point," Owen said.

We were a few hours down the interstate and still had to cross the Pikes Peak region. It was fun road-tripping with Owen. We talked a lot, listened to a podcast about talking with God. We even jammed out to tunes from the '60s and '70s. We stopped at a small market to get some sandwiches and then got back on the road.

"It's not much further," Owen said. "I don't like walking in the door saying, 'hey Ma, ya got any lunch for me?' So, I always stop here and get a sandwich."

"This is great, thanks Owen."

Owen was right, it wasn't much longer, and we arrived at his parents'. As Owen drove down the drive, I glanced over and there sat the most beautiful and magnificent barn. "Oh, my, Owen. That's some barn, whose is it?"

"Dad and Mom's."

"It's so beautiful."

"Yeah, it is," Owen said, nonchalantly.

As Owen came to a stop and put his pickup in park, two older folks stepped out onto the porch. They looked like a wonderful couple. Arnold was excitedly trying to get out. He couldn't wait for Owen to open the backdoor. He crawled across the console and he and Owen were getting tangled in Owen's arm.

"Alright, alright, ya crazy dog, here ya go."

"Hey guys," Dad said as he and Ma moved closer to my pickup after I was able to let Arnold out.

"Hi Ma, Dad."

"Ma, Dad, this is Karla Grainer, the woman I told you about."

"Karla this is my folks, Joe and Rosie Kaster."

"Hi Karla, glad to meet you. Nice that you could join us for Thanksgiving," Ma said, shaking her hand and then extending Karla a hug.

"Nice of you to have me, Mrs. Kaster."

"Thank you and call me Rosie. Owen says you're a marketing expert."

"Ah, well, I work for a marketing firm in Denver. I'm not so sure about the expert part."

"She flies all over the place and helps these companies market their products. So yeah, she's kind of a big deal."

"Owen, it's not that big of a deal."

"Well, come on inside, you two, you don't have to sell us on your girlfriend, Owen. We like her, she can stay."

I dang near crawled under the pickup. I figured this was only the beginning with the old man.

"Can I get anybody anything to drink?" Rosie asked as we sat down at the kitchen table. "I have tea, water, coffee, soda."

Karla and I unanimously answered with coffee.

"Oh, you're one of those, too," Rosie smirked.

"One of those?" Karla asked, looking at me confused.

"Yes, Owen's a coffeeholic, I usually never have enough coffee around when he comes to visit; it's kind of a family joke."

"MA!"

"Owen told me once he drinks gallons of it; I did find that to be a bit of an understatement, but not by much."

"Sounds like you've slowed down a bit, son. I remember in high school, Owen and his friends would stop at the Burger Barn—the other kids drank pop, and this kid was over here pouring down coffee like an eighty-year-old man."

"Thanks Dad! I wasn't that bad."

"Oh, I don't know, you've been pretty addicted."

"Seriously, Dad," I said, laughing.

"Oh, he's a good kid," Dad told Karla, grabbing my shoulder, shaking it a bit.

"Yeah, you hear that, Karla, I'm a good kid!"

"Grab your coffee, Owen. I want to show you something in the barn."

"Oh no, he's taking me out to the barn, now," I laughed at Dad, as he and I headed out to the porch. "You ladies enjoy chatting, and no more Owen memes, they're bad for my ego!"

His mom and I were both laughing at Owen when he went out the door with his dad.

"You have a beautiful home, Mrs. Kaster."

"Rosie, please, and thank you. It's been our home for nearly forty years now."

"Oh wow, forty years. That's an incredible feat."

"Yes, Joe bought this farm right before we got married."

"Ah, that's wonderful, and I noticed that barn out there when we first arrived—it's magnificent."

"Oh yes, Joe has done a lot of work out there in that barn over the years and run quite a bit of livestock through there."

"Does he have any livestock right now?"

"Just a few calves; nothing like he used to. He works on plane repairs mostly now. Joe and Owen both share a love for planes."

"Owen doesn't really talk about his work much; I gather it's pretty stressful."

"It might be, but he's very good at what he does. He's seen some tough stuff, but I think you've helped with that," Rosie said.

"Me, I don't even know much about what he does."

"I can tell a difference when we talk, he has a different sound to his voice, now. Especially when he started talking about you."

"Dad wants to know if you ladies want to ride along, into town," Owen asked when came in from the barn a while later.

"What's going on in town?" I asked him.

"Oh, I don't know. I think Dad has some errands to run. It's kinda his and Ma's thing, they ride around together.

"Yea, OK, sounds good. Can we visit any of your old haunts?"

"Actually, we mostly hung out in the barn," I said as we walked out the door. "My Dad's had various plane parts in there over the years and my friends and I thought they were cool; so, I didn't spend a lot of time in town after school."

Joe asked Rosie if she needed anything at the store for the Thanksgiving dinner when we got to town.

"I think I'm covered," Rosie told Joe. We drove around town a little; Joe made mention of a few things in town to Owen and then afterward we made a stop at the feed store and headed back to the farm. We had been in town about a half hour, I saw one gas station and no stoplights; it was a cute, charming town.

The next morning, I woke up and could hear quite a bit of activity going on out in the kitchen. I quickly got dressed and went to see if I could help. I figured Rosie was preparing Thanksgiving dinner.

"Good morning, Rosie."

"Good morning, Karla. How'd you sleep?"

"Oh, like a dream; it's so nice here. Are you working on dinner preparations?"

"Yes, a little here and there."

"Can I help with anything?"

"Yes, actually would you like to make the pie fillings?"

"Sure."

71

"What is your family doing today?" Rosie asked as I cooked peaches on the stove for a peach pie.

"I think they're all scattered a bit today. My brother's girlfriend Molly is an ER nurse, and a lot of her co-workers have kids, so she doesn't usually ask for holidays off. We just schedule our holidays around her work schedule."

"That's nice of her."

"My parents are at my aunt's house for a couple days; I'm not sure what my brothers are doing, they might just be catching football games. We're all going to have dinner at my house on Sunday."

"I'm glad you came with Owen," Rosie said, smiling fondly. "I think he was looking forward to it."

"Oh, I know he was looking forward to it," I said, chuckling. "He told me we'd leave about nine and I think he was at my house forty-five minutes early; raring to go! So, are Owen's aunts and uncles coming today?"

"Yes, some of them, they'll come today and stay through tomorrow or Saturday."

"Is this Joe's siblings or yours?"

"Both Joe's brother and my brother and sister and their spouses and a few of their kids are coming."

"You'll have a full house, then?"

"Oh, yes, but that is just fine by me. I certainly enjoy the holidays."

"Do you both have any other siblings?"

"I do, Joe just has the one brother. I have a sister living in the Philippines; we don't see her and her husband very often. We exchange emails quite often, though."

We had the meal just as good as ready when Owen came into the kitchen and said Aunt Kate and Uncle Martin were coming down the drive.

"Are any of their kids or grandkids with them?" Rosie asked.

"I don't know."

When Rosie and I followed Owen out onto the porch, there were five vehicles pulling into the yard.

"Time for a party," Owen said, putting his arm around me. "Just remember I warned you!"

72

"Oh stop," I said, slapping him playfully. "Your mom's been telling me about your family—they sound wonderful and I'm excited to meet them."

Everyone filed into Joe and Rosie's house and Owen started introductions. We eventually moved ourselves to Rosie's dining room and sat down to eat. Joe led everyone in a blessing over the meal.

"Bless us, O Lord, for the meal we are about to receive, we thank you for looking out for everyone traveling out here to the farm to join us for this blessed holiday. We ask that you bless us all over the next few weeks as we focus on your son's birth and keep your wisdom by our side. In your name we pray, Amen."

"Thank you, Joe," Rosie said. "Now everyone, dig in, there's plenty."

"Rosie, everything looks so delicious," Kate said. "I always enjoy coming here. You do such a wonderful job."

"I had some help this year, Karla helped me. I appreciated the help, and it was nice having someone in the kitchen to visit with."

"Oh, well, don't let this one get away, Owen, it's hard to find someone who can cook."

"Don't worry, Martin, she's not going anywhere. I drove her here."

Owen's comment prompted a round of chuckles from everyone including me, but really, I didn't have any reason to get away, I'm pretty content!

After the meal was over, Rosie and Owen's aunts and I went into the kitchen to clean up the dishes.

Owen's aunts tried to convince us that since we'd cooked all morning, we were off dish duty. It was nice visiting with these ladies while we all pitched in and had the kitchen cleaned up in no time.

That evening, everyone was sitting around Joe and Rosie's living room, probably devouring our third piece of pie. I think there were at least three separate conversations going on; there was a lot of

73

energy in this room. Owen leaned over and softly whispered in my ear, "Karla, would you like to go for a walk?"

"Owen, the girl doesn't need exercise," Joe said. "If you want to go hide out by the barn and kiss her; why don't you just announce that?" Joe's comment grabbed the attention of everyone in the room; they stopped their chit-chatting and clued themselves into what Owen and I were going to do.

"Thanks Dad, nice one."

"You're welcome."

The whole room was roaring with laughter.

I got up and stood beside Owen, holding my hand out. "I'd love a walk. I've eaten like eight pieces of pie today and sharing a kiss with you under the stars would just be the icing!"

Owen and I walked out to the porch, grabbed our jackets, and went outside. It was pretty chilly.

"Sorry about my dad's antics," Owen said, taking my hand in his.

"Are you kidding me! Don't be sorry, you've met my family?"

Owen wrapped his arms around me, holding me in his embrace. We didn't really see much of the stars, standing in the shadows of the moon. I'm not really sure if there were even stars shining in the sky. My focus was on Owen and his deep, luscious eyes.

"Shh," Owen said, sealing his lips around mine, holding it there, nibbling and pulling away at my bottom lip. Owen's kisses could set off a fire in the field behind me that would rage for days, it made me want to stand there and be held by him all night.

Owen stood back looking at me and released a breath of air and moved a wisp of hair from my forehead. "You're more than worth the grief I get from my dad."

The next morning, I heard quite a bit of activity in the kitchen again and decided Owen's mom and aunts must be having coffee. I got dressed in a nice pair of jeans and a cute sweater and went out to the kitchen to see what was going on.

"Good morning, ladies," I said, walking into the kitchen where they were all chatting.

"Good morning, Karla. Owen's out in the barn with the guys." Rosie said.

"That's OK. I'm fine having coffee with you ladies."

74

"Actually, Owen wanted you to get some coffee to go and meet him out in the barn, he's taking you on a little trip this morning," Rosie said as she coaxed me out the door. I could hear Owen's aunts speculating what Owen was up to; I, too, wondered the same thing.

"Thanks for the coffee, Rosie. I guess we'll see you later."

"Hey guys," I said as I walked into the barn. "Joe, you have a really great barn, here."

"Thanks, Karla."

"Good morning, beautiful," Owen whispered in my ear as he walked up and took the coffee, I'd handed him while slipping his arm around me.

"You know that's like his fourth cup of coffee this morning, Karla," Joe said, chuckling.

"Actually Dad, it might be my fifth."

"So, where we are going since you're all gassed up and ready to go?"

"Oh, a smart aleck you got there, Owen," Joe said as all the guys chuckled.

"On that note, goodbye everyone," Owen said, shaking his head again. "We'll see you all in a few hours."

"Bye," I said, following Owen out of the barn.

We drove away from the farm and out to the highway. Once we got to the highway Owen turned south.

"You're not taking me to Mexico; it's a little early for the wedding."

"No, we're not going to Mexico—my dad's right, you are a smart aleck. We're going out to the Flight School. Is that all right?"

"Are you going to take me flying?" I asked expectantly and excitedly.

"Would you like to go flying?" Owen asked, smiling at my excitement.

"Yes, yes, please. I mean I fly all the time, but not with you."

"I arranged to have a buddy of mine meet us here to use one of his planes," Owen said driving into the hangar airfield.

We drove up to the hangar and there was a young guy who jumped out of a jeep and walked over to Owen's side barely before

Owen put his pickup in park. Obviously, this friend was excited to see Owen.

"Hey, Owe! Good to see ya."

"Ty, how ya been?" Owen asked, shaking his hand.

"Doing good. Glad you texted me this morning; wondered when I was going to hear from you."

"How's the rescue business?"

"It's OK. Ty, there's someone I'd like you to meet. This is my girlfriend, Karla. Karla, this my good buddy, Ty."

"Hi Karla, nice to meet you. Did I hear you correctly there, Owe? Did you say this lovely young lady's your girlfriend? Are you telling me you found someone to put up with you longer than five minutes?" Ty stood next to Owen's pickup with a big smirk on his face, chuckling at his banter with Owen.

"Ah ha ha, funny," Owen said as he started getting out of the pickup.

"Yeah, I know I am. So, you guys going up this morning?"

"Yea, that'd be great."

Owen and Ty walked into the hangar, discussing a pre-flight check. I stood off to the side and watched Owen and Ty. It was incredible, they were like little machines, each one listing off what they'd taken care of; it was obvious Owen and Ty had worked together a lot and knew each other's routines.

"Are you ready to go?" Owen asked, breaking into my thoughts and taking my hand.

"Ever since we left the farm!"

"Well, alrighty then, let's go!"

"Owen, I've never flown in the cockpit before," I said, boarding the plane.

"I didn't figure you had. You can hardly see anything sitting in those commercial flights."

Owen prepared for takeoff and radioed into somewhere talking pilot talk.

"Owen this is awesome, the mountains are beautiful from up here."

We could see snow-capped mountains, rugged terrain, canyons and cliffs and frozen rivers. It was so breathtakingly beautiful. This was a whole new view of the mountains; I was completely taken by the beauty and rugged terrain and snow-cast trees standing like statues down there.

"Owen, how come you don't have your own plane—you could do this all the time?"

"It costs a lot of money to maintain a small plane like this for pleasure."

"How was it?" Ty asked when we climbed out of the plane, after Owen landed out behind the Flight School a few hours later.

"I enjoyed every moment of our flight across the mesas. It was so beautiful," I told Ty before Owen could answer otherwise. "That's a fabulous view up there."

"I think she liked it, Ty," Owen said, smiling at my excitement.

"Yep, looks like you got some brownie points on this one," Ty said jokingly.

"Well look at the time, better get back, Ma'll have lunch ready," Owen said. "Thanks for letting us use the plane."

"Anytime you want, Owe. You know that."

As Owen drove back to the farm, I thought about Owen and Ty. "You and Ty seem to go way back. He must be a good friend."

"Oh, you have no idea how far Ty and I go back," Owen said, seemingly lost in thought.

I could see the look on Owen's face—he and Ty had some history. I wondered about them: are they still as good of friends?

On Saturday afternoon, after about seven more pieces of pie and another five turkey sandwiches, Owen and I packed up to head for home.

Rosie had what looked like half her kitchen packed up and sitting on the counter when we walked through to load our luggage.

"Whatcha you got going on here, Ma?" Owen asked Rosie.

"Go put your bags in the pickup and then I'll explain."

Owen and I came back into Rosie's kitchen after loading our bags. "OK first, here's a cup of coffee for you both."

"Ah, thanks, Rosie, you read my mind."

"Yea, thanks, Ma, although Dad would just say you're feeding my habit!"

"Yes, I know. All right, there's three whole pies in here—Joe and I are certainly not going to eat them."

"Speak for yourself, Rosie, dear," I heard Owen's dad mutter as he sat down at the table.

"Karla, you take them for your family dinner tomorrow."

"Are you sure, Rosie? You don't have friends stopping by this week you'll need a dessert for?"

"Heavens no," Rosie said. "After this holiday I'm swearing off desserts for a while and so is Joe."

"This bags for you, Owen, there's some lunchboxes for you. You can have them this week or they can go in the freezer."

"Oh, nice, Ma!"

"And this bags for you, Karla," Rosie said, handing me a bag bigger than Owen's. "These are leftover salads from our dinner. I thought you could supplement them for your dinner tomorrow and you might not have to cook quite so much when you get home."

"Ah, Rosie, this is too much. You should keep these; you and Joe would have things for lunch this week."

"Uh huh, and the next and the next," Rosie chortled. "I have a few leftovers. But all this would just go to waste with just us two."

"This is very nice, Rosie. I'll be sure and get your containers back to you."

"Oh, I'm counting on it. A personal delivery, I insist. I want you to come back, anytime," Rosie said as she stepped up to hug me.

"We will, Ma." Owen said. "We'll be back for Christmas," Owen said, looking at me for verification.

"Thank you for everything, Rosie, it was nice meeting you."

I turned to say goodbye to Joe, sitting at the kitchen table. "Joe, thank you for everything. But I guess with no containers to return, well, this is it."

"Well lucky for me, Owen's pretty fond of you and after nearly thirty years Rosie's stuck with me, so when you guys bring those containers back, I'm likely to be here."

"Well good, I'd hate to miss you!"

"We better get on the road," Owen said. "Bye Ma, bye Dad."

"Bye son," Rosie said as she stepped up to hug us again.

"You guys be careful, love you," Rosie said as we headed out the door.

"We will, love you, too," Owen said.

We headed down the highway. I looked out across the mountains; it had snowed lightly this morning and the trees and mountain tops were glistening. Reminded me how close to Christmas we were.

"So, you survived my family—well, almost all of them," Owen said.

"It was great. I bet your brother's a big ole teddy bear; I'm looking forward to meeting him at Christmas."

"Yea, with the stuffing ripped out," Owen said laughing. "What time is your family getting together tomorrow?"

"Probably sometime after church."

"Can I come before church and help you with anything?"

", that'd be great, thank you. There won't be a lot to do, especially now that your mom sent so many salads. But I'm not about to turn down free labor, especially from a handsome guy."

"Hey! I can set a table like a pro; I'm not just some beefcake to stare at."

*Hmm we'll see about that...*I thought.

"Owen."

"Yes?" Owen said as he concentrated on the road.

"We talked about it awhile back, but are you planning to go Levi and Eide's wedding with me?"

"Do you want me to?"

"Yes, please! If you can get away."

"I'd love to go with you. A trip to Mexico, with you; well, that would just be awesome."

We got home that evening and Owen set my luggage in the foyer. "You're so good at this."

"Yeah, what can I say, builds my quads," Owen said, holding up his arm.

"Hey, my bags aren't that heavy."

"I'll take this food Ma sent and put it in the kitchen," Owen said, taking off with the bag from Rosie.

"Here, I'll help you. I need to run to the store and pick up a few things in a little bit and I have to get everything in the fridge."

"Well, how about we run the pies and Arnold to my house, and then go to the store together. I'll bring the pies back in the morning unscathed, I promise."

"I'm not worried about the pies, are you sure about going to the store?"

"Absolutely, let's go!" Owen said, motioning to the door. "What are we getting?"

"My dad likes ice cream with his pie, and I need to get some sweet potatoes and vegetables. Your mom supplied the rest and Levi's cooking the turkey."

"OK, sweet potato ice cream and vegetables coming up."

"Oh, yum. New seasonal flavor?"

"I'm glad the store wasn't too busy," I told Owen as he carried the groceries to the kitchen not long after we'd left.

"Saturday night after the big food day. I'd say everyone's probably in a food coma by now."

Owen swung his hands around me and we began dancing sweetly around the kitchen. Owen twirled me around the room, holding my hand up. Owen turned me around the opposite way and we both got tangled up in each other's arms. We were caught up in the moment and tripped over our feet. We both fell to the floor, laughing.

"Oh no, Karla. Are you alright?" Owen asked, chuckling.

We both recovered and leaned up against the cabinets, sitting on the floor. Owen put his arm around me.

"Are you sure you're alright?" Owen asked.

"Yes, I'm fine," I said, laughing hysterically. "Oh, Owen."

"I guess what they say is true," Owen said, laughing as well. "It's all fun and games..."

"Until you crash to the floor!" I said, interrupting Owen.

Alright, time for me to head out," Owen said, slapping my leg, attempting to get up. "I'll see you in the morning with at least some of the pies."

Owen left after he gave me a sweet kiss and an even sweeter embrace once we managed to crawl off the kitchen floor. *Owen certainly was crawling his way into my heart*, I thought as I went up the stairs.

The next morning, I'd barely gotten myself out of bed and was heading to the bathroom when the doorbell rang. *Well, so much for a potty break,* I thought as I made it to the front door and noticed Owen's pickup in the drive.

"Well, good morning," I said, opening the door to Owen standing on my porch, holding two cups of coffee.

"Am I too early?"

"At least you come bearing coffee. Have a seat here on the couch, I don't want to move too far yet."

Owen sat down beside me and set his coffee on the end table.

"Good morning, Karla," Owen said, whispering and nuzzling into my ear. "How are you this morning?"

"I'm fine, just very sleepy," I said, yawning and stretching.

"Did my parents wear you out?"

"No, of course not. I just haven't woken up yet; let me down this coffee and then I'll get moving."

I went upstairs shortly thereafter and got dressed while Owen waited on the sofa. I came back down, and Owen joined me in the kitchen to get busy prepping dinner items.

I was putting the sweet potatoes in the crock-pot while Owen took the plates and silverware to the dining room to start setting the table. I heard him holler back after he'd just gone into the dining room, "Hey Karla, can you come in here?"

"Yea, be right there." *He must have forgotten something for the table.*

"Yea, Owen?" I said, opening the dining room door. I saw Owen kneeling on the floor beside the table.

"Who ya praying for?" I asked Owen, chuckling.

"For you maybe. Did you know there is a large stain on your floor?"

"What? What is it?"

"Well, if I had to guess I'd say red wine."

"Did you drop a bottle of red wine here sometime?"

"No, I don't think I've ever brought wine in here, we always go out to the patio. For that matter, I hardly ever eat in here, anyways. Well, do you think if I got some carpet cleaner now it would help?"

"I wouldn't do anything with it today. It's dry and if you try to clean it without time to dry it'll just make it worse."

Good grief, where'd that stain come from? I thought as Owen and I stood there hunched over looking at the carpet.

"I can take care of this for you later," Owen offered.

"Well, I'm going wedding shopping with the girls next weekend; I won't be home for a night or two."

"That's actually perfect, you won't have any traffic through here."

"I don't have any traffic through here, anyways," I told Owen, and we finished up the meal prepping so we could get to church on time.

Shortly following the church service, everyone returned to my house. For all the food I'd eaten the last few days I was actually hungry. Mom, Eide, Molly and I put all the food out and Levi brought his turkey in.

"Oh Levi, that looks to die for, thanks for bringing it."

"Oh, yea, no problem."

"I think we got everything, who wants to say grace?"

"Didn't we just say our prayers in church?" Lane asked.

"No, Lane Kelly, I think you just volunteered," Mom said.

"OK, everyone bow yer heads, show some respect," Lane said as we all stood around my table holding hands.

"Lord God, we gather to humbly thank you for all that you have given us this past year. Not just the food before us and the hands that prepared it, but who is sitting around this table, the wealth of our family and friends. We thank you for the love and laughter you have given us, we cherish our health, happiness, relationships and memories and new memories yet to come in the years ahead. For that, you have our gratitude. Amen."

"Ah, that was nice," Mom said. "I think you just found yourself a full-time job."

"OK, thanks but I think we should dig in, it'd be a shame to let this food go to waste," Lane said, reaching for the bowl beside him.

"Yes, let's eat," I told everyone.

"Karla, you went to a lot of work, here," Molly said. "You've got like five different salads here, plus the staples. This is such a feast."

"No kidding, when did you have time to do all this?" Eide asked. "Didn't you go see Owen's family? What'd you do—stay up all night getting this ready?"

"We did," Owen said, chiming in before I could get a word out. "We got back yesterday evening and slaved away in the kitchen all

82

night, barely getting done in time to go to church. We're exhausted, right, hun?" Owen said, nudging my arm.

"Oh stop," I said, laughing at Owen. "Owen's Mom sent the salads."

"Hey, Kar. What's with the big ole bloody-looking stain over here?" Lane asked, looking like he was standing on his head.

"Oh yea, I found that this morning," Owen said. "I think it's red wine."

"How'd it get there?" Dad asked.

"I don't know. Sometimes I think I get so tired I forget half of what I do when I am home. Anyways, the salads came from Owen's mom. She had a lot of leftovers and said we should have them today."

"That was nice of her," Mom said.

"You don't know how it got there?" Dad asked.

"Not a clue. Owen offered to take care of it when we go wedding shopping—what, get a carpet cleaner?" I asked, looking at Owen.

"Yea, I thought it would be best if there was no traffic, it'll give it time to dry without disturbing it."

"Yeah, OK, let me know if you want help," Dad offered, shaking his head in agreement.

"Thanks, guys," I said, looking from Dad to Owen.

"Where do you women plan to go wedding shopping?" Levi asked.

"Denver," Eide said, looking at Molly and me.

"Don't look at me, this is your wedding. What you need and where we go is up to you. We're just along to make sure you don't buy an ugly dress." This caused an eruption of laughter.

"Ha ha, very funny."

"Don't forget Dad's cobalt-blue suit," Lane chimed in.

"Please do," Dad said as he reached for more potatoes.

"You keep eating like that, Dad, and nobody will know what size to get that suit," Lane joked.

"I think that's his plan," Mom said. "I bet he ate a whole pie at Jane's by himself."

"We did, too. Owen's mom had like a whole bakery for us, plus she sent three pies home with us for today."

"Ah pie, give me some," Levi said. "I haven't had any pie anywhere for like a year."

"Does anybody know what Garratt was doing this weekend—Dad, did you talk to him? I texted him and he just said, 'OK, thanks.'"

"No, I haven't seen him much this week," Dad said. "He's been in and out of the office lately, seems busy or preoccupied."

"Suppose he's got a girlfriend?" Lane chuckled.

"I wouldn't bring a girl around you two knuckleheads," Dad said. "You're all embarrassing."

"We are?" Levi muttered, questioning Dad's comment. "I think you invented embarrassing, Dad."

"Wrongo, buddy boy, I learned it from you two. Before you two came along, I was a calm, civilized individual. Right, Laur?"

"I'm pleading the Fifth," Mom said.

"Oh ho, you're busted, Dad," Levi said as I heard someone shouting my name.

"Kar, what in the name of Santa Claus is going on out there?" Lane questioned.

"Karla, Karla—are you home?" I could hear what sounded like my neighbor Marsha shouting in the kitchen. I stood up from the table to see Marsha rushing into the dining room looking very concerned.

"Marsha, hi. Can I help you?" I asked her as my family sat there looking stunned.

"Karla, I need to ask you to keep the noise level to a minimum around here. This isn't a party scene," Marsha said sternly.

"Oh, well, I'm very sorry. I didn't think we were getting out of hand."

"Things have most certainly been out of hand. What do you expect with everyone around?" Marsha said as she turned and left the room. We all sat there stunned and staring at the swinging door to the kitchen.

"Alright, who put a bee in her bonnet?" Lane asked.

I started to walk into the kitchen when I heard Levi call out and tell me to bring the pie back.

"Levi, quiet down, you heard Captain Ahab," Lane joked.

When I got to the kitchen and looked out the window, I saw Marsha walking across the yard back towards her house. I turned around shaking my head to find Owen standing behind me. "Everything OK?"

"Honestly, I have no idea what that was all about, very strange." Owen and I grabbed the pies and ice cream as we stepped back into the dining room.

"Who's ready for pie?" I asked everyone when Owen and I returned to the dining room.

"Well, did you get Captain Ahab all calmed down, now?" Lane asked.

"I honestly don't know what she's talking about. You couldn't even hear us from the yard if you tried."

"Has she ever done that before?" Dad asked.

"No. Well, yes, she has. She just wasn't exactly yelling at me. She came into the yard and eventually invited herself for a tour of the house the first night I lived here. And a couple other times when I was out in the yard coming back from a walk or something. She's a very interesting woman."

"What do you mean she came in?" Owen asked, looking confused.

"Oh, it's no big deal, I stepped onto the porch, and we were having a very choppy conversation, at best. She started looking around, stepped into the kitchen and eventually made her way around the rest of the house. I didn't think much of it at the time. She had mentioned her friends living here and I figured she was just remembering old times."

"You better watch that one," Lane spoke up.

"I think she harmless, just lonely."

"I think we're all in a food coma," Molly said later that afternoon when everyone was preparing to leave. Owen, you be sure and thank your mom for all that food, it was wonderful."

"Yes, it was very nice. All of it was," Mom said as she put her coat on.

"It's all good," Owen said. "She and Dad wouldn't have finished it anyways."

"Eide, what time are we leaving Friday?" Mom asked.

"We might as well go catch a game! These women could be awhile," Dad said, prompting a round of laughter from the guys.

"Hush, Darren, or I'll make you walk home," Mom said.

"I don't know, you think mid-morning. Nine-thirty or ten?" Eide said, looking at us.

"Sounds good to me," Molly said.

"I'll drive," I volunteered. "I'll be around to pick you all up."

"Thanks for the food and entertainment, Kar," Lane said, hugging me as he and Molly stepped out the door.

Chapter 8

It was a cold and snowy start to our Friday morning shopping trip when I left to pick Eide up. After I went around to get Eide I swung by for Mom and Molly.

"Are we ready to shop, ladies?" I asked as Molly made her way into my SUV.

"Yes," Eide said, sitting in the front seat, turning back to look at Molly and Mom. "I've been ready. You people are just too busy for me."

"Alright, Eide, what's on your list—we're here for ya, right, ladies?"

"OK!" Eide said. "Obviously, some dress shops, maybe some other clothing stores. I want to find some things to wear the rest of the time we're in Mexico."

"Oh, tell me about it, I went out with Owen a couple weeks ago to a play and you think I could find something decent? I finally picked out a black dress I think I've had since high school and didn't make me look too frumpy. I decided my wardrobe could definitely use some updating. I'm actually surprised you didn't throw some of those things out when I moved."

"I should have," Eide said.

"Please," Molly said. "You have a really nice wardrobe."

"Right, I do if I'm at work and wearing business suits. I don't have anything that says 'fun Friday night casual date.' Everything in that department is a good ten to fifteen years old or more."

"I probably bought you that stuff," Mom said.

"Probably, good grief, that's just sad."

"You got nothing on me," Molly said, chuckling. "At least you don't have scrubs in your wardrobe. It's all blue, all pink, all some other color.

"Thank God no one sees what I wear to work," Eide said. "I could sit in a bra and panties and send off a draft to the home office and no one would be the wiser."

"See, you've got it made, Eide."

"Well, maybe at least on that front," Eide said, laughing at her joke.

We arrived in downtown Denver and found Eide's first stop. It was a small, elegant shop with numerous dresses displayed in the window. The dresses displayed in the window didn't really scream Eide's style, I thought as we all walked into the shop.

We didn't stay very long. Just as I thought, these dresses weren't right for Eide. Eide walked down one aisle and back up another. "Alright, ladies," Eide said, heading to the door. "I've seen all I need to see here."

We drove to another part of town for Eide's next stop. This shop didn't look as elegant as the last one; there were several dresses displayed in the window but not quite as princess-y.

"This looks promising," Mom said as we walked in, looking around. Soon Mom cut off and went to another part of the store.

Eide started in on what I assumed was her mission. She would pick dresses off the rack and look at them, hold some of them up and then hang them back up. Molly and I followed Eide around like this for almost an hour.

"It doesn't seem to be here," Eide said.

"Why don't you tell us what you're looking for? Molly asked.

"I want something that's got spaghetti straps, floral bodice, maybe split down the leg and a flowy, thin gown. Does any of this make sense, what I'm envisioning?" Eide asked, looking at us with a questioning look.

"Makes perfect sense, sounds like a beautiful dress for you, Eide. Let's ask a sales associate."

Before we were able to talk to a sales associate, Mom came walking up the aisle towards us with a dress laid over her arm.

"Eide, this is basically open all down the back, but I think you'd look lovely in this dress."

"Laurel, that's the dress. I was just telling Karla and Molly about a dress almost identical to this one that I was envisioning but couldn't find it."

"Well, try it on, already," Molly said, coaxing Eide towards the fitting room.

We stood at the dressing room door waiting for Eide. I could hear her struggling and it sounded like she fell to the floor. "Eide, you OK in there?" I asked her. Eide grumbled something back.

Eide finally opened the door with disheveled hair, waltzing out of the dressing room.

"I might need it hemmed a little." The dress was a little long even for Eide.

"Eide, you look fabulous."

"I don't know about the fabulous part, right now, but this is the one, right?" Eide asked.

"Yes, you're right." I told Eide. "Go buy it."

"Well, she should probably take it off first, before she takes a header with it," Molly suggested, laughing at Eide's eagerness. "Perfect, one down. Now what are you and I going to wear?"

"Um, that part's easy—we just need to look like the ugly stepsisters," I said, laughing.

The salesclerk took Eide's dress and set it aside as Molly and I continued our search.

"You made that look easy, Mom. You wanna pull two more out of your back pocket?"

"No, you two are on your own. But I found this one for me."

"Mom that's beautiful, I love the beadwork at top and the chiffon covering. Go try it on."

"I already did; I'm buying it."

"Molly, we're going to be wearing shorts and tanks to this wedding if we don't get our butts in gear. My mother's making us look bad, maybe we need to hit up the aisle she keeps going to."

We left the dress shop with Eide and Mom's dresses and went in search of another dress shop on Eide's list. This store was in a strip mall with lots of great shopping choices.

As we got out of the vehicle and started walking to the door, I heard my phone ringing at the bottom of my purse; I dug it out and noticed Owen's number on the caller ID. "I'll be right in, Owen's calling me."

"Hey, make it snappy, you and lover boy can talk later," Eide said, laughing.

"Hi, Owen, how goes it?" I said, laughing at Eide's joke.

"Hey Karla, sorry to interrupt, just had a question?"

"No problem, we're on our third dress shop so a little interruption is welcome. What's up?"

"Were you expecting someone to stop by today?"

"Stop by? What do you mean?" I couldn't figure out what Owen was talking about.

"I came to your house a little while ago to clean the dining room carpet."

"Oh, gosh, I'm sorry. I forgot about that, thank you. Wait, how'd you get in? I didn't leave the door open for you."

"I got a key from your dad, no big deal. Anyways I was cleaning the carpet and this guy comes walking in with a duffel bag, very strange."

"He just came walking into my house?"

"Yeah, he just looked at me and said, "Oh, sorry, I'll wait. I asked him if he was looking for you. He said he wasn't. Then he just turned around and left."

"Sounds very random. Did he say who he was?"

"No, probably some relation to your crazy neighbor."

"Hmm, very strange. But thanks for taking care of the carpet."

"No problem; good as new. I didn't want to keep you too long, I just wanted to ask about that guy."

"Nope, no visitors."

"All right. Bye, Karla."

"Thanks, Owen. Bye."

"How's lover boy?" Eide questioned me when I joined them in the dress shop.

"He's been busy."

"Oh?"

"Yea, he's been cleaning that stain in the dining room. I forgot he was going to do that today."

"And so, he just called to tell you about it?" Molly asked.

90

"No," I said, chuckling. "He had sort of a random encounter and wanted to run it by me. Some guy came walking into the house with a duffel bag. Owen thought he was looking for me, but he said no and then he left."

"Weird, probably your neighbors' doings," Eide said.

"That's what Owen said. So, any good dresses here?"

"Yes," Molly said. "While you were chatting it up with your handyman, I found us these dresses."

"Oh, cute. I love the color—did you pick that out, Eide?"

"Hmm, sort of a group effort. It was a toss-up between orchid and aqua, and the orchid won out."

"Good, this color will look fabulous on me."

"Now that we got that knocked out, now what?" Molly commented after we tried on the dresses and paid for them. "What's next?"

"There's a clothing store a few doors down; I saw it while I was on the phone with Owen. You know, the whole frumpy wardrobe."

"Lead the way," Eide said, pointing to the door. "Hopefully they've got some great bargains."

"This was a great stop, lots of sales. I think I have five bags coming through," I said, waiting for the clerk to finish ringing up my purchases.

"Yea I know, but let's just hope no one checks that bank account anytime soon," Eide said, chuckling.

"Oh, come on girls, you're having fun. Let's go have some lunch," Mom suggested. "My treat, what are we in the mood for?"

"Champagne, booze, white wine," Eide said sarcastically.

"Don't dress shops usually pump champers into the bridal party when they're trying on dresses?" Molly asked.

"Not when you only pay $118.95 for a wedding dress and the rest of the bridal party runs across town to get their dresses. Trust me, neither dress shop made a killing off this bridal party."

"Oh, Eide," I said, laughing at her. "It's not the price of the dress, it's how lovely you look in it."

"I know, and Levi is going to drop his jaw when he sees me."

After lunch, we checked into a hotel room. We were all stretched out across the beds.

"What's the next adventure?" Molly asked.

"Shoe shopping," Eide reported.

"I veto," Molly said. "Let's look online, I doubt many stores in Denver are selling beachwear this time of year. I vote we go to a spa."

"That's a fabulous idea, Molly. Sound good to you, Eide?" I asked, looking for her reaction.

"Yes, absolutely," Eide said. "I haven't been to a spa in ages."

On the drive home the next day, Eide decided she wanted to have lunch at the fish taco shack outside of town.

"We should invite the guys to join us. It would be nice, being we left them to fend for themselves," Mom said.

"They're grown, capable men," Eide said, laughing. And yet here she was on the phone talking to Levi.

"Sucker," I whispered to her, interrupting her conversation.

"Are they going to meet us?" Mom asked Eide when she hung up.

"Yea, there all in Darren's garage working on something. Levi said they'd head over and meet us there."

"Here," I said, holding up my phone. "Would someone call Owen and see if he wants to join us?"

"Me. Me," Eide said, grabbing for my phone. "I'll take care of that."

"Be nice, Eide!"

"I'm always nice," Eide insisted.

"Um yes, Owen Kaster?" And there it was: Eide's bad, front and center, again.

"Eide, be nice," I whispered as she continued.

"This is Eide, soon to be Eide Grainer, calling you on Karla's behalf. She requests the honor of having you join us for lunch at the fish taco shack just outside of town in about twenty minutes."

"Thanks, Eide. I knew that was a bad idea—he's probably going to think we're calling for a booty call; you have such a seductive voice. Why'd you say it that way? Give me my phone back, if he calls back Mom can talk to him."

"You should give that boy a booty call, it'd be good for both of you," Eide said.

"Never you mind about booty calls."

The guys were waiting for us at the fish taco shack. I could see them sitting at the tables just inside the door when I pulled in.

"I guess your boy didn't get the message," Eide said. "I don't see him."

"Me either, your message probably sent him walking."

"Hey guys," I said as I walked in and sat down next to Dad.

"Hi, how was the shopping?" Dad asked.

"Anybody got any money left? That's the real question?" Lane joked.

"Nope, not a dime," Molly said. "That's why we called you in for lunch."

"Oh, the truth comes out, boys. We're only here for the money."

"What's Owen doing today, he should come down and join us," Dad asked me after Lane was done ranting about money.

"I tried. Actually, Eide tried while I was driving and probably scared him off. She left him a half-seductive phone message."

"Good grief, call him back, he probably thinks Eide's pulling a prank."

"Good point." I tried to call Owen back, but it went to voicemail again.

"Hey Owen, this is Karla, for real this time, and we truly are having lunch down here at the fish taco shack. So, if you're not totally freaked out by Eide's message come down and join us. Otherwise, I'll talk to you later. Bye"

"Did you get all your shopping done?" Levi asked, looking at Eide.

"I hope so," Lane said sarcastically. "When is this wedding again?"

"About a month, Lane. You'll survive!" Eide said.

"You'll survive, Lane. Me, on the other hand, I don't know," Levi said, half hugging Eide and kissing her forehead.

"Do you guys have any Christmas plans, yet?" Mom asked.

"Yep, a wedding in Mexico," Levi told us, chuckling.

"We could just attend church services this year, Laurel," Dad said. "With the wedding later and everybody's busy, let's just play it by ear."

"Yea, you're right," Mom said, almost defeated.

93

We finished lunch and I dropped off Mom, Molly and Eide with their haul and went home to unpack, too.

I carried my purchases upstairs and was hanging up the new clothes when my phone rang.

"Hello."

"Hi Karla, sorry I missed your, uh, messages," Owen said skeptically.

"Well, I only left you one, but lunch was over hours ago."

"Yea, I'm sorry I missed you. I was at work."

"I'm sorry, tough day?"

"It's OK, we're all good."

"Anything I can do for you?"

"No, I'm fine. Just tired. I wanted to let you know I wasn't ignoring you all day."

"Oh, no, I didn't even think that for a minute."

"I'm going to go home, shower and zonk out for the night. Can I call you tomorrow, maybe get together?"

"Sounds good. Rest well, Owen."

"Bye, Karla."

Chapter 9

"Eide, what's wrong, you don't freak out. I can barely understand you. Don't go all Bridezilla on me now; we fly out this afternoon." And here I thought this was going to be such a good phone call.

"Why did I agree to run away with Levi and get married?" Eide asked, crying.

"Because you love him, you goof."

"Maybe your mom's right; maybe we should stay here and get married at the church with Pastor Tim. This is going to be a disaster."

"This is not going to be a disaster; this is going to be a wonderful wedding."

"Do you know what it takes to get ready for a wedding like this?" Eide said, half yelling, half crying.

"Eide, stop, you're getting married in a few days, everything is going to be just fine. Do you need help getting packed?"

"No, I'm fine." I could hear Eide sniffling, trying to turn off the water works. "We'll see you at the airport."

I heard the doorbell ringing and I hollered down for Owen to come in. I grabbed a couple suitcases and went down to meet him in the foyer.

"Hey, are you ready?" Owen asked, kissing my forehead before I hurried back upstairs.

"Mexico or bust, baby," I said as I set my bags down. "I have a couple more items to grab upstairs. I should never unpack, I'm always packing/unpacking, packing/unpacking."

"No," Owen said. "I barely get to see you as it is, at least this is for an awesome trip. I'll take these out to the pickup while you grab the rest of your things."

Owen put the rest of my bags in his pickup and backed out of my driveway. Driving down the street, I noticed a large van full of people driving by. "Looks like my neighbors are getting some visitors," I commented off-handedly.

"Hey everyone," I said as we all gathered just inside the terminal doors.

"Are we gonna make this flight?" Lane joked.

Don't joke, Lane," Eide scolded him. "Levi, here, about can't make it as it is."

"Do we need to find a minister for you two?" Lane joked, making googly eyes at Levi.

"Laugh now. But when it's your turn, I'll be plenty prepared with a sack full of jokes to pass out."

"Hah! Joke's on you, Molly and I are eloping."

"Don't say that Lane, you'll give your mother a heart attack," Molly said, scolding Lane. "Besides, who said we're getting married; I'm just here for your money."

"Oh, burn, little brother."

Garratt came rushing into the terminal, just as we finished checking our bags.

"Garratt, where've ya been, buddy?" Levi asked.

"You know, around," Garratt said breathlessly.

"I wondered if you were going to make it," Lane said, slapping Garratt on the shoulder.

"Of course, I wouldn't miss this," Garratt said, still breathless from his marathon trip getting into the terminal. I'd hate to see how he drove; that could have been dangerous.

"You keep ditching us, dude. You got yourself a girlfriend?" Lane asked.

"Something like that," Garratt said with a small smirk.

"You heard it here, folks, Garratt here's a ladies' man!" Lane said, slapping Garratt's shoulder. "You should have brought her along," Levi said.

"What and subject her to this abuse? I think not," Garratt said.

We landed in Cancun, Mexico, to beautiful sunny weather, and crisp coral beaches. It felt so good, being that we left the eight-degree Colorado weather behind this morning.

Levi and Eide chose a small, low-key resort overlooking the ocean. Our rooms had private balconies with a postcard-worthy view. There was a spa on the main level.

"I booked us an appointment to the spa in the morning," Mom said, walking by.

"Nice, thank you, Laurel," Molly said. "I always look forward to some time at the spa. You guys picked a great place, Eide."

We checked into our rooms and rode the elevator up to the sixth floor. The balcony held a wonderful view of the beach; you could see the beach, and the ocean seemed to go on forever. The sun was reflecting off the water and felt good for the soul even just looking out the hotel window. After the guys dropped their luggage in their rooms, they immediately decided it was time to hit up the beach pub. I walked down along the beach, the sand squishing through my toes after I'd taken my flip-flops off, it was so relaxing. I had walked down the beach looking out into the ocean when Owen came walking up alongside me.

"Hi, care for some company?" Owen asked, putting his arm around me.

"Always. Did they run out of drinks down at the tiki hut?"

"I just wanted to walk along the beach with you. Or should I say, kiss you, like my dad says, because you don't need the exercise."

"Your dad," I laughed. "Probably cut from the same cloth as my dad."

We walked way down the beach until we made it to some private cabanas.

"Follow me," Owen said, taking my hand again. Owen walked up and spoke with the hostess and shortly thereafter, we were shown to a private cabana and seated.

I think Owen must have set this up earlier, there was no way we would have gotten seated so quickly by randomly walking up. A waiter showed up shortly after the hostess left. He brought us a large jar of lemon water and a bottle of chardonnay. They both looked very fancy. We had a private meal of sautéed scallops and pasta catered to us. It was a very delicious and romantic meal.

Owen and I were able to sit and watch the sun go down, held in each other's arms.

"How was your meal?" Owen asked.

"This was so nice, Owen. You're pretty incredible, I can't believe you set all this up."

"What, you think I'm not capable of something like this?" Owen asked, laughing.

"Yes, I know you're capable, but to go to the effort for me."

"Oh stop, you're worth every effort and more," Owen said, kissing my forehead. "By the way, you're exceptionally beautiful this evening, you know that?"

The next morning, Mom, Molly, Eide and I met downstairs to go to the spa. We had hot stone massages, facials, and hydrotherapy. It made me feel like I needed a nap after the massage, but that's just getting all the toxins out of you. It was so relaxing.

"Ah, so relaxing, right, ladies? Thank so much, Laurel," Molly said.

"That's quite the ringtone, Karla," Mom mentioned when my phone started ringing. Thinking it was probably Owen calling to see where I was, I didn't really pay attention to the caller ID. I pushed the button and said, "Hello."

A pre-recorded message came on the line and said, "*This message is for Karla Grainer, calling to inform you an alarm has been activated at 2176 Trail Ridge Road. Law enforcement has been notified and will update you of the situation, soon.*"

"Seriously, Owen can wait," Eide said.

"That's odd," I said, looking at my phone as I hit "end call."

I must have had a confused look on my face because Mom, Eide and Molly were all staring at me when I looked up from my phone.

"What was that all about?" Mom asked. "You look a bit disturbed."

"I don't know, the call was from my security system company; they said an alarm was triggered at my house," I said, relaying the message to them.

"I wouldn't worry about it," Molly said. "It's probably just a sensitive system, and an overeager salesman is there, a deputy will call you shortly."

"Yea, probably," I told Molly. We finished at the spa and went to meet the guys for lunch.

We met up with the guys for lunch after their boat came in from a chartered fishing expedition Dad arranged. Later, when I went shopping down along the boardwalk, I saw a deputy talking to someone on the sidewalk. I still hadn't received a call from a law enforcement officer, like the message said. Weird, I thought. Must have been some kind of system error.

We walked in and out of stores almost all afternoon. It was so nice, the ocean view and the mild temperatures made you want to stand on the beach and soak up the sun and melt your cares away.

While the guys were snorkeling this afternoon, we sat outside of the resort basking in the sun waiting for their return. I could see them all down the beach coming this way. The guys came walking up, commenting on the beautiful view. Funny, I don't think they were looking out at the ocean, though.

"We'll go in and clean up and then there's a pub down on the beach—thought we'd check it out," Dad said.

"Lane's suggestion, I suppose?" I asked.

"Hey hey, stereotyping there," Lane said. ", Owen here picked it out. We're just happy to oblige."

When the guys went into the hotel, Eide suggested we start walking in that direction. My phone rang again as we were walking down the beach.

A pre-recorded message came on the line and said, "*This message is for Karla Grainer, calling to inform you an alarm has been activated at 2176 Trail Ridge Road. Law enforcement has been notified and will update you of the situation, soon.*" I listened to the message and clicked "end call." What was up with this company, I thought.

After we all arrived at the pub, Dad ordered us burgers and fries and I think the guys were already working on a hangover considering the number of drinks coming to our table.

I finished my burger and was looking out towards the ocean. It was so beautiful, the moon reflecting off the water. I walked out to the beach watching the waves and felt someone walk up behind me.

"Owen, I thought you were enjoying the pub, you picked it out."

"I did, to distract them so I could distract you," Owen said, smirking.

"Oh, sneaky," I said, shaking my head in agreement.

"How was your day?" Owen asked, looking out towards the ocean.

"It was actually pretty good. How was yours?"

"Uh well, I didn't drown," Owen joked.

"Well, that's good," I said, setting my hand to the side of Owen's chest. Owen took my hand, twirling me around.

"You better watch yourself there, pal. Last time we were dancing we ended up in a pile on the floor," I said, laughing at Owen, remembering our random dance.

"Yeah, yeah. We got this," Owen said as he continued shuffling us around in the sand. "What'd you guys do today?"

"We went to the spa and did some shopping along the boardwalk. You know, girly girl stuff."

"Good. I'm glad you all got to hang out, take a break from work."

Owen and I swayed back and forth on the beach, listening to the waves come in. "Doesn't that sound incredible, Owen?"

"Where did you and Owen disappear to last night?" Eide asked me as we sat in the salon getting our hair done the next morning. "We barely finished eating and you two were gone."

"Yeah, I know," I said, smiling.

"I thought it was Owen's idea to go to that pub?" Molly asked.

"It was. He got what he wanted out of it," I said, smirking.

"Hey, I was going to ask—did a law enforcement officer ever contact you yesterday?" Molly asked.

"No. I figure it's just a system error, they had the wrong address, wrong phone number sort of thing. I live in a pretty quiet neighborhood so I'm guessing not much is going on."

"Right," Mom said. "According to your neighbor you're the rowdy one; I never thought that'd be the case. I always thought it'd be Lane that's accused of being rowdy."

100

The hairstylist was putting Eide's hair up into a side sweep and putting little lavender orchids up the side.

"Eide, your hair is looking great. You're going to love it; she's doing a beautiful job."

I chose a loose bun style, with some tiny ringlets coming down the sides. We all had our nails done; Molly and I chose a light purple color to match our dresses. Eide had hers done in an opaque; she was going to knock Levi's socks off.

Owen was sitting at the patio tables overlooking the ocean in front of the resort when we came walking back from the salon.

"Hey, good-looking," I said, walking up beside him.

Mom, Molly and Eide went on to their rooms and I took a seat on Owen's knee.

"Who are you callin' good-looking? I take it you were the only client in the salon."

"No, why do you say that?"

"Because you're the most beautiful woman in town. If there wasn't this little business about a wedding going on tonight, I'd be tempted to sweep you away. I'd hate to steal the thunder away from the bride, it is her show."

"Exactly, and she's waited a long time for Levi to get his butt in gear and give her a diamond."

"So, Karla, why isn't Eide's family here for this? You've never said anything about them?"

"Well, she doesn't have any that she knows of, besides us. Eide's dad left before she could walk—she doesn't even remember him or know if he's alive anymore."

"Hang on a sec. Hello," I said, answering my phone.

A pre-recorded message came on the line and said, *"This message is for Karla Grainer, calling to inform you an alarm has been activated at 2176 Trail Ridge Road. Law enforcement has been notified and will update you of the situation, soon."*

"Oh geez, not this again," I muttered.

"What's the matter?" Owen asked after I ended the call, looking concerned. "Eide freaking out about something?"

"Eide doesn't freak out—well, she had a slight rattle the day we left but she's good. No, this call was supposedly from my security alarm company. I think it's a systems error of some sort."

"What?" Owen asked, looking perplexed.

"Yeah, my security system company has been calling with a pre-recorded message. It said an alarm has been activated and law enforcement would update shortly. I've gotten this message a few times since we left home and then nobody's calls to update me. It's nothing."

"That doesn't sound like nothing," Owen said, creasing his brows. "I think you should have somebody check it out."

"No, it's fine. What were we talking about? Oh yeah, I was telling you about Eide's family."

"So, Dad's gone, her mom got into drugs terribly and OD'd when she was a sophomore in high school, her grandpa tried to help her for a while, but he passed away when she first got into college. We started hanging out in college and even more so after her grandpa died."

"Oh wow, that's just sad," Owen said. "You're a good friend, Karla. Eide's lucky to have you."

"I'm really the lucky one. But now we need to get ready for the wedding, the photographer will be looking for us."

"You, not me," Owen said, smiling.

"Oh yes, you're coming along," I said, extending my hand for Owen to come along.

Owen and I arrived at the wedding area down on the beach before any of the others. There were a few small white chairs with the backs wrapped in tulle and an orchid-colored bow attached facing the ocean. Small deep-purple flowers were scattered along the way to the altar.

"This is a beautiful setting for a wedding; simple and elegant," I told Owen, looking things over.

"Yeah," Owen said. "Really makes you think, huh."

"Eide's going to love this; simple, yet elegant. I need to go meet up with Eide and Molly, do the wedding march thing, ya know."

"Oh, you wedding march, can't wait to see that," Owen joked. "Do you suppose it could include cartwheels coming down the aisle? Oh, can I record it?"

"That'd be a hard pass, no recording."

102

Eide came walking down the aisle as Westlife's "I Want to Grow Old with You" played in the background. I was standing there next to Molly watching Eide take her walk down the aisle; she was glowing. The orchids in the side of her hair were the perfect touch that tied everything together. Her dress was elegant in its own way, just right for Eide. It was a perfect day for a beach wedding.

The gentleman presiding over the ceremony did a wonderful job—you would have thought he'd known Levi and Eide their whole lives the way he talked of their love and commitment towards each other. You really could see the love Levi and Eide shared as they stood together, exchanging vows. He really did capture the spirit of their love for each other and their relationship. The minister shared the quote, *"Life takes us to unexpected places and love brings us home."* This truly was Levi and Eide in every aspect of their lives, I thought, brushing a tear away.

We ushered out of the wedding area, after the minister pronounced Levi and Eide husband and wife. Levi and Eide went over and thanked Mom and Dad and then completely disappeared. Garratt took my arm and we walked partway down the aisle and Garratt stopped where Owen was sitting and held my hand out to Owen. "I think she belongs to you."

"Oh, good, I was missing her," Owen said, taking my hand.

"Thanks guys, when did I become property!" I said, laughing at their joke.

We moved on down the beach to a private cabana for a reception dinner for Levi and Eide. While we waited for them to return, we all ordered a drink. As we were being seated and offered menus, Levi and Eide returned to join our party. We all offered our congratulations. Well, except for Lane! Lane stood up and proceeded to make what some would call the "best man's" toast.

"Did you make it, Levi? Congratulations, little brother, I'm happy for you!" Lane said, slapping Levi on the back. "It's great seeing you two finally tie the knot and thanks for bringing us on this great trip. Just make sure to pick up the tab on the way out!" A round of laughter ensued and everyone raised their glasses. "Hear, hear!"

We had a wonderful meal and the party soon turned into a dance celebration. Owen came and took my hand and shuffled me out on the dance floor.

Owen and I danced alongside the rest of my family. It was fun, and other beachgoers started to join in the fun as well.

After a while, Owen and I took a break and went and sat off to the side with Garratt.

"You two want a drink?" Owen asked.

"Yes, thanks, Owen. I'll have a glass of wine."

"Garratt?"

"I'll take a Corona."

"Coming right up," Owen said.

"How's it going, Garratt? We haven't seen you much lately. Levi wasn't even sure you'd make it to the wedding."

"I'd never miss this in a million years."

"I'm glad you're here. What happened to you at Thanksgiving? I texted, and you said OK. I thought you'd make it."

"I've just been busy," Garratt said.

"Here we go," Owen said, handing us our drinks.

"How's work, Karla?" Garratt asked. "Last we spoke you were traveling a lot?"

"Yes, I am," I said, rather unenthused.

"She's on the go all the time," Owen said. "I feel like the only time I see her is when I'm dropping her off and picking her up at the airport," Owen said, chuckling.

"He's right, I've even canceled dates on him. It's a wonder he even puts up with me."

"Ah, you're alright," Owen said as he half-hugged me.

Mom and Dad stepped up to our table. I'd been watching them; I think they had secretly been enjoying themselves.

"You guys form your own party over here?" Dad asked.

"Well sort of—come join us."

"Yea, we need a break. I think your mother about danced the pants off me," Dad said, causing a round of laughter.

"I don't know, Dad. I think you were having a pretty good time, too. I saw you kicking up your heels out there."

Lane and Molly and later Levi and Eide joined our party at the table.

"Is everybody having a good time?" Eide asked.

"Yes, we are. Are you?" I asked Eide. "You're such a beautiful bride."

"Oh, the best time," Eide said with the biggest smile I think I've ever seen her share.

"Eide, you did a nice job arranging all this," Mom said. "I'm sorry I overreacted when you guys shared your news. I thought it was going to be a cheap, dirty affair, but this was a beautiful wedding, and you look stunning, Eide!"

"Laurel, it's OK," Eide said, taking Mom's hand and hugging her. "We didn't exactly give you much reaction time, but now it's past us, and on to the next Grainer wedding," Eide said, looking at Lane and me, holding up her glass.

"Don't look at us!" Lane said. "We're eloping."

"Stop doing that to your mom," Molly said, slapping him. "Besides, I told ya I'm just after your money, honey." All joking aside, Lane and Molly were a great couple and may very well be the next Grainer wedding event. Owen flashed his million-dollar smile at me. God, I loved that smile.

Lane commented how lucky Dad was that mom couldn't locate a cobalt-blue tux, so she claims. We continued to discuss the wedding and this wonderful vacation. As we were laughing about Dad and the cobalt suit, my phone rang.

"Come on, Karla, this is a party," Eide exclaimed. "Work can wait a few more days."

I looked at the caller ID and let out an unrelenting sigh.

"Same call as before?" Owen asked.

"Yes, I swear I'm going to cancel this service; a lot of good it's doing me," I said, clicking the phone to speaker.

"What's going on?" Dad asked.

"This message is for Karla Grainer, calling to inform you an alarm has been activated at 2176 Trail Ridge Road. Law enforcement has been notified and will update you of the situation, soon."

I let the message finish out and clicked "end call." "This is about the fourth time I've gotten this message since leaving home. I have yet to receive an update. I assume there's some sort of system error."

"That's ridiculous," Dad said.

"I think someone should go check on your house," Owen said.

"I think you should call the sheriff's office and ask them if they've been dispatched to your house," Dad said.

"I don't think any of that is necessary," I said, brushing off Dad and Owen's suggestions.

"NO! Call them now," Dad said, rather sternly.

"OK, fine, Dad," I said as I started dialing the phone.

"Boulder County Sheriff's Office," the lady on the other end of the line answered.

"Hi, my name is Karla Grainer. I've been notified several times in the last twenty-four hours of a triggered alarm. It stated that law enforcement was notified, and a deputy would contact me. There hasn't been a deputy contact me. I was wondering if a deputy was dispatched and if I could get an update."

"What's your address?"

"2176 Trail Ridge Road."

"Your name again?"

"Karla Grainer"

"OK, please hold and I'll see what I can find out."

"This is taking long enough," Lane said as the seconds the call was connected continued to add up and the melancholy music I'd been placed on hold with, held us captive.

"Ma'am, are you still there?"

"Yes, I'm here."

"OK, sorry for the wait. The file hasn't been processed yet, so it took a minute to find it. It looks like a deputy was dispatched to that address, and the deputy notes he spoke with the owner. They were just having trouble with the system."

"There must be a mistake, I'm the owner and I'm out of town right now. Is the deputy available? I'd like to speak with him?"

"No, he's off duty."

106

"Can I leave a message to have him call me?'

"I can leave a note for him and ask him to call. What's the best number he can reach you?"

"970-518-2418."

"OK, I'll put it on his desk."

"Thank you."

"Now, I think we should send Todd to look things over."

"I hate to bother him, Owen. I still think this is some sort of system mix-up."

"Don't worry about Todd, I'll give him a call," Owen said, getting up from the table.

"Let's have a drink and forget our troubles," Lane offered. "I'm buying the next round, what's everyone want?"

We took our drink and migrated back to the dance floor, and Eide went and cranked up the music.

"I think we scared the other guests with our dance moves—they're probably wondering where these hicks came from," Eide nearly shouted over the music. We all danced together for a while, doing the macarena, the chicken dance, the twist. Even Lane and Levi danced it out. I realized Owen hadn't returned from going to calling Todd. I walked down the beach and noticed Owen; he was looking up at where we'd been dancing. He took my hand, pulling me into one of his loving embraces and kissed me.

"Whatcha doin'?" I asked.

"I was watching you having a dance-off with everyone, it was great. You looked like you were having a great time."

"Eide thought we were going to scare the rest of the guests with our dance moves."

"Not a chance," Owen said.

Holding me around my back, Owen bent me over and kissed me. It was an incredibly passionate kiss that left me completely lost of all my senses. It was a good thing Owen was holding me, otherwise I'd have been lying flat on my back in the sand.

"You've got this sexy thing going with your hair and this dress, just beautiful."

"Owen."

I was lying in bed the next morning contemplating getting up and reflecting on Levi and Eide's wedding last night. It was late last night when we returned to our rooms.

We all agreed to meet out front and find a place down the beach for lunch around eleven or eleven-thirty. I wondered if anyone would actually make it. Eide and Levi might actually be holed up in their room all day! I chuckled at my musing. I had a few hours before meeting everyone for lunch. I decided to go for a walk on the beach. It was so nice out there.

Just before I headed out the door, my phone buzzed.

"Are you awake?"

"Yes."

"Thought I could hear you. What are you up to?" Owen replied.

"I was headed out for a walk on the beach...want to join?"

"Yes, see you in five," Owen fired back.

In less than five minutes' time, I heard Owen gently tapping on the door. "Are you alive? Can you even walk this morning?" Owen asked after I opened the door for him.

"Yes, remarkably well, in fact. The side effects might not actually surface for a few days."

"Yea, just in time to return to civilization," Owen said.

Owen and I walked down the beach holding each other's hand, enjoying the other's company. Owen stopped short and turned around, looking at me with those dark, bold eyes of his. Owen moved in for a kiss, sealing his lips over mine; he tipped me back, still smoking in his passion. Owen tipped me back even further and I ended up falling backwards into the sand. Owen fell right alongside me and never missed a beat and stole a kiss as I squealed in delight.

"I told you this was going to happen, Owen!" I said, laughing hysterically. We laid there together for a moment before Owen jumped up and grabbed my hand, giving me a boost out of the sand. We started walking towards the front of the resort to meet everyone for lunch. Lane texted me and said he and Molly were a no-go on lunch. I replied, "FIGURES." Make him feel guilty for ditching us.

Turns out Owen and I were the only ones to join Mom and Dad for lunch; Eide also texted and said they were passing on lunch—although I never really expected her and Levi to make it to lunch. And Dad said Garratt flew out early this morning, wasn't sure what that was all about. Guess he had something come up or maybe I just didn't know he was going back a day sooner than we were.

"Are you guys a little hung over?" Dad asked.

"Not so much as alcohol hung over, but lack of sleep hung over."

"I think Lane may still be recovering into next week," Dad said. "At the rate he was going."

"Oh, he'll be fine," Mom said. "He's just having fun."

"Did you hear any more about the security system?" Dad asked.

"My buddy Todd did a drive-by and didn't see anything suspicious," Owen said. "Maybe Karla's right and it is just a system error."

"Well, that's good to hear, I guess. Thank your friend for us," Mom told Owen.

"Yea," Dad said. "That is good to hear." I could see the gears spinning when I looked at Dad. I didn't think he was really satisfied with this answer.

That afternoon, we lounged around on the beach soaking up some vitamin C, definitely a must. I think some of us even took a nap. Eide and Levi made an appearance later in the day.

"Hi guys, glad you could join the party," Dad said.

"How's your day been?" Lane asked, punching Levi in the arm.

"Never you mind, little brother, your time's coming."

"What's everyone been doing?" Eide asked.

"Not a darn thing and enjoying every moment of it," Molly said.

"Speak for yourself. Some of us behaved ourselves last night," I said, looking at Owen.

"Where's the fun in that?" Lane asked.

"I've had fun, I just didn't feel the need to fund the National Corona Cash Cow Fund, Lane Grainer!!!"

"I haven't funded anything, just mildly boosted the local economy; and besides, you're not supposed to drink the water down here, remember? I'm just trying to be safe."

Chapter 10

Early the next morning, we all boarded the plane for home. Except for Levi and Eide, who were extending the honeymoon and changing venues to Jamaica. It'd been a great vacation, but I was still ready to get home. I slept on the plane some; I think everyone did. We didn't hear too much out of Lane during the flight, either. We had a lengthy layover in Salt Lake City, and it was getting dark when Owen pulled into my driveway after finally getting to the airport in Denver.

"Wow, Karla, look at your dumpster; it's running over. Did you have that much trash when we left?"

"Um no, I never have that much trash. I don't even think that's my trash. Who would use my dumpster?"

"I don't know, maybe your neighbors as a runoff—you were gone for several days," Owen said, looking around the backyard.

"Something doesn't seem right, Karla. I don't feel comfortable leaving you here alone.

"It's just trash, Owen."

"No, it's not just trash. Especially after the situation with your security system and the sketchy answer from the Sheriff's Office. I don't think you should stay here alone."

"Oh, come on, Owen, I'll be fine."

"No," Owen said, looking concerned. "It's either my house or Lane's or your parents'."

I reluctantly gave in and went to Owen's house for the night. Neither of us were in a big hurry to head to bed, since we'd slept on the plane. We settled in on the couch and just stared at each other, not sure what to say or do.

Owen finally spoke up. "You want something to eat or drink."

"Maybe just something to, I think I ate enough in Mexico to last a week."

"Something to drink, something stronger to calm your nerves?" Owen asked.

"Water's fine. This isn't the only odd situation I've come home to."

"What do you mean?" Owen asked, looking at me concerned.

"It's no big deal—I've been coming home to weird stuff for a while now. I've decided I must just be tired."

"What do you mean by weird things?" Owen asked.

"Well, there's the weird stain in the dining room. Oh, the really weird one, that night you picked me up at the airport really late a couple months back. I must have been completely wiped out; I thought an upstairs light was on."

"There was a light on up there, Karla, I saw it," Owen said, looking perplexed.

"Later that night, after you'd left, I'd been in bed awhile and thought I'd even fallen asleep. I woke up and heard the front door open and close and then again early the next morning. I'm not even convinced I could hear the front door open or close from my bedroom."

"I'm not so convinced it's a tired thing," Owen said. "I think we should go talk to the responding deputy. At least see why he hasn't returned your call."

"It's not a big deal," I said, shrugging my shoulders. "I'm just tired from traveling."

"That may be, but I don't call a stain or a light being on for a while and then magically be shut off a tired thing."

"Yeah, the stain's weird."

Karla had fallen asleep while we sat there talking and not talking, I leaned over and covered her up with a throw blanket from the back of the couch. I sat down in the chair next to her and watched her sleep. She slept so peacefully. Despite everything going on at her house, she just chalked them up to being tired. I'm sure she was tired; she goes nine-O around the clock; but this wasn't turning out to be a tired thing. I watched her sleep a short

112

time, her long curly brown hair draped across her face. The way she had her hair fixed for the wedding was so beautiful, I could take a moonlight walk on the beach every night. Hmm, so lovely, I thought, going into the kitchen. I made a pot of coffee and started reading 1: Peter in my bible. I grabbed a cup of coffee and sat down at the table and continued with my scripture reading. I noticed the sun coming up. I let Arnold out and refilled my coffee.

"Good morning, how'd you sleep?" I asked Karla as she stepped into the kitchen later that morning. "I'm good, how are you?"

"Cups are above the sink, help yourself to some coffee."

"Sorry, I crashed on ya."

"Don't be, you looked exhausted."

"Did you get any sleep?" Karla asked.

"No, I sat in the chair beside you and watched you snoring."

"I don't snore," Karla said, sitting down next to me.

"I disagree, I sat in that chair over there and listened to you. It's a cute snore, but a snore, nonetheless."

"Oh, please, nobody's ever told me I've snored."

"Well, I'm not nobody."

"Ya got me there. I need to go home this morning and get some clean clothes and shower."

"Sorry, not going to happen, at least not yet" I said, taking a drink of my coffee.

"You have things from the trip, and I have a shower back there somewhere," I said, pointing down the hall. "You looked great in that dress you wore to the wedding, wear that."

"Ha ha, very funny."

"You'll find something to wear, but you and I are going to the Sheriff's Office first. I want to talk to deputy what's-his-name about his report and find out why he never called you back. I'd even like him to do a walk-through of the house with us."

"That's sweet, Owen, that's probably not going to happen; he'll just tell you I'm crazy."

Karla came back in the kitchen after showering. Her hair all wet and curly framing the side of her face was a sexy look. She had her hair down and wrapped across her shoulder. "I see you found some very nice clothes to wear today," I said, handing her some toast and refilling her coffee.

"Thanks, Owen."

The Sheriff's Office appeared to be busy when we arrived, I noticed, as Karla and I approached the desk. No one stepped up immediately to see if we needed assistance; we stood there waiting before a deputy finally approached the counter.

"Have you folks been helped?"

"No," I said, "we haven't. We'd like to talk to the deputy that took a report at her house a few days ago."

"OK, what's your name and address?"

"Karla Grainer, 2176 Trail Ridge Road," Karla told the deputy as he keyed the information into the computer.

"It looks like Deputy Greenly took that report, but he's off duty right now."

"That's what I was told when I called in. Do you know when he'll be back?"

"No, sorry, ma'am', I don't. Is there a problem?"

"Yes, there is," Karla said, a bit short with the deputy. "I was told his report indicated he spoke with the homeowner following several triggered alarms at my home. I didn't talk to him, so who did he talk to when he took the call?"

"I'm reading that here on the report as well, but I don't know who he talked to. I will see if I can get that answered and get back to you."

"OK, thank you, Deputy," Karla said reluctantly.

"I told you we wouldn't get anywhere. Now you have to take me home," Karla said as we walked back to my pickup.

"Yes, I will take you home. We'll do a walk-through together," I said, taking her in my arms and hugging her.

We drove up to Karla's house and everything appeared the same as it did last night. The trash was still overflowing by the garage.

"Here, give me your keys," I told Karla as we walked up to the front door. Karla followed me as I handed her keys back after opening the door and we walked into the living room and then the kitchen.

114

"Well, everything looks fine."

"Yea, maybe, but I'm still not convinced," I said, rubbing my chin. "Something's not right."

"I want you to come back and hang out at my house a few days and see if the security alarm goes off again, and then we can come over together and check it. I don't want you here alone if it does."

"I don't think that's necessary, Owen."

"I do, so go pack a bag."

After three days at Owen's and no additional alarms, I told Owen that morning that I needed to go home and get out of his hair.

"I don't have much hair for you to be in."

"Well, you know what I mean—it's time I get back with it."

"Hmm, I suppose." This was still an interesting situation but with no additional alarms, he knew she was not concerned with it. "Can I at least take you out to supper tonight?"

"I tell you what, you take me home this morning and then when you get off work, I'll make you supper."

Owen conceded and dropped me off before he went to work. He took my luggage in and looked the house over again.

"It's OK, Owen. I'm fine—besides, I have things to do."

"You need to call me if something comes up, OK?" Owen said, holding my hand in the foyer and sounding as stern as Owen could muster.

"I will. Come hungry."

"Bye, Karla," Owen said as he slightly kissed my cheek and reluctantly went out the door.

I went and started some laundry and dove into cleaning the kitchen; everywhere I turned was another mess. How did I miss all this when I cleaned before going to Mexico? There was even mud on the patio—now how'd I get that there?

I went back to change the laundry and start another load. I opened the dryer door and saw a few articles of clothing. *I don't remember leaving these in her*e, I thought, grabbing them, and adding the load from the washer. I threw the clothes from the dryer in the basket and went back to cleaning.

That afternoon, I'd finished cleaning the kitchen and bathrooms and sat down in the living room to fold the laundry I'd finished earlier. I had towels on top and worked my way through to the bottom of the basket and there sat the forgotten clothes. Two shorts and a shirt. *These aren't even my clothes*, I thought, holding them up. *Why would these be in my dryer?*

It was just after five that afternoon when Owen rang the doorbell, with Arnold standing at his side. I heard Owen walking through the foyer.

"I'm in the kitchen," I hollered out to Owen.

"Hi guys, how was your day?" I asked Owen.

"It was ho-hum. How was yours, anything unusual?"

"No, pretty boring. House cleaning, laundry and now I'm just working on some supper fixings."

"I can help with that," Owen said, rolling up his sleeves a little.

"Actually, yea, you can. Would you chop up the salad?"

"Sure, where's your cutting board?"

"Third drawer on the left, by the fridge."

"OK," Owen said. I heard him moving items around. "Um, Karla, there's no cutting board in here."

"What? I always put it there. Let me see."

"Oh, don't worry, I'll make do."

I turned the water on to boil for lasagna noodles and Owen started chopping the lettuce.

"How was work, Owen?"

"Terrible, I missed you the whole time."

"Oh, come on. You spent the last nine days with me. You're probably sick of me."

"Not a chance. I offered to take you out tonight, remember?"

"I know, but we ate out a lot when we were gone. I wanted to cook something for us."

"That's OK, I like this idea better."

Once the lasagna noodles were finished cooking, I went to get the colander out of the cupboard only to find it wasn't there.

"This is strange."

"What's that?" Owen asked.

"We couldn't find the cutting board earlier and now I can't find the colander. You'd think I don't know my way around my own kitchen."

"Don't worry about it, I put stuff away all time and forget where. The black hole!" Owen said, laughing.

I pulled the noodles out of the water with tongs and assembled the lasagna. I put it in the oven as Owen finished the salad.

"Would you like a glass of wine?" Owen asked when he put the salad in the fridge.

"Hmm, not yet. How about a walk down to the water? I know it's cold, but I could use some fresh air."

"Sure. Arnold, come on, boy, we're going outside."

Arnold came up alongside Owen, looking at him excitedly.

"Owen, thank you for going to Mexico and helping me out the last few days, it means more to me than you'll ever know.

"Are you kidding me?" Owen said, taking my hand walking across the yard. "I had a great time in Mexico. I'm glad you invited me; I'd hate to think I'd have missed out on all that. The moonlight walks alone with you were worth it; I could do that every night. Have you heard from the newlyweds?" Owen asked, changing the subject.

"As a matter of fact, yes! Eide texted me this morning, after you let me off. I told her you held me hostage for three days; she didn't have any sympathy for me."

"I bet not," Owen chuckled. "When do they get back?"

"I think over the weekend."

"Should we have a welcome-home dinner for them?" Owen asked.

"You're becoming one of the Grainers, it seems. You're right, we should have a welcome-home dinner for them."

"I guess you're rubbing off on me some, but I'm a Kaster through and through."

"Let's plan a dinner a few nights after they're back. But now, we should go get our dinner out of the oven before it burns the house down."

"I'd rather eat it." Owen said chuckling.

"This is a great lasagna, Karla. A much better idea than going out."

"Yea, I thought so, even though I couldn't find my dishes. I'm going to have to clean my cupboards out and reorganize them."

"Oh, you'll be fine." Owen laughed.

Owen and I finished eating and cleaned up the supper mess and moved to the sofa in the living room. We discussed the wedding and the trip to Mexico some more. We laughed so hard about things; I think we even woke up Arnold.

"It's getting late," Owen said as he stood from the couch. "I better get going—you'll call if anything comes up?"

"Yes, I will, Owen. I think it's all good, now."

"I'll call you before I go to training tomorrow. Can I pick you up for church Sunday?"

"It's our standby; I wouldn't have it any other way."

"Good night, Karla," Owen said, standing with me on the porch before he left. Owen caught a sweet kiss just before stepping out the door.

Chapter 11

I stood there looking at myself in the mirror that afternoon; Owen and I was actually getting a Saturday evening out. It was rare for us to align our schedules. He had training sessions some Saturday's and I had a full line of travel on my plate. So, since Eide and Levi's wedding, which was nearing two months now, geez times flies, Owen and I were back to our airport drop off/pickup dating again. I heard the doorbell ring interrupting my thoughts; and Owen called out to me. At least we've come this far in our relationship; he just let's himself in now.

"Hello, Owen." I said coming down the stairs meeting him in the foyer. Owen gracefully took my hand, kissed my cheek, and whisked me out the door as I grabbed my keys from the hook.

Owen took me to a dance down in the village that evening. Owen and I dance hand in hand for hours. I felt like we were back in Mexico.

I walked Karla to her door later that night. It was great we'd gotten a night out together. It was nice seeing friends I'd made at work and church the last year but spending the time with Karla was more special. Had we really been seeing each other a year already. "So, church in the morning?" I asked Karla.

"Yes, looking forward to it. Thanks for a great night, Owen."

"You bet." I said before taking her back in my arms and kissing her fiercely, tipping her ever so slightly back. I released her and stepped away, "good night, Karla."

"Good morning," Owen said, handing me a cup of coffee when I jumped in his pickup. I think I was actually early getting ready this morning. Owen barely put his pickup in park.

"Thank you and good morning."

"Oh, I see where your priorities are this morning," Owen said laughing.

"Yes, need the coffee this morning."

"Rough night?" Owen asked.

"No, just haven't made any this morning."

After church, Owen took me to the coffee shop we went to the morning Eide slapped us together last summer.

"You know, I nearly skipped church that morning Eide wanted us to meet?" I told Owen as we waited for our coffee.

"What? You? I don't see you backing down from a challenge. Are you glad you ended up going that morning?"

"Best decision I've made in a long time."

Once our coffees were ready, we grabbed them off the counter and left the coffee shop. Owen drove up the mountain to a beautiful lookout spot in the park.

"Ah, this is a beautiful spot. I just love it here, Owen. Too bad we didn't bring a picnic lunch—even though it's cold, it's nice here."

"Don't worry, I got ya covered," Owen promised.

Owen drove down the road to a little sub shop. We each got a sub and a cup of coffee. Owen drove us back to the viewing spot. Owen pulled blankets out of his backseat and threw them in the back, and we jumped in and sat down together.

"You do pretty good at this dating thing, Owen."

"Ah well, I'm not so sure others would agree with you. I've made a mess a time or two."

"Don't worry, Owen, you're doing great."

We were eating our subs, taking in the view, when Owen's phone rang.

Owen dug the phone out of his pocket, looking at the caller ID. "Sorry, I've got to take this. Hi, this is Owen."

"Yes, sir. No problem, I'll be there soon."

"Sorry, Karla, we have to go," Owen said, putting his phone back in his pocket, breaking away from the coziness.

"No need to be sorry. Your call sounded important."

"It was, there was an avalanche up at the pass and my team was called out."

"Oh, that sounds terrible."

"Well, I hope it's not too bad. I'll drop you off and then go."

"Owen, if it would be quicker, you can go on in. I can get a ride," I told Owen as he drove down the road rather quickly, but steadily.

"I hate to do that to you, but it would be quicker, though."

"Did you text anyone about getting a ride?" Owen asked as we drove into the Mountain Rescue airfield hangar. I could see in the building the other guys getting gear ready. I knew Owen worked here but didn't really think about what he did and how dangerous these situations could be.

"Hey, Karla," Owen said, breaking into my thoughts.

"Hmm."

"Hey, it's alright. I train for this all the time. Did you get a ride?"

"No, not yet. I'll call my dad."

"Why don't you take my pickup?" Owen said, handing me his keys. "I've gotta go." He kissed my forehead and walked away. He took a few steps and then turned around.

"Oh hey, can you go let Arnold outside? Bye, Karla, I love you."

Owen just said "I love you"; even before I agreed to let Arnold out. He's never said that to me before. I sat there watching his team pack their gear to get ready. They were all calm but seemed to know danger loomed.

I finally moved to the driver's seat and left the parking lot feeling numb. It had finally sunk in what Owen was about to go do. I stopped by Owen's house and let Arnold run around outside. I decided to take him home with me for a while. Owen had to get his pickup later anyways. "Come on, boy, get in the pickup—want to go to my house?" Arnold barreled in the pickup like he was getting to go on the adventure of a lifetime.

It was almost eleven-thirty, and I still hadn't heard from Owen. I sat in the kitchen sipping a cup of coffee. I didn't really know what to expect when he went out on a rescue. I only heard him talk about them after the fact and he'd always been adamant they were no big deal; or he'd say they had a successful outcome. I finally gave in and decided to go to bed around one a.m. I dumped the rest of the coffee in my cup down the sink, it had long since gone cold. I went upstairs and Arnold followed me in and jumped up on the bed, lying at the foot of the bed like he owned that portion of the bed.

"I see how this works: Owen lets you sleep in his bed, spoiled dog."

A few hours later, I woke up and grabbed my phone, looking at the screen. Still no call or text from Owen. *Just great, I sit here wondering about you, Owen. I don't even know if you're home or still out in the field.* I sat up in bed and Arnold looked at me expectantly. "What, I suppose you want to go outside?" I went to move off the bed and Arnold made a beeline for the door. As I came down the stairs, I could hear him sliding across the kitchen floor. "Better stop, Arnold, or you're going to run into the cabinets." I was too late; I saw Arnold skid into the kitchen cabinets just as I got to the kitchen. I let Arnold out the back door and stood on the patio looking at the stars. *I hope you're OK, Owen.* I stepped back into the kitchen and decided to make a pot of coffee.

I filled my cup and went to my office to check my email. I had been assigned a client in Tennessee. "Oh yeah," I said sarcastically. "Won't this be a fun trip." I reviewed the client's files and their poor-performing product. I worked up an agenda and prepared the files. At this point, I could take care of these items in my sleep; this client wanted to re-brand a product that came out a few years ago in hopes of revitalizing it. I added my travel information to Dad's calendar and booked me a flight. I already had a bad feeling about flying out again. Between the flight and Owen, I was consumed with worry.

My phone rang shortly before seven that morning; I don't think I was ever more relieved to hear the chimes of my ringtone.

"Owen, hi, thank God. Are you OK?" I asked in a rush.

"Yes, Karla, I'm fine. I knew you'd be worried even though I told you I'd be fine." I could hear how tired he was even in the few words he'd spoken.

"I know, I didn't know what to expect when you left."

"Nothing to expect, really. It's just like going to work."

"I know but I thought you'd call like in a few hours, not a day and a half later."

"I take it you didn't have a very good night."

"Well not really, but it's alright. I was working on files for a new client."

"How's that going?" Owen asked.

"This new clients in Tennessee."

"Well, it should be warmer there"

"I suppose. Did you know I kidnapped your dog?"

"I didn't, I haven't been home yet. Can I pick up him and my pickup later?"

"Oh, right, do you need a ride?"

"No, I'm good. Todd's just finishing up and then he's going drop me off. Do you mind if I sleep for a while, and we get together later?"

"Of course. Arnold and I will be by later with supper."

"That sounds great. Thanks, Karla."

"You bet; I'll see you later. Sleep well."

After I hung up with Owen, I finished the client files and decided to make a pot of chili soup and some cinnamon rolls. I figured Owen could use a good hot meal to warm him up.

I stood at the stove, stirring the soup that afternoon. I was thinking about Owen; he was out so long and sounded so tired. I hadn't thought much about Owen being out in the past and now he told me "I love you." I just sat there; my mind too jumbled to say anything in return.

I pulled the rolls from the oven and packaged them both to take to Owen's. I loaded them in Owens's pickup while Arnold roamed in the backyard. It was late afternoon when we left for Owen's house, I was taking a chance on Owen being up and ready for company. It's almost like Owen and his team needed time to

123

recover physically and emotionally. I prayed to God for their health and safety always.

I rang the doorbell and stood on Owen's porch holding the soup pot and cinnamon rolls. When Owen opened the door, Arnold barreled in the house, racing around Owen.

"Wow, I guess somebody's excited to see you."

"Yea, guess so," Owen said, watching Arnold dance around him and then look back at me, smiling. "Oh wow, something sure smells good. Do you want me to take something?"

"How about taking this pot; I made some chili and cinnamon rolls. I thought you could use a good hot meal to warm you up."

"Ah, you read my mind, I was just thinking how good a big bowl of chili sounded, it's been a while."

I watched the back of Owen as he carried the pot of chili and headed to the kitchen. His jeans fit him stylish, and perfectly sculpted his backside, I couldn't help but notice, I thought, chuckling to myself. I was also following in the air of his sweet and musky cologne—oh, it smelled so good.

"Did you get some sleep today, Owen?"

"I did, slept very well. Oh man, I haven't had chili and cinnamon rolls in, I don't know how long. You went to a lot of work here," Owen said as he pulled me into to a hug and then twirled me around. "Did you get a nap in this afternoon, or did you just cook all afternoon?"

"I worked on client files. I don't really understand why they want our services, so I was studying up on the company and their product."

"Where's your new client?"

"In Chattanooga, Tennessee," I said, mustering as much enthusiasm as I could afford.

"Oh, yea, you said that earlier. Don't sound so thrilled," Owen said, chuckling. "When do you have to leave?"

"A week from Sunday. How was the rescue?"

"Not much to tell, really. We flew out to the pass; my team did a search from the sky and provided some ground coverage and had a successful outcome."

"Well, that's good, but sounds dangerous."

"They can be dangerous, but we train for these all the time to handle the unexpected." There was Owen's predictable answer, I thought.

"I knew the Mountain Rescue Center was out there, but I didn't really think about what they did until I watched you guys getting ready to leave and then waiting for you to call. It all kinda hit me."

"I'm sorry, Karla, I shouldn't have let you worry like that."

"I need to know these things, Owen. Make me take the rose-colored glasses off and open my eyes."

"That's what makes us stronger. This chili smells amazing, and I bet it tastes even better—can we dig in?" Owen asked.

"Of course."

Chapter 12

Owen and I planned to attend church services this morning before I had to fly out this afternoon. I was getting better about being on time. Sometimes I wondered how I ever make it to work on time. I still didn't feel good about taking this trip, the closer I got to this day, the worse my attitude became.

"Good morning," I said as I answered the door.

"Good morning, sunshine!" Owen said. "Ready for church?"

"I'm ready for church; just not another work trip. This one has really been nagging at me."

"Let's just enjoy the services first," Owen said lightly kissing my forehead.

When the services ended and we walked back to Owen's pickup, we still needed to run back to my house and get my things.

"I'm going to swing by and pick up Arnold before we head to the airport," Owen said. "It won't take long."

"Yeah, that's fine. He's going to the airport with us?"

"Well, yea," Owen said. "I was thinking last night about running down to the farm for a day or so after I drop you off at the airport, since we didn't make it at Christmas."

"Oh, that sounds nice. Be sure to tell them hello from me. Now I'm really dreading this trip. I'd rather go with you."

"I know, we'll make another trip, soon." Owen said. "We'll plan a weekend after you get back from the Volunteer State.

"We haven't had a chance to have a dinner for Levi and Eide either; they'll no longer be considered newlyweds by the time I get this done. I'm just a terrible sister and friend."

"No, you're not," Owen said. "You're just busy. I tell you what; you text them, invite them and I'll take care of the rest."

"What do you mean you'll take care of the rest?" I asked him, eyeing him suspiciously.

"I'll have dinner at my house. I'll shop, cook, everything."

"Really?"

"Don't act so surprised! It was my idea in the first place, it's only fair I take care it. Besides, you can't even find your own cutting board!" Owen said, laughing at his own joke.

"I did find it; it was stuffed in a drawer across the kitchen."

"Weird, why was it there?"

"Don't ask me. Sometimes I think I'm losing my mind. I had other things moved around, too; the whole kitchen was a disaster. One day I found a few articles of clothing in the dryer; I didn't even think they were mine."

"Hmm. You should quit cooking in your sleep. Well, anyways, tell everyone to be at my house about seven Friday. I'll have everything ready and then I'll pick you up at the airport."

"No way, if you're cooking for everyone, I'll take an Uber."

"I can do both."

"No buts, Owen."

I dropped Karla off at the terminal doors around four that afternoon for her flight. I grabbed her luggage from the back and set it on the sidewalk. "What time is your flight scheduled to arrive?" I asked her.

"About eight-twenty, eight-thirty."

"It looks like there's some weather coming in," I told Karla as I looked the sky over.

"Oh, don't tell me that."

"You'll probably be OK, just have some extra turbulence. Call me when you land, OK?"

"Oh, pilot talk, sexy. I'm digging it."

"You like that?"

"Um huh," Karla said as I pulled her into a passionate, steamy kiss.

"Bye, Owen, I gotta go."

"Bye, Karla, text your family and call me," I said as she walked into the terminal.

127

I jumped back in the pickup. "Are ya ready to go to the farm, Arnold, buddy boy?" Arnold picked his head up off the seat as if he knew just where we were headed. "Should we get some coffee, first?" As soon as I suggested the coffee, Arnold dropped his head back to his snoozing position.

I traveled down I-25, headed south with the music cranked up. It didn't really matter what was playing on the radio because I had one thought on my mind, and she had left her lingering taste on my lips for another week and was now some thirty thousand feet in the air. I was worried about her. The sky looked ominous this afternoon and she could be in for a rough flight; I wish I could be her pilot.

Just as I was pulling down the drive to my parents' farm, my phone started ringing.
I parked in the yard and answered the phone as I let Arnold out to do his business.
"Hello."
"You and that pilot talk," Karla said.
"I take it you just landed."
"Yea, a little later than expected, just headed to baggage claim now. You were right, there was some bad weather over Missouri and we had some rough turbulence, but it wasn't that bad."
"Well good, I'm glad you made it safe."
"Did you make it to your parents'?"
"I did, just drove up."
"OK, well, I won't keep you. Tell everyone hello."
"Call me sometime this week, if you have time. Love you."
"I will. Love you, too. Bye, Owen"
"Bye, Karla."

As I sat in the yard talking on the phone with Karla, I looked over at the big old barn and into the field where Arnold had run to. I already missed Karla, just looking at this barn and how she loved it. When she came to visit at Thanksgiving we walked all around the barn; she looked it all over and told me how magnificent she thought it was. I missed her something fierce every time she got on a plane. I noticed Dad coming out of the barn talking to Arnold, motioning in my direction. After I hung up with Karla, I jumped out of the pickup as Dad and Arnold were making their way towards me.

"Hi, Dad, how ya doing?"

"Good, Owen, how are you?"

"Oh, fine."

"Who was you on phone with?" Dad asked, pointing to the pickup, referencing I had been sitting in there.

"Oh, that was Karla, she just landed in Chattanooga for a work meeting this week. The sky didn't look too friendly when she boarded and I figured her flight might run into some weather, so I told her to call me when she landed."

"So, she did?" Dad asked. "Was there bad weather?"

"Yea, a little over Missouri they had some rough turbulence."

"But she landed, and you got your call then and everything is, OK?" Dad asked, eyeing me skeptically.

"Yes, Dad, don't look at me that way," I said, shaking my head and smiling.

"Um hum, whatever you say, Owen. Let's go in the house, I need a piece of the pie your mother made today. Might have something to do with your impending arrival; you could call her and tell her you're coming home more often, maybe I could get some more pie."

"Dad! That's not nice."

"What's not nice?" Mom asked as she greeted Dad and me on the porch. "Hi, Owen, nice you could finally make it home."

"Hi, Ma, nice to see you too. I'll let Ward Cleaver over here tell you what's not nice; but if I was you, I'd send him to bed with no pie tonight."

"I simply made a suggestion." Dad said, holding his hands us feigning innocents.

The next morning, I grabbed a cup of coffee and headed out to the barn. It seemed no matter how early I got up, Dad always seemed to be in the barn, already working on something.

"What are you working on this morning?"

"Hey, mornin', Owen. Is your mom up yet?"

"No, I didn't hear her. But you're up pretty early, what are you working on?"

", Ty brought this over from the Flight School a few days ago; this panel needs some structural repair of the engine pylon upper skin. An area of the exfoliation is corroded. Ty found it in the forward edge of the skin during an inspection awhile back. He took it out of service, which is a good thing; the corrosion's very extensive and caused a hole in the entire panel, weakening it.

Ty called around and tried to find someone to repair it; he even called out of the country but was unsuccessful in getting the logistics arranged. I was closer, and he seems to think I can repair it."

"Of course, you can repair this, Dad. Don't sell yourself short; you're great at it. Ty was right by bringing this to you; you do far better work than anyone else."

"Right, and I'm *free* is what you're saying."

"Of course, and I picked a good time to show up. I'll help you. I want to work on this bad boy," I said, excitedly rubbing my hands together.

"Well, let's get busy," Dad said. "It's not going to finish itself. Besides, you can tell me about that phone call you had last night."

"The one with Karla? I already told you, I had her call when she landed, I figured she'd run into some weather."

"Good grief, Owen, that's not what I'm getting at. You brought her home for Thanksgiving and went to a family wedding in Mexico with her."

"I haven't bought a ring yet, if that's what you're getting at, Dad."

"That's what I'm getting at, Owen. What are you waiting for?"

"Don't worry, Dad, I'm thinking on it."

Dad and I worked on the plane panel for several hours that morning. My thoughts kept returning to Karla. She wasn't exactly thrilled to be taking on this client in Chattanooga. Occasionally, Dad would pipe in with his opinions about my relationship with Karla.

"You-hoo—" Ma said, stepping into the barn. "I got some lunch ready."

"Hey, Ma, didn't realize what time it was."

"Yea, well, that's what happens in this old barn. Time just gets away from you," Mom said.

"How've you been, sweety?" Mom asked as she came up to the bench where I was working, and half-hugged me.

"I'm good, Ma. How about you?"

"I'm fine, you guys going to come in for some lunch soon?" Mom asked.

"Yes, Rosie dear. We'll take lunch if you're offering. Do you have any more pie?"

"Pie, is that all you want, old man?"

"Well, maybe a little, Rosie," Dad said, putting his arm around Ma. "Come on, Owen, let's go get some pie."

After lunch, Dad and I returned to the barn, working on the side panel until late in the afternoon. I could see the sun slowly falling beyond the horizon when I looked out the window because I heard someone drive in the yard. Dad and I were both holding the panel up and neither of us could step out to see who had pulled up.

"Are you expecting someone, Dad?"

"Oh, I don't know, could be anyone. It could be Ty, it could be Old Man Erving from up the road, Max, or simply the UPS driver. Some days, it's like Grand Central Station around here."

"How is Mr. Erving? You haven't said much about him in a while."

"I think he gets along alright. Maybe a little lonely since his wife passed and I don't think the girls come home very often. You and Ty don't run go-karts through his back field anymore."

"That's right, I forgot about that," I told Dad thoughtfully. Hmm, those were the days.

"Gentleman thought I'd find you in here," Ty said as he came through the barn door.

"Hey, Ty, I heard someone pull in, but couldn't let go of this."

"Yea, how's it coming?"

"It's quite a project, we have to machine the area and fuselage the pylon skin and reposition; it'll be a challenge."

"I bet," Ty said. "But you guys are up for it. How much longer before I get the plane back in service, you think?"

"Ah, I'm heading back tomorrow. But Dad's your guy."

"Oh, it'll take some time," Dad said. "Have some patience there, Ty."

"What else is new?"

"Hey. Dad just mentioned Old Man Erving from up the road—remember the go-karts we used to ride through his field?"

"Ah yes, yes," Ty said, chuckling. "Remember how he used to get all crabby with us? Secretly, I think he used to like watching us."

"I do remember that." I said, laughing with Ty.

"I haven't seen Ol' Erv in a while, how is he?" Ty asked.

"I was telling Owen I think he gets lonely since his wife died and the girls don't come home all that often. And he did like watching you guys out in that field; he's told me that," Dad said. "Don't ever tell him I told you that, either; he liked knowing that he could berate you boys like the sons he never had."

"Where's the girls at now?" Ty asked.

"Don't go down that road, again, Ty. You missed your chance. Little Miss Katy gave you the cold shoulder so much I figured you wither up and die. It was kinda funny how little attention she gave you," I said, chuckling.

"She might have shown a little more interest than you noticed," Ty said. "Speaking of interest, where's that brown-eyed beauty? Did she finally get smart and dump your sorry butt?"

"Owen's going to buy that girl a ring," Dad interrupted.

"No kidding, Owe, that's big, my boy."

"Reel it in, guys, let's not get ahead of ourselves. All I said was I was thinking about it, that's all. Let's just focus on this panel."

Mom stepped in the barn just then. "Hey guys, how ya doing out here? It's time you all came in and wash up for supper. Max, Elaine, and the kids are coming over for supper and should be here soon. Ty, you're staying, right?"

"Wouldn't miss it, Rosie, thank you."

"We'll be along just as soon as we secure this," Dad said.

As we were walking to the house, Max drove in. He and Elaine started unbuckling the kids.

"Gampa, Gampa, Gampa" was all we heard.

"Well guess we know who she wants to see," Max said, laughing.

"Well, I am her favorite."

"Hi, Max, Elaine, how ya doing?"

"Hey, Owen, how are ya? Sorry we missed you at Christmas."

"Me too; I'm sorry I didn't get here. There was a terrible accident up on the pass and my team flew out; we spent eighteen hours up there."

"Yea, that's what Mom said. So, you flyin' solo today? I was supposed to meet this terrific gal at Christmas, Mom said you her brought her to Thanksgiving, and you all had a nice time. Now all I get is this ugly mug," Max said, grabbing Ty's shoulder and roughhousing him. "So where is she—please tell me you haven't totally abolished this relationship, too."

"Word on the street is he's going to buy her a ring," Ty said.

"Do you guys ever listen," I said, shaking my head. "Besides that, it was just barn talk. I'm only thinking about it."

"You'll buy," Max said, shaking his head and laughing. "Once you start thinking, it's a done deal. Let's just go to town tomorrow and wrap this puppy up!"

Mom stepped out on the porch, apparently just in time to hear the end of Max and Ty's bantering.

"Who's going to town for a puppy?" Mom asked.

"Nothing, Ma," I said, laughing, as I walked towards the house. "Let's eat, I'm starved!"

"Owen, right, let's eat."

As the rest walked into the kitchen, I heard Ty walk by Mom in passing. "Owen's going to buy that girl a ring."

Ma just flashed me a smile and told everyone to take a seat.

We finished eating and everyone cleared their plates from the table and put them in the sink and then headed to the living room.

"That was good, Ma, thanks," I said, putting dishes in the dishwasher while Mom was putting the leftovers in the fridge. "I can do that Owen; you can go in with the others."

"I'm good, I listened to them all day. I've only seen you a few minutes today."

133

"Ty told me something on the way in for supper."

"I know, I heard him."

"You're going to buy Karla a ring?"

"Dad asked me earlier today if I'd bought Karla a ring yet. I said I was just thinking about it. Now those guys have it turned into a big thing and Max has it in head to go to town and buy the ring tomorrow. All I'm doing is thinking."

"Well, whatever you do, Owen, just be happy, and I think Karla would be a great addition to the family whenever the time is right."

"Thanks, Ma. Speaking of Karla, she's calling me," I said, looking at my phone. "I'm going to step out back and talk to her."

"Hey, Karla, how's it going?"

"Hi, Owen, my day hasn't been very good at all. How are you?"

"I'm great. I worked on a challenging side panel for a plane with my dad today. But what happened to your day?"

"Oh, this client is the pits, to say the least. I'm not so sure he even remembered I was coming. I had to wait on him when I arrived and that wouldn't have been so bad but then he didn't even seem to think he needed to assemble a team. We didn't get anything started until two that afternoon."

"I'm sorry, Karla, do you think things will get better now that they have an idea of what to expect?"

"I hope so. Tell me about your day, sounds way better than mine."

"It probably was. Everyone says to tell you hello, by the way. They all thought I made you run for the hills when you didn't come with me."

"Not a chance," Karla said. I could at least hear a smile in her voice, a little better than when we started the conversation.

"That's good to hear. Ty brought my dad a plane panel that needs some major work. It's good working out there with Dad, we haven't done that in a while. Ty even stopped by and helped. Then Max, Elaine and the kids came, we all had supper."

"Ah, that sounds like a good time. I won't keep you any longer; you can go see your family."

"OK, I hope everything goes better for you tomorrow."

"Me too, love you, bye."

"Love you too, Karla."

"Where've you been?" Dad asked when I came back into the living room.

"I was on the back step talking to Karla." I sat down on the couch and realized telling this audience I was talking to Karla was probably a big mistake.

"Oh yea?" Dad said, looking at me suspiciously.

"You can't go twenty-four hours without talking to her—hmm, you're in trouble, my boy," Ty said.

"Oh, never you mind. She called me anyways; she had a bad day at work."

"Even worse, she wanted to share her day with you. You're in so deep," Ty said, shaking his head and smirking.

"Yeah, so I'll take it. I don't see anyone knocking on your door."

"Not that you're aware of," Ty said, smiling.

"Where'd you say she's at?" Dad asked, interrupting Ty's commentary.

"Chattanooga, Tennessee."

"You going to go visit her on this trip?"

"Dad?"

"You went to visit her on a work trip, Owe? You are so married," Max said, snickering.

"It was my birthday; she had a two-week session in San Francisco, so I flew out for the weekend. No big deal. Dad, you need to learn to mind your own business."

"Oh, this is so a big deal, brother, you're a goner," Max said. "We should just plan the wedding right here and now."

"More like the bachelor party," Ty said.

Driving home the next evening, I was thinking it was too short of a visit. It was good to spend the time with Ma and Dad, albeit the razing from everyone. Working with Dad in the barn had been a longstanding thing for us and since I'd moved, we hadn't gotten to work together as much. It was even better that Ty stopped over; he's taken the Flight School in a whole new direction since I stepped back. And who knows, they all might be right; I kinda think I am ready to propose.

"Hello," I said, nearly dropping my bags to answer my phone just as I was about enter the client's office building. This morning was so not starting off on the right foot.

"Hello to you, too—you don't sound very good."

"Sorry. Hi, Eide."

"What's up with you?"

"I'm irritated with this client, and this morning is not helping anything. Why are you up so early?"

"I have to get up early If I want to check in with you. Leaving us lowlifes to fend for ourselves back here in the 'hood."

"Yea, well I'd like to be a lowlife back at home."

"Man, you are in a bad mood. What's wrong?"

"It's this client. They are terribly disorganized and dysfunctional. They haven't gotten a single thing done this week. I just want to scream at them."

"Oh, wow, Karla, calm down."

"I know, I'm sorry. None of this is your problem and here I am unloading on you."

"That's not why I told you to calm down, you're going to give yourself a heart attack."

"No, I'm not, I'm fine."

"Just take it easy, Karla. Will ya? Hey, Owen invited us to supper."

"Yeah, I know, I texted you."

He invited us, too. That's a big deal!"

"Not really, he brought it up after the wedding and then time just got away. So, when I was headed down here, he offered to take care of things."

"Ah, that's so nice"

"He's a pretty good guy, if I don't say so myself! Do we need to bring anything?"

"We never really discussed it, so I'm going to say no. And if that's not what Owen had in mind, I'll take the blame."

"I'm going to tell him you said that." Eide said, laughing.

"Yea, yea, you're always telling on me. Owen said he'd take care of everything, so I'm taking it literally. I have to go, it's time to meet the dysfunctional clan; I'll talk to you Friday."

"OK. Hey, Karla, try not to get too worked up."

"Yea, I'll be fine. Bye, Eide"

"Bye, Karla"

I went into the conference room and there was hardly anyone there. I shouldn't be surprised; Mr. Jones had been almost two hours late when I first arrived and didn't even act like a team was needed. We couldn't even have a proper recap the next morning. Somebody said, "I was here, was a recap necessary?" I tried to explain the benefits of having a recap, but he made it impossible. *What an annoying group*, I thought as I was getting my information ready. I know, very unprofessional thoughts. This team has really tanked my attitude. I was supposed to have an exit meeting with Mr. Jones on Friday but at this rate, I'd be surprised if he even showed up or if we had any accomplishments to discuss. It was Wednesday afternoon, and we were only able to start a few agenda items, let alone finish anything.

That evening I lay on the hotel room bed staring at the ceiling, growing more frustrated. I was tired of traveling to these things. I was trying to come up with a solution to this client's lack of motivation when my phone rang.

"Owen. Hi."

"How are you?"

"I'm tired and frustrated."

"Dang it, I take it things haven't improved with your client?"

"Owen, what's that noise?"

"That would be Arnold, he's picked up a new habit since he spent the night with you. He howls when I talk on the phone or the doorbell rings, I think he misses you."

"No way, that's funny," I said, laughing." "Oh, Arnold buddy, you'll be fine."

"So, what happened with this client that has you so frustrated?"

"It's gone from bad to worse. I've been lying here trying to figure out how to make the most of the last two days. I just want to scream at them to get their butts in gear."

"Ha ha," Owen chuckled. "You'll figure something out."

"Don't laugh, it's not funny."

"Hang in there. You're great at this; you'll get it figured out. I talked to your mom tonight."

"You did? This ought to be good."

"It was good talking to her. She called to thank me for the invitation and to see if they needed to bring anything."

"And what did you tell her?"

"They don't need to bring anything. Why?"

"Oh, nothing, Eide called asking the same thing. I told her you said you'd take care of everything."

"Yep, I got this, hot dogs and chips."

"Yes! My favorite. How was your trip—did you finish the plane panel?"

"Oh, the farm never disappoints. As far as the plane panel, that's a big project; Dad won't finish it for several weeks, but I was glad I got to tear into it with him. Ty looked all over to get a repair shop to take it on; he even tried out of the country, but it was a no-go. So, he took it to my dad. But hey, you can listen to me rattle on about that another time; I should let you get some sleep."

"It's nice listening to you rattle, but yes, I need to get things ready for tomorrow."

"Don't work too hard, Karla."

"I won't. Good night, Owen."

"Bye, Karla."

As I was walking into the conference room Friday morning, I saw Mr. Jones in the hallway and reminded him that we needed to meet at two today to have a recap meeting.

"OK, Ms. Grainer, thanks for the reminder."

Great, he didn't even say he'd be there. The guy really needs a calendar— or use it. I don't get it, this company seems to be doing well despite its bumbling, dysfunctional boss.

I went to Mr. Jones' office a few minutes before two that afternoon. Just as I'd thought, Mr. Jones was a no-show. *Now what,* I thought, sitting down, hoping he'd be along soon. Soon being twenty minutes later when he finally came rushing through the door.

"Ah, Ms. Grainer, very sorry to have kept you waiting; it has been quite a day."

"Good afternoon, Mr. Jones. Actually, it's been quite a week."

"How are things coming?

"Well, unfortunately not very well. Your team has made very little progress."

"Hmm, what seems to be the problem? Something with your program?"

"No," I said, shaking my head. "No, there's nothing wrong with the program. This program has a very proven track record. I've tried all week to work with your team; they are disorganized and don't even seem to care that I'm here. It doesn't help that you don't participate, either. We haven't even been able to follow the agenda. I feel as though your team thinks I'm here to prepare the campaign material for them. I'm here for guidance and analysis and at this point I don't even have enough information to start the portfolios."

"Well, we have all been busy around here this week, Ms. Grainer," Mr. Jones said, quite angrily.

"I can understand being busy, Mr. Jones. I, too, have a schedule to keep." Well, this was not turning out to be a very professional discussion at all.

"I understand, Ms. Grainer. What can we do to amend this?"

"I've been thinking this over today and I think I've come to a solution. I'm leaving here shortly to catch a flight home this weekend. If your team can read over the proposal my firm sent and get a better idea of the meeting requirements, I will come back on Monday so we can start fresh. I need your team to be organized and willing to follow the terms of the proposal."

"OK, Ms. Grainer, I'll see what I can do. Thank you for your advice and cooperation," Mr. Jones said, standing and extending his hand to me. "I'll email you later today and we'll see you Monday morning."

"Thank you, Mr. Jones."

I grabbed a taxi and made it to the airport in time to board. I laid back in my seat to rest my eyes. What was I thinking making a commitment to return next week? I didn't even have the desire to take on another client.

I was looking forward to getting to Owen's and the dinner he'd planned. Even though I told him I'd get an Uber, I half-expected him to be waiting for me when I landed. As I was walking to baggage claim and trying to pull up the Uber app, my phone chimed.

"Since you refused to let me pick you up, I sent Lane and Molly, they were thrilled. They should be waiting out front for you. Love ya, see you soon!"

As I was waiting for my luggage to come through baggage claim. My phone chimed again. *"Hey Kar, Owen sent us to come pick you up; we're out front."*

"Hi Lane, just got in, waiting on luggage. I'll be out soon. Thanks."

As promised, Lane and Molly were waiting out front when I walked out the door. "Hey guys, how's it going?" I asked them, jumping in Lane's pickup.

"We're good, how are you?" Molly asked.

"Do you need to stop anywhere?" Lane asked as he merged out into traffic.

"No, I just want to get home. It's been a terrible week and now I'm going back on Sunday."

"That don't sound good," Molly said. "What happened?"

"This has been the worst client; I've berated myself so many times for not being professional. What's up with you guys, anything new here?"

"Well, you might have to smooth things over with Dad," Lane said.

"Why what's wrong?"

"Oh, he called about twenty minutes ago and wanted to know what I was doing. I said we were headed to the airport; I think he would have liked to pick you up."

"Oh, well, if that's all his problem is, I can have them drop me off on Sunday."

"Geez!" Lane said. "Must be nice being so popular, you are the favorite daughter."

"Right, *only* daughter."

"Still the favorite, and very popular among the masses," Lane said, smirking. "Are we supposed to bring anything to this shindig tonight?"

"I meant to call you or Owen," Molly said." But didn't get a chance."

"No worries, Owen said he had it all covered. So, I guess you're off the hook."

"And the favorite daughter's ranking rises a bit higher. The boyfriend cooks dinner for the whole family."

"You better believe it; he cooks some darn good meals.

"Here ya go, thanks for taking Lane and Molly's airport shuttle today, don't forget to tip your driver on the way out," Lane said as he rolled into my driveway. "Do you want us to swing back around and pick you up on our way to Owen's?"

"No, you idiot," Molly said, punching Lane in the arm.

"What, why are you hitting me?"

"We're going to her boyfriend's; she might stay later," Molly said.

"Geez, OK. I was just offering her a ride," Lane said, rubbing his arm.

"I'm good, guys, thanks for this ride. I'll see you later."

I took my luggage inside and set it by the stairs, I was going to grab a quick shower before going to Owen's. Before I headed upstairs, I decided to grab a bottle of water. I opened the fridge, thinking I had bottles of water but didn't see any. So, I went to the sink to get a glass of water. As the water filled my glass, I thought, *Was there a bottle of champagne in the fridge? I don't ever buy champagne, that's odd.* I finished filling my glass and went back and opened the fridge door. Sure enough, there was a bottle there. I grabbed it, looking at the label. By the looks of it, it was some very expensive champagne. The label said, "Moët & Chandon." I bet Eide brought it over; somebody probably gave it to them as a wedding gift. *Talk about regifting.* I stuck it back in the fridge and went upstairs.

I showered, redressed, and attempted to do something with my hair. It looked a mess, and I was getting tired of holding the brush up. I gave up on it, grabbed my phone and purse and left. I was ready to see Owen, anyways. I was driving down the street a few blocks from Owen's when my phone rang.

"Hey, Owen!"

"Hey, yourself, you better be on your way over here. Lane texted me over an hour ago and said you've been delivered."

"Come on guys, I'm not a piece of furniture."

"His words, not mine. Are you on your way over here yet?"

"Yes, I am, do you need anything?"

"Not a thing, just that exciting, beautiful, brown-eyed beauty I left at the airport last week. You know where I can find her? I miss her."

"Hmm, I might be at your doorstep in five-four-three …"

I rang Owen's doorbell a few minutes later, I could hear Arnold howling. "Oh Arnold," I called out. "It's alright, you're OK, buddy."

"Hey, how are you?" Owen asked, grabbing the door and my hand all at once. He pulled me in for a nice long hug, kissing me softly along my neck.

"Thanks, I needed that. How are you, Owen?"

Arnold came up, circling me and sniffing my legs. "Hello, Arnold, what's up with the howling, buddy?" I asked, leaning down, scratching around his ears and head. "Did you miss me? I missed you and your master."

"I think he missed you and his master certainly did," Owen said. hugging me again after I stood up from talking to Arnold.

"So how did things end up with your client?"

"Black hole. Now I'm going back Sunday."

"Seriously, Sunday already."

"Yes, I told Mr. Jones he needed to visit with his team. They need to follow my agenda and the company's proposal. He said he understood and agreed to visit with his team to help turn this around."

"How'd that go over?"

"Well better than expected. At first, he blamed the program, he thought there was a problem with it."

"So, did you set him straight?"

"I don't know, I suppose the offer to return helped." I sighed. "So, we'll see how things go Monday."

"Way to kick butt, Karla," Owen said, putting his arm around me, slightly dancing.

"Yea, sure, it might be my butt that's kicked."

"How was your week, other than Arnold's newfound trick?"

"It's been pretty busy since I got home from the farm; but otherwise, OK."

"Busy as in training, or?"

"No, we had to fly down into Powder River Canyon and provide some ground coverage, but it's all good."

"That don't sound good."

142

"Well, none of them are really that good, but everyone's OK, including me."

"Owen," I said. turning to hug him, "you should have canceled on us."

"Not a chance, we've put this off long enough. I'm going to check things in the kitchen," Owen said as his doorbell rang. I looked out the window and my family was standing on Owen's porch. Was he really having supper for everyone? I opened the door and stood there looking out at them. "Hey, guys."

"Hmm, answering the door, I see," Eide said sarcastically.

"Owen's in the kitchen, he'll be out soon."

"How are you guys?"

"Hey Owen, you notice that?" I asked him when he came in the living room.

"What's that?"

"Arnold, he's quiet?"

"Well, ya, you're here now. I suppose when you leave, he'll take up howling again. You'll probably have to take him with you."

"What's this all about?" Mom asked.

"Hi, Owen, how are you?" Dad said, extending his hand to shake Owen's.

"Darren, I'm good," Owen said, shaking Dad's hand and then turned to Mom. "Mrs. Grainer, good evening."

"Hi Owen, nice to see you again. Laurel, please and thank you for having us."

"Hi, Garratt, long time no see. How ya been?" I asked.

"OK, how's things with you?"

"Come have a seat," Owen said. "Drinks, anyone?"

"Pale ale?" Lane asked.

"You're still drinking after the wedding?" I asked Lane.

"Yea," Lane said, looking confident.

Levi, Dad, and Garratt also took a pale ale.

"Ladies, what can I get you?"

"I'd take a glass of wine, if you got it," Eide said.

"Same here," Mom said.

"Molly?"

"Yes, please."

"Karla?"

"I'd just like a water, thank you."

143

Eide was sloshing the wine around in her glass and smelling it when Owen returned with my water and his beer. "Hey, Owen?"

"Yes, Eide."

"This is really good wine—what is it and where did you get it?"

"It's a Sanceree by Sibylle, or something like that, not sure I'm saying it right. I can show you the bottle. I got it at the market; I wasn't sure what to get so I'm glad you like it."

"Oh, hey, that reminds me, Eide, thank you for the champagne you left in my fridge. Owen and I will pop into it some night when I get back from Tennessee."

"What champagne?" Eide asked, looking at me skeptically. "I didn't put any champagne in your fridge."

"Oh." I looked around the room at the others and Owen. "Did one of you put champagne in my fridge?"

Everyone else looked as confused as I felt. "Owen?"

"No, sorry, hun, I didn't."

"OK, guys, jig's up. Who put that bottle in my fridge?" No one spoke up. "Really, no one knows about the bottle of champagne."

That is so strange, who else has access to my house that can put a bottle of champagne in my fridge? I thought.

"Well, on that note, we should eat," Owen said.

Owen sidled up to me as we were walking into the kitchen. "Is everything alright?"

"I guess, it's just been a long week. I'm tired."

Owen put his arm around me, smiling brightly. "Everything will work out."

"You're right," I said, looking up at Owen.

"Now let's go eat, I made a feast."

"A feast? No hot dogs?"

"Hey, Owen, you can play tonsil hockey with my sister later, how about we eat now?" Lane hollered as we walked into the kitchen.

"Lane!" Molly said, knocking him in the gut.

"Hey, don't hit me—it's good for 'em!"

"Owen, you got a really nice cut of beef here, nice and tender," Dad said, complimenting Owen on his meal.

144

"It's all very good, Owen, you're a very good cook," Mom said. "You should have let us bring something; then you wouldn't have had to go to all this work."

"Oh, it's no problem, Mrs. Grainer."

"Owen, this is really good meat, where did you get it?" Garratt asked.

"I've been going down to that little meat market in the village."

"Oh, yea, I know about that place," Garratt commented. "I was talking to a guy a while back and he recommended it. I checked it out and the meat choices are much better and more reasonably priced than the places in Denver."

"I don't think I've been there, but this is really good," Dad said. "I'll have to check it out."

Everyone agreed it was a good idea to go check out Owen's meat market in the village.

Funny, I'd check out Owen's meat market anytime. Oh geez, come on, Karla. Terrible thoughts during a family dinner, but I couldn't quite quell them, looking into his deep, dark eyes and that incredible smile.

"All right, Eide and Levi, tell us about the honeymoon," Molly said.

"Oh, Jamaica was absolutely wonderful, wasn't it, Levi."

"Well, when we left the hotel that is," Levi said, looking sly and smiling at Eide.

"That's my boy," Lane said.

"Did you guys take any tours or outside activities?" Molly asked, trying to avert Lane's comment.

"We took two," Eide said. "We did a café sunset cruise and went snorkeling. The rest of the time we just hung around the beach, and it was blissful."

"Sounds wonderful," Mom said. "Glad you guys had a nice time."

"Who's in for a game of pitch?" Lane asked after Eide, Molly and I finished cleaning up Owen's kitchen. Owen tried very hard to get us to leave the dishes or at least let him help, but Molly put up a bold fight.

"I think we'll pass; we're going home," Mom said, turning to Dad. "Thank you for everything, Owen, it was a delicious meal and a lovely time."

145

"It was great! Thanks, Owen. And thanks for the tip about the meat market," Dad said. "We'll see you all soon." Dad called out as everyone gathered around the table.

"I'm going to pass on the cards, too." I told everyone.

I heard several "what's and whys'" that I couldn't hang for a card game; but I was feeling a headache coming on.

Owen came over, taking me in his arms. "Are you sure you don't want to stay and play cards with us?"

"No, I'm sure. Thank you for everything."

"Can I call you tomorrow and we get together?" Owen whispered to me as he placed a delicate kiss upon my lips.

"Yes."

"Good night, Karla, I hope tomorrow's a better day."

"Karla didn't hang very long tonight," Lane commented as we were all getting settled to play cards.

"She didn't have a very good week."

"Yea, she mentioned that on the way back from the airport, plus she looks stressed-out," Molly said.

"Well, what do you expect. She's the human plane," Eide said. "You know, I've been having recurring dreams about her, that someone's following her. I've called her trying to tell her I'm worried about her, but she keeps brushing me off. Hey, why'd you play that card, Owen?"

"You better watch what you're eating, Eide," Lane said. "It can really affect your sleeping habits."

"She's really affecting my sleep habits," Levi said, laughing. "She even gets up in the morning and is sick over it."

"It's not a joking matter guys, I see someone following her— kinda looks a lot like you, Garratt."

"Me? Why are you draggin' me into your dreams, Eide?" Garratt asked.

"Owen, you shouldn't play that card; we're playing for points here, that's a slough card," Eide said.

"I followed suit."

"I wanted the three, you should've played that," Eide said.

"That not always the case," Lane said.

"Oh please," Eide said. "Besides, Lane, you're a terrible player."

"You always say that Eide. I think you're just intimated by how good of a player I really am. Besides, I play more often than you do," Lane said, playing the winning card. "And that, my friends, is how it's done."

As I drove home, I grew more tired and didn't really feel the best. I'd had a headache that was trying to set in. *This week has totally hit me, and I'm just wiped.*

I grabbed a couple aspirin from the medicine chest, and I looked at my luggage. *Eh, forget it*, I thought. *It can wait until tomorrow.* I was just going to need to repack again Sunday anyways. I brushed my teeth and crawled into bed.

I woke up quite a while later to my phone ringing. Good grief, who's calling this late?

"Hello?"

"Hey, Karla."

"Owen? Are you alright?"

"Yes, I'm fine. But are you alright?"

"Yes, why wouldn't I be?"

"I tried calling you a few times this morning, but just got your voicemail."

"Yea, I was sleeping, what time is it?"

"Almost ten-thirty."

"What? No way." I sat up in bed looking toward the windows, but the curtains and blinds were shut. Looked like the middle of the night in here. "I don't sleep this late."

"Well, you did today. I guess you needed it."

"No, I didn't need it. I have so much to do. I have emails to send, book a flight, revise the agenda, and laundry. I've gotta go, Owen."

"OK, I'll call ya later. Bye, Karla."

Good grief, I can't believe I slept this long. What's wrong with me? I thought, heading to the shower. *I haven't slept this late in I don't know how long.* I quickly showered and threw in a load of laundry before going to my office to check my email. I should have emailed my boss yesterday. Once my email opened, I saw he'd already emailed me. Seems Mr. Jones contacted him.

Good afternoon, Karla,

Seems you had a rather difficult experience with our new client this week. Mr. Jones emailed me this afternoon and expressed his displeasure with you at first. It seems by the ending of your meeting he'd changed his mind. I'm pleased you came to a solution.

Let me know if you need anything on my end this next week. Thank you for handling the situation, whatever it may be, that benefits the clients as well as our firm. If you need to talk, give me a call, I'm available.

Thanks again,
Craig

Hmm, well, thanks, Craig, I thought. *That was an interesting note. You've always had my back.* I hope things are better come Monday; I can't take another week like this one.

Hi Craig,

Sorry I didn't get you emailed earlier. Yes, this has been a rather difficult week with this client. I did have a visit with Mr. Jones regarding the firm's proposal and my agenda for the sessions. I hope we can adhere to them this coming week, when I return to complete the project. In the end, he did seem pretty receptive to my plans. I fly out again tomorrow afternoon and will be back the following Friday, I'll try to stop by your office and discuss this with you.

Thanks again,
Karla

I booked another flight back to Chattanooga for tomorrow afternoon. It's a good thing the firm picks up the tab on these flights. This one comes in at $972.00 for booking on such short notice. *Almost a year of bouncing across the country, I was tired of being a beach ball,* I thought, laying my head across my keyboard. I raised my head and continued through my emails.

By the time I had my emails taken care of, a flight booked for Sunday, and added my schedule to Dad's calendar, the afternoon was nearly shot, and I hadn't even taken the time to work on any marketing files or a new agenda. And I still needed to call Mom and Dad about giving me a ride tomorrow.

"Hi, Mom."

"Hi, sweety, how are you?"

"OK, how are you guys?"

"We're good, had a nice time at Owen's last night. Is he there? I'd like to thank him again."

"No, he's not here. He called me and woke me up this morning. I had a lot of things to do today, and we haven't made plans for tonight."

"He woke you up. How early did he call?"

"About ten-thirty; I thought it was the middle of the night."

"You don't usually sleep that late."

"You're telling me. With all the work I needed to get done, I feel like I wasted the whole day."

"Ah honey don't worry about it. With your schedule, you needed the extra sleep."

"A little extra sleep would be fine, but not half the day," I said irritated. "Is Dad around?"

"I think he just came in the back door. Why, what's up?"

"Lane said Dad was a little miffed that Owen didn't ask you guys to come pick me up. So, you want to drop me off at the airport tomorrow?"

I could hear Dad in the background asking who was on the phone. And then Mom must have switched over to speakerphone.

"It's Karla."

"Oh, hey, kiddo, what's going on?"

"She asked about taking her to the airport tomorrow but we're going to Jane's in the morning."

"I vote for the airport," Dad said jokingly.

"No, Dad, go to Jane's."

"We can pick you up," Mom offered.

"Let's do both," Dad said, chuckling again at his jokes.

"Hey guys, it's fine. I'll get Owen to take me. Tell Jane hi and I'll talk to you guys' next week."

"OK, bye, honey."

"Bye, kiddo."

"Hi, Owen."

"Hey, Karla, things better now?"

"Yes, I'm fine."

"Did you get everything taken care of?"

"Some, yes, well almost—would you take me to the airport tomorrow?"

"Sure, hon, what time?"

"I need to be there about four."

"Yea, that's no problem, how about church, and lunch first?"

"That'd be great. Thank you, Owen."

"What are you doing tonight?"

"I hate to tell you this, but I'd rather not do anything. I just want to stay home. You can come do nothing with me if you'd like?"

"How about pizza and a movie?" Owen asked.

"Sounds great."

"OK, well, I better get a move on it, I'll see you in a few."

"OK, bye."

I heard the doorbell ringing awhile later; I had vegged out the couch and so I just hollered and told him the door was open, and here came Arnold barreling in and dive-bombed me on the couch with Owen following him.

"Arnold, get down, you know better; lay on the floor," Owen instructed him.

"Hi, how are you, besides the dive-bombing dog in the lap?" Owen asked as he leaned in for a partial hug and kiss.

"I'm good, how are you?"

"Good, ready for some pizza?" Owen asked, holding up the pizza box.

"Sure, let me get some plates and drinks," I told Owen as I started to get up off the couch.

"No need, you look comfortable," Owen said. "I'll get us some."

"I see you haven't indulged in the mystery champagne," Owen said when he came back from the kitchen.

"Oh, yes," I said, shaking my head. "I still don't know where it came from; guess I must have put it there sometime and forgot. What movie did you get?"

"I just brought a movie from home; I hope that's OK?" Owen asked.

"Works for me; which one is it?"

"*Dead Poets Society.*"

"Oh, ya, I remember that movie."

"Yea, you like it?" Owen asked.

"Yea, good choice."

"OK, let's dig in," Owen said after he started the movie and was sitting down next to where I was laying. I started to move so Owen would have room to sit beside me.

The movie started and Owen handed me some pizza when I hadn't taken any yet. I took the piece of pizza and had a small bite but wasn't all that hungry. I set the plate with the pizza on the coffee table and focused on the movie. I was super tired, I thought, yawning.

I woke up later and Owen was gathering up the pizza and plates.

"Hey. I was going to wake you after I cleaned this up."

"Is the movie over?" I asked, leaning up from the couch.

"No, I shut it off," Owen said. "I put the pizza in the fridge in case you want some later."

"You don't have to leave; I can sit up and we can finish the movie."

"No, that's OK. We'll watch it another time; you're tired. I'll be by to pick you up for church in the morning."

I started to get up as Owen headed out the door. I was going to tell Owen good night, but he leaned down, hugged, and kissed me.

"Don't get up," Owen said. "You look beat. I'll let myself out." Owen said, leaning down to kiss me. "Good night, Karla, love you."

"Hmm K. Bye, Owen. Love you, too," I said, leaning back on the couch thinking I'd get up and go upstairs in a few minutes.

"Come on, Arnold. Arnold, let's go, buddy," I heard Owen whisper to Arnold as they went out the door. I heard Owen latch the door.

I must be dreaming, I thought as I stirred in my sleep. *Was I dreaming?* I hear a phone. I think that is my phone. *Where is my phone anyways?* I thought, sitting up. *Oh man, that hurt so bad, why am I sleeping on the couch? That's a bad idea.* I could hear my phone ringing out again. I got up looking for my phone and found it in the kitchen. I guess I left it there earlier. Oh crap, it was almost ten in the morning, I realized looking at the screen.

I had three texts and now two missed calls from Owen. Church services started in less than half an hour; so much for getting there this morning. I still had to pack.

I called Owen on my way upstairs to get in the shower.

"Hey, Owen." He answered on the first ring; he must have been waiting for me to call. "Sorry I missed your calls and texts."

"Yea, I was getting worried," Owen said. "I'm just about to your house; are you about ready to go?"

"No, actually I'm not," I said, yawning. "I just woke up a little bit ago, I could hear my phone ringing."

"Are you going to be ready in time for church?"

"No, and I'll be lucky if I'm ready when you come to pick me up."

152

"Oh, OK," Owen said, sounding dejected. I'm going to go to church, and I'll swing by when it's over and we can go to lunch."

"Can we just grab a sandwich on the way; is that OK?"

"Yea, sure. As long as you're OK, you don't sound very good."

"Yes, I'm fine. I just woke up, I've got sleepy voice, I've slept too long."

I was just bringing the last of my luggage down when Owen rang the doorbell. I had spent the better part of the last two hours trying to find some clothes that didn't need washed. Packing this morning was a challenge in more the one way.

"Hi, how are you?" Owen said, stepping into the foyer, handing me a cup of coffee. "You had me worried this morning," Owen said, looking concerned.

"Thanks, I needed this. I'm sorry I worried you."

"It's OK," Owen said, taking me into his fold, gently laying my head against his chest. "You sure you're, OK?"

"Oh, yes. Well could have done without sleeping on the couch."

"Yea, bother your neck?" Owen asked as he briefly rubbed my neck.

Ugh, talk about a crook in the neck, but it's fine, I need to get going. I'm going to hit the bathroom, and then I'll be out?"

"OK, I'll take your luggage and get it situated."

Owen grabbed my luggage and headed to his pickup.

As I was headed through the front door out to Owen's pickup, my phone rang. It was Mom.

"Hi, Mom."

"Don't 'hi' me. What's up with you, Karla? Owen said you were sleeping and wasn't coming to church, what's wrong?"

"Nothing, I just overslept and didn't make it, I had to get ready for my flight."

"Your mom?" Owen whispered as he pulled out of my drive. I shook my head yes.

"I've never known you to oversleep," Mom said, sounding concerned.

"Well, I did and now I'm headed back to Chattanooga," I told Mom, rather shortly.

153

"No wonder you're tired, you never stop."

"Well, what can I say, I have two speeds: go and stop; and now I gotta go, I'll call ya later."

"OK. Bye, Karla."

"Bye, Mom," I said and clicked the button to end the call.

"She asked about you at church, she thought it was out of character for you to sleep this late."

"Oh, well, she'll get over it. She's just concerned. I thought they were going to Jane's, anyways."

"Oh, I don't know, she didn't say anything," Owen said.

Owen drove through a drive-thru and ordered us some sandwiches and coffee before hitting the highway. Once we got to the terminal, Owen pulled up out front and set my luggage on the sidewalk in front of the terminal doors. He stood there looking at me like I was going to break. Don't get me wrong, it was not a hardship staring back.

"Karla, are you sure you should be leaving; you don't look like you feel very good." Owen put his arms around my midsection, gently kissed my forehead and along the side of my neck.

"Yes, I'm fine," I said, brushing off his concerns. "Thank you for being so sweet, but I gotta go." I quickly grabbed my luggage and headed into the terminal.

I drove away from the airport terminal and down to the coffee shop before getting back on the highway. I felt as though Karla was as stressed as Molly mentioned other night and she didn't look like she felt very good; I prayed to God this would be a better week for her. After I got my coffee, I headed back to the pickup to text Karla. As I sat there in the parking lot getting a message ready for Karla, my phone rang, interrupting my message.

"Aaron? Yes, sir."

"OK, I'm about forty-five miles out but I'm on my way. See you then."

"Yes, I'll be careful. Thanks, bye."

Chapter 13

A while after the plane took off, I woke up with a humongous headache. I should have just gotten my files out and reviewed them. Now, wowzah, my head hurt terribly, probably from sleeping on the couch last night—or there might have been a lot of turbulence. I'm surprised Owen didn't have a comment about the weather before I left. I sat up, putting my head between my knees.

"Excuse me, Miss, could I get some water?" I asked the flight attendant when she asked if I was alright. I could have used some aspirin, but I left them in the bathroom cabinet after I took them the other night. The flight attendant brought me a bottle of water. I drank some and laid back, closing my eyes again.

I heard someone make an announcement over the intercom later, saying something about being cleared for landing into Metropolitan Municipal Airport in Chattanooga. "It's a breezy sixty-four degrees here this evening, local time is seven-ten. We hope you've enjoyed your flight with us today."

I saw a text message from Owen as I walked to pick up my luggage.

"Hey, Karla, hope you've had a good flight and you're feeling alright. Take care and call me if you need anything. Talk soon."

As I waited for my luggage to come through baggage claim, I replied to Owen's text.

"Thanks, Owen, just landed. Talk later."

I got an Uber and directed them to the hotel.

When we pulled up, I remembered I hadn't made reservations. I asked the driver to wait to see if I could get a room. I was able to check in and sent the driver on his way after I retrieved my luggage. I went to my room and laid down wishing I had stopped to get some aspirin for my headache. I checked my messages, thinking Owen would have texted back or called by now. We can catch up tomorrow, I was going to sleep.

The next morning, I got up and headed back to Mr. Jones' office. The headache I had last night was a little better, which was a good thing if things hadn't changed with this office. I didn't need a lingering headache to contend with.

"Hi, Mr. Jones, please. He should be expecting me," I told the receptionist.

"Your name, please?"

"Karla Grainer, I was here last week and worked with him."

"Oh, right, please hold and I'll give him a call."

"Mr. Jones will be with you shortly," she said when she hung up the phone.

"OK, thank you." *At least I wasn't told to take a seat*, I thought. Mr. Jones did arrive moments later, I was impressed.

"Good morning, Mr. Jones," I said, extending my hand to shake his.

"Good morning, Ms. Grainer," he said, shaking my hand. "Thank you for making the return trip."

"Sure, is your team ready to continue?"

"They are," Mr. Jones assured me. "We had a staff meeting Friday after you left and reviewed the materials you mentioned."

"Thank you, I appreciate that. I hope things go smoothly this week. Will you be joining us, Mr. Jones?"

"Yes, sometimes, Ms. Grainer."

We stepped into the conference room, and I was nearly in shock, almost everyone was there and looked ready to go—*was this even the same group?* "Good morning, everyone, does anyone have any questions before we get started?" No one indicated any questions, so I reviewed a somewhat off-the-cuff agenda for the week. I didn't take the time to prepare a new one or even revise last weeks. I decided that last week's agenda would work just as well.

As the morning wore on, my throat became drier all the time and I seemed to have picked up a cough. *Hmm*, I thought, *must just be a slight tickle*. I excused myself to the restroom. When I got to the restroom, the coughing seemed to have gotten worse after walking down the hallway. The coughing didn't seem to help my head, either, as it decided to gear up, again. I wiped my face and headed back to the conference room; the cough continued. *What was I going to do?* I thought, standing there looking at everyone in the room; many of whom were staring back at me.

"Can someone point me in the direction of a vending machine?" I asked.

"Yes, there's one in the front lobby, can I get you something?" asked the gentleman in the front row who'd thought a recap was unnecessary.

"No, thank you," I said between coughs. "I'll be back shortly; I'm just going to grab a water."

I returned to the conference room, where I did more drinking and coughing than presenting. I was having a hard time getting my message across because of this cough. Between the coughing and the headache, I gave up early in the afternoon. I'm sure they couldn't understand me, anyways. I told the team we needed to break for the afternoon, I wasn't doing any one of us any good.

I was glad I had remembered to ask the taxi driver to stop off at a pharmacy to grab aspirin and throat lozenges, I thought, riding the elevator up; and now I planned to go soak in a hot bath and lie down.

By five the next morning, I felt so terrible and had the worst night, I had decided Owen was right. I probably shouldn't have come. I'd spent the better part of the night coughing and my head was throbbing. I grabbed my computer to see if I could change my ticket home.

The airline had a flight available at ten-forty this morning. Something sooner would have been better. I emailed my boss and Mr. Jones, explaining that I was sick and would be taking a flight home this morning. I would schedule something with Mr. Jones soon to finish the project. I laid back down feeling drained and exhausted from the cough, which seems to have gotten worse. I got up a couple hours later, washed my face off in the bathroom and called the front desk to request a taxi. I packed my belongings and went down to the lobby.

I stepped up to the front desk and asked the clerk if the taxi had arrived.

"Yes, I think I just saw him pull up," she said, looking at me perplexed.

"Thank you," I said and tried to explain I would need to check out this morning, through a breathless coughing fit.

"Yes, ma'am. I'm sorry to hear that, should I charge the credit card on file?"

"Yes, please."

"Would you like a receipt?"

"Just email me one," I said as I went out the door.

"Metropolitan Airport," I told the driver as I got in the taxi.

"Yes, ma'am, Metropolitan Airport," the driver confirmed as he drove away.

On the way to the airport, I texted Owen and told him that I was sick, had changed my flight and wondered if he could pick me up. I was surprised Owen didn't just call me right away, but he didn't even text back. Oh, well, he's probably busy at work this morning. I called Dad but only got his voicemail; I left him a message of the same nature. I arrived in Denver feeling worse than when I left this morning. This cough had gotten worse, my head hurt, and now my chest was starting to hurt and burn, probably from all the coughing. All I wanted to do was go to bed.

I checked my phone as I headed to pick up my luggage. That's strange, no call or text from Dad or Owen. I figured one or both of them would have left a message by now and be waiting out front. I grabbed my luggage and pulled up the Uber app to request a ride. I hadn't used this service in a while and the way my head hurt I couldn't get the stupid thing to work right. I finally got it, and a confirmation message back. That was stupid hard to get done.

I was leaned back, resting my head against the seat in the Uber driver's car. After we'd been on the road awhile my phone rang.

"Hello?"

158

"Oh, geez, Karla, you sound awful. I'm sorry I missed your messages. Did you get a ride?"

"Yes, I got an Uber. We're about halfway, I'd guess," I said, coughing.

"So, what's going on with you, are you alright? I knew you shouldn't have left Sunday; you just didn't look like you felt very good," Owen said, rambling on, concerned.

"I don't know, probably just a cold. I just want to go home and go to bed," I said through a breathless coughing fit.

"OK," Owen said. "We have a few things to take care of here at work and I'll meet you at your house."

"OK, bye," I said, laying my head back against the seat. I didn't have the energy to argue with him, but I didn't really see the need for Owen to stop by when I got home. I was just going to bed; but I could tell him when he got there.

Owen was sitting in his pickup when my driver pulled into the other side. Owen jumped out of his pickup and came over to my side of the car.

"Hey, hon, how are you?" he asked as he took a hold of my face and neck. "Oh wow! You're burning up."

"Oh, it's nothing."

Owen grabbed my luggage from the car and walked up the steps.

"I just...want...to…go...to bed," I said through a breathless coughing fit.

"You should go to the doctor and get checked out first."

"I'm fine," I said, after coughing and feeling like I was choking.

"This don't sound fine," Owen said.

"I'm just going to go to bed, and you can get back to what you were doing."

Owen carried my luggage, stepping into the foyer.

I set Karla's luggage near the stairs. We were both speechless at the state of her living room, there was luggage and belongings laying around. There was even a child's pack 'n play set up in the back of her living room.

"Did you leave these things out when you left?"

"No." Karla was coughing so hard, almost sounding like she was having a hard time breathing.

"Where did all this come from?" she asked, running her hand through her hair. "I don't even have a pack 'n play."

"I don't know, why don't you have a seat on the couch. I can look around and check things out. You seem like you can't breathe, and that cough is terrible."

Karla shook her head at me and followed me as I went into the kitchen. The counters had a few bags of groceries and a just-cooked-in vibe.

"I take it those aren't yours, either?" I asked, pointing to the bags on the counter.

Karla shook her head we stood there looking around. I left the kitchen and went upstairs. I could hear Karla walking behind me. Her breathing was worse with every step she took—man she needed to see a doctor and soon.

"Owen, this is weird," she said, coughing almost to the point of not being able to understand her.

"Yes, I know. I wish you'd sit down and let me handle this before you pass out." We looked in every room and saw several bags of luggage and even some air mattresses.

"Owen, it's like there's people staying here."

"Do you have people drop in when you're gone?"

"No, never," Karla said in a short tone.

Let's go downstairs, I'll call the Sheriff's Office.

"All I wanted to do was come home and go to bed, now I have to take care of whatever this is," Karla said, sitting on the couch.

"I'm going to take care of this. Do you want to go to my house so you can get some rest—or better yet, a trip to the doctor?"

"No," Karla said, coughing harder and now that I was sitting next to her, I could hear some terrible congestion going on.

"I wish you'd get checked out," I said as I dialed the phone.

"Owen, do you remember all the security system alarm issues and the messages I got when we were in Mexico?"

"Yea," I said, shaking my head. I couldn't continue that thought with Karla, someone had picked up on the other end and I started talking on the phone.

"Hi, I'd like to report a break-in at my girlfriend's home."

"Your name and address?"

"Owen Kaster, 2176 Trail Ridge Road."

"Is there an intruder in the home?"

"No, but I think they may return."

"OK, sir. I'll send a deputy out there."

"Thank you."

"They're going to send a deputy; now would you go to the doctor and go to my house so you can go to bed?"

"No, I want to talk to the deputy," Karla said, still breathless and looking very rundown the more I looked her over.

"You can't even talk you're coughing so much."

I should have pushed more for her to stay home from Tennessee when she left Sunday. I knew she wasn't feeling well even then.

"Hang tight," I told Karla when the doorbell rang. I got up to answer the door.

"Hello," I said as I opened the door to a uniformed deputy.

"Hi, I'm Deputy Montez. I'm responding to a call that there was a break-in at this address."

"Yes, I called. I'm Owen Kaster; my girlfriend owns the home. Please come into the living room and I'll explain the situation."

"Karla, this is Deputy Montez."

"Deputy, this is Karla Grainer."

"Ma'am, sorry for your troubles," the deputy said as he shook our hands.

"I understand you've had a break-in today; would you tell me about it?"

Karla began to tell him about coming in and finding the luggage and belongings strewn about, but then she had to stop because she was coughing so hard and couldn't go on.

"You see, Deputy," I said, continuing while Karla was coughing. "Karla was out of town on business this morning. I met her here when she was dropped off, we came in and found all this," I said, gesturing my hand around the room. "It's like someone's staying here."

"Have you seen anyone around the home?" Deputy Montez asked.

"No," I said, shaking my head.

"This isn't the first problem Karla's had of this nature. She had some security alarm issues back in January; we tried to visit with the deputy who took the report."

"What happened in January?" Deputy Montez asked while jotting notes on his pad.

"Karla received some messages from her home security system company that said an alarm had been triggered at her residence and a deputy would contact her for an update, but the deputy never contacted her. She called the Sheriff's Office and while the deputy's report states he spoke with the homeowner, she didn't speak with a deputy. When we got back from our trip, we stopped by the station, only to find out the deputy was off duty; we asked to have him call us when he returned. I think it just got swept under the rug, no one ever called. She didn't have any more messages so we kinda let it go."

"Hmm, interesting. Who was the deputy?"

"Green, Greenley, Greeley, something like that."

"It was probably Deputy Greenley, and he's no longer with the department."

Karla was trying to tell us about other things that had been going on when she traveled but the coughing wouldn't relent and kept interrupting her. She couldn't continue and eventually laid her head on her knees. This was getting worse, she needed to see a doctor. We were interrupted by the front door opening. We all looked stunned at each other. A group of gaily chattering people of varying ages from young children to older adults came through the front door and were gathering in the foyer, taking off coats and hats. Deputy Montez and I approached them. I could hear Karla come up and stand behind me.

"Can I help you?" I asked.

The group went dead silent, staring at the deputy and me standing there. "Excuse me, Deputy, is there is a problem?" an older gentlemen asked.

"Well, there seems to be," Deputy Montez said. "It seems you folks are trespassing."

"Trespassing—trespassing? I don't understand," a stunned looking, distinguished older gentleman said, stuttering.

There seemed to be a stunned and confused consensus among the group.

Another adult male in the group stood out from the group, looking to the deputy for direction. "I don't understand, what do you mean we're trespassing?"

Karla moved out from behind me. I could tell she was very tired and upset, having terrible coughing spells, and breathing harder all the time. She loudly yelled through a croaked voice. "YES, YES YOU ARE. THIS IS MY HOUSE AND I COME HOME SICK WANTING TO GO TO BED ONLY TO FIND YOUR THINGS LAYING AROUND. I'd say you're trespassing."

I'm not sure anyone even understood her with all the coughing and then she turned and walked away. *This is not going to be good*, I thought, following her into the kitchen.

"Karla," I said, coming up behind her as she stood over the kitchen sink with her head down. I put my arms around her. "Karla, you're burning up, your coughing is terrible. You obviously have pneumonia. Let's just go to the doctor and take care of all this later."

"Just stop it, Owen. You don't need to worry about any of this, I told you to go home," Karla shouted as she backed out of my embrace and stormed out the back door to the patio, still coughing. I could see her through the window; she was bent over, coughing. I stood there watching her for a moment; I was just about to go out after her when I saw Darren walk into the yard.

"Karla, are you OK? What are you doing back here? I could hear coughing all the way out front."

"Dad?" I said breathlessly, lifting my head.

"Yea, what are you doing out here? Why is there a cop car here? Is Owen here?"

"Honey, you sound awful," Mom said as she came and stood beside me. I had my hands on my knees, bent over; I just shook my head. I couldn't talk and I certainly couldn't keep up with their questions.

"Is Owen inside?" Dad asked.

I shook my head, to indicate Owen being inside.

"OK, you need to go to the doctor," Dad said. "I'll go tell Owen and you take her to the car, Laur," Dad said, going into the house.

Dad came back to the car as we were getting settled.
"Ah listen, Owen's got a bit of a situation. You take her to the doctor, and we'll catch up later."
"OK," Mom said skeptically.
"What's going on in there?" Mom asked when she pulled out of the driveway and drove down the street.
"Break-in," I said breathlessly.
"Oh goodness."

Mom took me to the walk-in clinic at the hospital. A nurse came and showed me to a room, while Mom answered registration questions. She took my vitals and asked me what was going on.
"I have a cough; my chest is on fire and my back hurts," I said breathlessly and coughing.
"Yea, I can hear that cough. I'll tell the doctor; he'll be in soon," she said, handing me a gown when she went to leave.

I sat there on the exam table, cold and coughing. All day, I'd been trying to get back to my bed, I was willing to guess I wouldn't be getting there tonight. I barely heard the light knock at the door, interrupting my thoughts when the doctor and nurse stepped into the room.
"Hello, Ms. Grainer," the doctor said, looking at the chart. "How are you doing?"

"Cough, burning chest and my back hurts," I said as a coughing fit took over.
"Where does your back hurt?" the doctor asked.
I pointed to an area just below the back of my neck, showing the doctor.
"OK," he said, listening to my chest and lungs. "We're going to get a chest X-ray, some blood work, and Nurse Dalpha here is going to start an IV; she's the best nurse for the job," the doctor said, joking.

As the nurse was cleaning up from starting the IV, I noticed someone was waiting with a wheelchair by the door. "This is Trent," Nurse Dalpha said. "He'll take you to X-ray."

"Your chariot awaits, miss," Trent said as he helped me maneuver the IV tubing as I moved from the hospital exam table to sit in the wheelchair.

Trent rolled me down to X-ray, trying hard to carry on a conversation, but I couldn't keep up with it.

Trent helped me get settled for the X-ray and then stepped out of the room. He returned when the technician was finished. Trent rolled me back down the same hallway we'd come through earlier. As he entered the room, I could hear Mom talking on the phone, but then said she needed to go pretty quickly when I got in the room.

"That was your dad, he was telling me a little about what happened to you today."

I just shook my head and laid my head on the pillow after Trent helped me from the wheelchair back to the bed.

"Would you like a blanket, miss?"

"Yes, please."

Trent left the room and promptly returned with a warm blanket, spreading it out for me.

"Anything else, I can get you, miss?"

I shook my head and closed my eyes.

The doctor came into the room shortly thereafter. "How are we doing? Here's what I know and what we're going to do. I don't have your blood work back yet; we can review that later. I'm pretty sure I know what it will say, anyways. Your X-ray shows a severe case of pneumonia and some fluid in your lungs, which would contribute to your chest and back discomfort. I'm going to admit you with some orders for high-dose steroids and IV antibiotics. If the steroids don't help the fluid on your lungs, we'll need to drain it off, but we can cross that bridge, later. Sound, OK? Any questions?"

I shook my head.

"OK," the doctor said. "Hang tight, Trent will be back to take you upstairs, and hey, you got the hard part done, you already got the IV started."

Please, I thought, *as though the IV was the worst of my worries."*

"Owen?" Darren said as he came in the back door.

"Hey, Darren," I said, lifting my head up from my knees.

"Hey, Owen. You, OK?" Darren asked, touching my shoulder as he took a seat at the table next to me. long day?"

"Yea, like two or three long days."

"Laurel's taking Karla to the doctor."

"Good, I tried several times since she got home, but she kept refusing me. I didn't think she even looked like she felt very good Sunday. I should have pushed her not to go."

"She's stubborn, Owen, you couldn't have changed her mind. Now what's going on here? Why's there a cop here?"

"Karla texted me this morning and told me she was sick and coming home. She asked for a ride, but I was out on a rescue and didn't get back to her until she was almost home. If I'd have been able to pick her up, I would have insisted she go to the doctor before coming home."

"She called me, too," Darren said. "I was in a meeting all day, and my phone wasn't charged. I didn't get the message until about an hour ago, so I went and got Laurel and we came over. I heard her in the backyard, she sounded terrible."

"Yes, she's coughed almost non-stop since I got here, I don't even think she can breathe very well, and then she blew up at those people and then at me."

"Who are these people?"

"We came in here and found all this stuff scattered about, so I called the Sheriff's Office."

"I'd blow up at them, too," Darren said, laughing.

"She was trying to tell the deputy about things that have been going on, but she was coughing too hard."

"What do you mean? Has she said anything to you about this stuff?" Darren asked.

"Yes," I said, shaking my head. "She told me some things after we came back from Mexico, but then she brushed them off as being tired. And then there's the problems with the security alarms. And now here we are. I didn't do anything to help her and everything's worse," I said, rubbing my face and eyes.

"Hey, kid," Darren said. "Don't beat yourself up. When's the last time you slept, anyways? You don't look so hot yourself."

"It's been a while. I got called out as I was leaving the airport Sunday after I dropped Karla off. But that's beside the point. What are we going to do about this?"

"We'll get this figured out. It's a wonder she hasn't gotten sick before, she runs herself silly. Hang on, Owen," Darren said, pulling his phone out of his pocket.

"Hey, Laurel, everything OK?" Darren asked, flipping his call to speaker.

"So, the doctor's admitting her for high-dose IV antibiotics and steroids, she has pneumonia and fluid on her lungs. If the steroids don't help the fluid, they'll need to drain it later. What's going on there?" Laurel asked.

"We're trying to figure that out," Darren said. "The deputy's in talking to the others, now. When we finish up here, Owen and I'll swing by."

"OK, see you soon," Laurel said.

"Yea, bye, hon," Darren said, ending the call, and then stood up and stuck the phone in his pocket. "Let's go find this sheriff and see what he has to say; we can figure this out later." Before Darren and I left the kitchen, the deputy came into the kitchen.

"Deputy Montez, this is Darren Grainer, Karla's dad," I said, gesturing from Darren to the cop. "Karla's getting admitted to the hospital."

"OK," the deputy said, looking at me perplexed.

"Is there a problem with that?" Darren asked.

"Well, I had some questions for her, and I need to get a statement for my report."

"Well, that's not going to happen tonight," Darren said roughly. "First order of business is getting these people out of my daughter's house."

"It's not that simple, sir," the deputy told Darren and me.

"What do you mean it's not that simple? Sure, it is," Darren said. "They're squatters and you need to send them on their way."

"I can't do that," Deputy Montez said. "They've rented the house for a week."

"Excuse me," I said. "What do you mean they rented it for a week? From whom?"

168

The deputy pulled his phone out and made a few navigational moves and showed Darren and me a website. "Darren, that's Karla's house," I said, pointing to the deputy's phone.

"What the— Who put that there?" Darren asked, looking as confused as I felt. "It says it's completely booked; this is ridiculous. I don't know about this site, but I can show you paperwork that proves my daughter owns this house and it's not for rent. These people need to leave. You need to find out who posted this or I'm going to talk to your supervisor."

"They did pay for a whole week and wondered what happens to their week's rent," the deputy mentioned after Darren had given him a bit of the what-for; I've never seen Darren that cranked up before.

"Do I look like I care?" Darren asked. "Tell them to contact whomever they rented from. And don't forget we want that post removed."

"I actually want it left up," the deputy said. "I want to have the department IT guys do some investigating before it comes down. We'll be checking on things; and you be sure and bring Miss Grainer in for a statement, OK?"

"Yes, we'll be in when she's up to it," I told the deputy.

"Darren," I said after the deputy left the kitchen. "How are we going to make sure no one else stays here?"

"You answer your phone, and I'll make sure the deputy gets the keys from them people before they leave," Darren said, leaving the kitchen.

"Hey Eide, what's up?"

"Owen, finally. I've called and texted Karla several times today. I know she's out of town, but she can still answer her phone."

"Eide, hey, calm down; what's wrong?"

"I've just been trying to get a hold of Karla."

"Well, you can stop, she won't answer her phone—at least not until tomorrow. She's home—well, not home—she's in the hospital."

"She's in the hospital? What happened? I knew something was wrong."

"She's sick, she took a flight back this morning. She's had a terrible day—not only is she sick but her house was broken into."

"What? Oh my gosh, what about the hospital?"

169

"She was admitted for pneumonia and fluid on her lungs. Darren and I are going up there shortly."

"Is there anything I can do?" Eide asked.

"Yea, actually you can. I'm planning to come back here to clean tomorrow, the place is going to need it."

"What do you think you're planning to do?" Darren asked, interrupting. I hadn't even noticed that he'd come back in the kitchen.

"Hold on, Eide, I'm putting you on speakerphone."

"Hey, Darren," Eide said.

"Like I was saying, Karla's not going to want to come home unless the house is cleaned, she'll just want to clean it herself and that's the last thing she needs to do when she gets out of the hospital."

"I agree, but you're not going to be the one to clean it," Darren said, interrupting. "You need to sleep tomorrow; you're going to be in the same place as she is if you don't take a breather."

"Hey guys, h e l l o! Molly and I will clean her house. She'll want to know about Karla, anyways. Tell Karla I'll be by to see her tomorrow."

"Hey, wait, Eide, why were you trying to call Karla, did you need something?"

"Nope, not important tonight. We'll talk tomorrow. Bye, guys."

"Bye, Eide," Darren and I said in unison.

"Alright, let's go to the hospital," Darren said. "We have a few things to discuss."

"Darren, what are we going to do to make sure no one else shows up?"

"I know, I've been thinking about that," Darren said as I drove down the street. "I'm not sure that deputy's going to be much help and not sure Karla should be alone after she gets out of the hospital."

"We can run up and see how Karla is and then go grab a bite to eat," Darren said as we walked through the hospital parking lot. "I texted Laurel, she's in room 342."

"I'm just going to say a quick goodnight to Karla and pass on supper," Owen said. "I just want to know she's alright—last I saw her, well, she was pretty upset with me."

170

"Hey, Laurel," Darren whispered as he stuck his head just inside the hospital door. "Is she awake?"

"Not much," Laurel said. "She's been trying so hard to sleep, but then she coughs."

"Maybe the meds will kick in soon and she can finally get some decent sleep," I said, stepping in the hospital room behind Darren.

"Hi, Owen, how are you? Thank you for helping with this whole mess."

"That's fine, Laurel," I said, walking over to Karla's bedside.

"We should probably go, Laurel, she needs to rest, and you're my ride."

"Owen, are you going to come eat with us?" Laurel asked.

"No, I'm not. I'm just going to see Karla for a minute."

"He's been up since Sunday; he was just getting in from a flight," Darren said, nodding in my direction.

"Oh, Owen, I'm sorry," Laurel said as she stepped over and hugged me.

"Thanks, Laurel," I said hugging her back.

I turned back to Karla after her parents left the room. "Hey Karla," I said, brushing some of her long curly hair off the side of her face and brushed a kiss on her cheek. She was still super-hot; I knew she didn't feel good all day. I should have convinced her to get checked out sooner.

"Feel better, tomorrow's a new day."

"Hmm...Owen, people...house, gone."

"Shush, it's OK. Go back to sleep. I'll see you tomorrow, love you."

I got home that night after being gone over fifty hours this week, today being the worst of all. I stood in the steaming shower with sprays of water running down from my head and back, soaking, letting the warm water melt the muscle tension away. *Dang*, I thought, hitting the wall of the shower, *I couldn't keep her safe. She's become my world and look what I let happen to her.* I stepped out of the shower after the water long turned cold. I laid down in bed and tried to get comfortable; I turned several times and only ended up making the bedding a complete mess. After being in the field all that time, I should have had no problem crashing tonight, but I

171

couldn't, I was worried about Karla. I knew when Karla left, she didn't feel good that day. I finally decided to call in quits lying here. I went to the kitchen and made a pot of coffee. I received a magazine in the mail sometime while I was gone. When the coffee was done brewing, I grabbed the magazine and sat down at the table. I started flipping through the magazine to see what was new and exciting in the world of aviation. I closed the magazine after skimming the first page.

"Dear Lord," I said, bowing my head. "Father of goodness and love. Please comfort and provide healing to Karla. Lift Karla up in your wisdom so that the challenges she faces are no longer weighing on her. Please, Lord, provide Karla with joy and blessing."

I gave up at the table when I was done praying to God. I took my coffee and sat on the couch and turned on the TV show I'd been watching about the Wyoming sheriff. The show didn't hold my interest, either; my thoughts kept turning to Karla. Why didn't I insist she stay home Sunday? She got on a plane twice; all that pressure in her lungs didn't help her, either. And her house was a completely different mess. Who would do something like this? She'd made some comments about things she was noticing; heck, I knew things were going on. Every time something came up, she'd convinced me that all it amounted to was she was tired. Why didn't I push for more information? I finally gave up with the show, I tried lying back on the couch and closing my eyes.

Later that morning, I woke up. I looked at my watch. It was just before noon. I got ready and went back to the hospital. When I arrived, Karla wasn't in her room. I stepped out to the nurse's station and a nurse told me she was down at X-ray and would be back shortly. I took a seat in the chair near the window in her room to wait. I laid back in the chair, soaking up the sun streaming in the hospital window. The sun was warm; made me think back a few months ago to the time Karla and I spent on the beach in Mexico.

"Hello," the guy that was pushing Karla's wheelchair into the room said. I stood up and watched him help Karla navigate the IV tubing and other cords that monitored her as she got back in bed. "We made a little trip to X-ray."

"Yea, that's what the nurse said. How do you feel?" I asked Karla after she was settled back in bed.

"Tired. But I'm fine," Karla said.

"Are you all set, miss?" the guy pushing the wheelchair asked after Karla was settled.

"Yes, thank you."

"OK, have a nice day. See you on the next trip," he said, leaving the room.

"Are you feeling better?" I asked, putting my head to hers, brushing a light kiss across her forehead.

"Some," Karla said as she laid her head back on the pillow and closed her eyes.

I stepped back and watched her for a moment; she was still pretty warm, and the cough was just terrible. I sat back in the chair and noticed that Karla had fallen asleep; she wheezed in her sleep, and I could still hear some serious congestion.

I sat with Karla all afternoon. She'd wake up, coughing terribly and then fall back asleep. I even dozed a few times. I pulled my phone out, pulling up the site that Karla's house was posted on. Sure enough, there it was. Yesterday wasn't a dream, that was for sure. I read the post over and over; they had no opening "but email us and we'll let you know when we have a cancellation." That's just weird.

"Hello, I'm Dr. Keen," the doctor said as he came in the door, interrupting my thoughts.

"Hello, I'm Owen. She's been sleeping off and on this afternoon."

"Ah good, she needs that," Dr. Keen said. "Unfortunately, I'm going to have to wake her now so I can listen to her lungs. Hello Ms. Grainer. I'm Dr. Keen. Remember me from this morning?" the doctor said as he stood next to Karla's bed.

"Yes," Karla said.

"How are you feeling?" the doctor asked, sitting on the edge of Karla's bed.

"My back still hurts some and my chest burns."

"I'm not surprised, with that fluid and infection built up your lungs. The blood work shows your white count coming down and the X-ray also shows some a reduction of the fluid. So, I think we're on the right path."

"When can I go home?"

"I'll have another X-ray ordered for morning and we'll go from there."

"Hello," Laurel whispered as she stepped into the room. "Oh sorry, we didn't mean to interrupt." Laurel and Darren came in and stood near me as the doctor finished visiting with Karla.

"That's OK," Dr. Keen said. "Were about finished here. I was just saying that we'll recheck the X-ray in the morning and if there's still improvements then we'll see about sending you home tomorrow afternoon."

"That's good news," Laurel said, smiling.

"If you don't have any questions, I'll see you in the morning. Call if you need anything."

"Hey kiddo, how are you doing?"

"I've been better, Dad," Karla said as she tried to sit up, but started coughing.

"Yea, I bet."

"What's going on with my house?"

"Hopefully, nothing at the moment," I told Karla. "Why don't you rest now, and we'll talk about it later?"

"Eide and Levi cleaned it today, she was going to come see you but decided to wait a day," Darren commented.

"I thought Molly was going to help?" I asked Darren.

"Yea, she was but she got called to work early this morning. Molly said she stopped up earlier, but you guys were both sleeping and didn't want to wake you."

Karla looked like she could crash at any moment, her eyes were black and sunken in. Even though the X-ray showed some improvement, *I could tell Karla still didn't feel well*, I thought to myself as Darren continued to talk about her house.

"I told everybody what happened and that we'd have a discussion sometime, see if we can't figure this all out." "But we need you there and feeling better," Darren said.

174

"I think we should go and let her rest," Laurel said. "I'm not sure Karla heard much of what you just said."

"Yea, we'll get into this later," Darren said, glancing at me. "Owen, are you going to pick her up tomorrow?"

"Yea, I was planning on it."

"OK, I figured so but wanted to check," Darren said. "We'll check on you tomorrow, kiddo," Darren whispered towards Karla, but Karla didn't even stir in her sleep. "Did you get any sleep, Owen?"

"Yea, I dozed off and on today."

"You better go home get a decent night's sleep; I'll call you later," Darren said, looking concerned.

"I will. Thanks, guys," I told Darren and Laurel as they stood at the door to Karla's hospital room about ready to leave.

"Bye, Owen," Darren said.

I sat back down in the chair after Darren and Laurel left and closed my eyes. I was still thinking about this post—who would do something like this? We really had to make sure that no one else showed up at Karla's house with that post still up, and that was the only post. This wasn't the only homeshare site on the web. I pulled my phone out and looked them up. As I was scrolling through another site, I heard Karla start coughing. She was still coughing very hard, almost to the point of choking and not being able to breathe. That must hurt something awful.

She sat up some and that seem to help, but then she looked over at me.

"Owen why are you still here?" Karla asked me. "You've been sitting in that chair dozing off and on all day; you should go home."

"I was going to leave when your parents left but then you fell asleep, and I didn't want to leave you while you were sleeping."

"I'm good, you can go home," Karla said, turning over and covering herself up.

I stood up and looked her over; she just looked miserable. "I love you," I said, leaning over, kissing her lightly on the cheek. At least she didn't feel as though she was burning up quite so bad. "Good night, Karla."

Chapter 14

"Oh, hey, Mark. Do you know where Justin is? I was just in his office, but I didn't see him."

"Sorry, Mr. Hightower, he's out this afternoon getting some quotes for the Pierce account. I don't think he'll be gone that much longer. Is there something I can help you with? I thought you were going to be out of the office this week, anyways?"

"That's what I wanted to discuss with him; can you send him to my office when he returns, please, Mark?"

"Will do. Hey, while you're here, did we ever get the funding to move forward on the Stepping Up project? I think this is a great opportunity and I have some ideas I'd like to contribute; I think Justin does too."

"Yes, I think we did. I saw an email this morning but didn't read it completely. Why don't you talk to Justin and you guys set up a meeting with me next week and we can go over your ideas, I look forward to hearing them. Thanks, Mark."

"What ideas are those?" Justin asked as he was walking toward us.

"See there, Mr. Hightower, told you he wouldn't be gone long. Mr. Hightower was looking for you and I asked him about the Stepping Up project."

"Oh yea, did we get funding for it?"

"Yes, I believe so," Mr. Hightower said. "But I'd like to discuss another matter with you."

"Oh, sure. Let me just drop my things off in my office and I'll be right over."

"Thanks, Mr. Hightower," Mark said as he walked off.

"Weren't you scheduled to be out of the office this week?" I asked Mr. Hightower as we walked into his office.

"Yes, actually, that's what I wanted to talk to you about."

"OK," I said, looking skeptical.

"Have you had any problem with that house rental you referred to me?"

"No, not a thing. In fact, I was thinking about seeing if they had an opening in a few weeks and see about getting some fishing and hiking in. I just love it up there."

"I'm not so sure that'll happen."

"Oh, sure, no problem, I understand. I know we're busy."

"No, it's not that. I took the whole family there this week, and there was a bit of an incident. The cop isn't sure what the situation is, but a guy and a woman who was clearly very sick were there when we came back Tuesday afternoon and claimed we were trespassing."

"Someone called the cops on you?" I said, chuckling. "Sorry, that's just hard to imagine. So, is this house not for rent on the homeshare site?"

"I don't know, it seemed to be," Mr. Hightower said. "I got an email notifying me of a cancellation like you said. I checked with the family and the dates worked so we took it. And then this happens."

"That's wild. It's also kind of a letdown—that's a great place."

"It is a nice place," Mr. Hightower said. "Well, I'll let you know if something further develops. Oh, Mark's going to schedule a meeting about the Stepping Up project."

"Yea, that's good, I have some ideas for that I'd like to share."

"Yea, that's what he said. I look forward to getting started. Thanks, Justin."

"Yes, Mr. Hightower," I said as I left his office. I couldn't believe it—someone called the cops on Mr. Hightower. That's just unbelievable, must be a mistake of some sort, I thought shaking my head and chuckling to myself.

"What was that all about?" Mark asked when I came back to my office.

"Get this, seems our very own Mr. Hightower had a little run-in with the cops the other day, so he hightailed it home."

"What?" Mark asked, looking about as stunned as I felt.

178

"Well, no, not really. He did have a visit with the cops." Mark still just looked at me in shock.

"Some guy and a woman accused him of trespassing in the house I recommended he rent."

"Oh, wow, did he go to jail?" Mark asked.

"No, I think it's just some sort of mix-up, which is a bummer. I was going to head back up there in a few weeks."

"Dude, come on!" Mark exclaimed. "What is up with you—you goin' soft on me? You've taken more vacation these last few months than in the eight years we've worked together."

"Feel good to be home?" Owen asked as we walked into the foyer.

"Hmm, yes and no. All I wanted was to get home and go to bed the other day and now that I'm here I'm not even sure that I even want in my own bed."

"Levi and Eide cleaned yesterday, you have clean bedding. So, whenever you're ready, it's ready for you."

"I know, Eide told me yesterday when she came to the hospital."

"I think she wants to talk to you about something—did she say anything when she was at the hospital?"

"No, she wasn't really there that long, and she mostly wanted to know about me, why?"

"I don't know, she called me and said she'd called and texted you several times, but then when she found out all this out, she clammed up. I asked her about it, and she said nope, not important, we'd talk about it later."

"Hmm, I don't know," I said, shrugging my shoulders, looking around.

"So, bed or couch?" Owen asked.

"Couch for now—you promised to tell me about the sheriff's visit and those people."

"I know I did, I just didn't expect it to be the first five minutes after you walk in the door. Have a seat, and we'll talk about some things," Owen said, getting his phone out.

"What are you doing with your phone?" I asked.

"I'm going to show you something," Owen said, turning his phone around. "Here, see this."

"What's this?"

"This," Owen said, handing me his phone.

"What's this, what are you showing me?"

"It's a homeshare rental site."

"I know, I've seen them before."

"Look at the house on this posting."

"That's my house. Why is a picture of my house there?"

"That's what I said. We haven't figured out what to do about it, yet. The deputy wants the post left up so the department's IT people can review it before contacting the website."

"I want to talk to the deputy, now."

"We will, probably tomorrow. I told him I'd bring you to the station when you're feeling better."

"Well, I'm out of the hospital and I'm not coughing as bad. Let's go talk to him about this," I said, getting off the couch.

"I understand," Owen said. "But not today. You have to let them investigate this; we'll go tomorrow."

"Seriously, I have to just wait around and see if someone up and decides to come spend the night? I don't think so."

"We don't have to stay here," Owen said. "I have some things I want to check; but then we can go to my house, or I can take you to your parents'."

"What are you going to do here, don't you have to go to work?"

"No, I'm not going in until later next week."

"Why?"

"I want to hang out with you," Owen said.

"Sounds like babysitting to me," I said, shaking my head.

"No, that's not it; I just want to hang out with you and make sure you're safe."

"Well, it's not like you're going to change your mind anytime soon and I don't have the energy to argue with you so I'm going to go to my room and lie down."

I went upstairs and crawled in bed. I'd wanted to come lie here for days, and now that I lay here, coughing, my mind wandering, I wonder how many people have stayed in this bed. I wonder what Owen plans on checking—he said he had some things he wanted to check. Do I really need a babysitter? I sat up and tried to help the coughing, I sat there in bed staring at the wall; what on earth was Owen doing downstairs? I finally gave up on the wall-starin' game, I just coughed anyways. I came down the stairs to find Owen standing at a window in the living room. "What are you doing?"

"Hey, just checking the locks, did you have a good nap?"

"No," I said, shaking my head.

"I wondered; I could hear you coughing up there. How are you feeling?"

"Not as lousy. I'm sorry I snapped at you, Owen. I know you're just trying to help and ..."

"Hey, Karla, it's OK," Owen said, interrupting me, taking my arm. "You haven't had the best week, and you have all this stuff going on. I can handle a little crabby."

"I shouldn't take it out on you, though. I'm sorry."

"It's OK, you're going to be OK, we're good."

"What exactly are you doing to the windows?" I asked Owen, looking at the window and the tools he had.

"I'm checking all the window locks to make sure they're locked and in working order."

"Oh," I said letting what Owen said sink in. "I guess that's a good idea; I never checked them when I moved in."

"I also changed your door locks—well, except for your garage. I'll go out there later."

I stood there looking at Owen. "I guess I never would have thought of these things."

"I didn't either, until yesterday afternoon."

"Owen, I don't know what to say. Thank you."

"It's all good. I have a few more windows to finish in here and then I'll get us some supper ready. Eide made some food and left it here when she cleaned yesterday."

"Geez, she's good, that was nice of her. I'm going to text her while you finish the windows and then I'll meet you in the kitchen."

"Are you done with your phone call?" Owen asked as he walked into the kitchen and sat down next to me.

"Yea, I texted Eide. But she didn't text back, she just called me instead. She said they're coming over Saturday."

"Yea, well maybe," Owen said. "Your Dad thought we could get everyone together and visit about what's been going on, if you feel up to it. We all have questions, and you can tell us some of the things that's been going on. Maybe we'll have some information from the deputy by then. Now, how about something to eat? Eide brought a soup, a hamburger casserole and something else but I can't remember."

"I'll take the soup and maybe some coffee?" I asked hesitantly.

"Well, that goes without saying. Coming right up."

I moved into the living room and sat on the couch while Owen heated the soup. I turned on the TV but didn't find anything that caught my attention. Owen came in carrying a bowl of soup and a cup of coffee.

"What are you watching?" Owen asked, setting my soup and coffee on the coffee table.

"Nothing really, I was just flipping through channels."

"Do you want to watch *Dead Poets Society*—I left it here last week?"

"Yes, let's watch that," I said, picking up the bowl of soup and stirring it. I took a couple bites but wasn't really that hungry. I set the bowl back on the coffee table and laid my head back against the couch.

"Owen?" I heard him picking up dishes and moving around the living room.

"Hey, sorry I woke you. Do you want to go up to bed?"

"Yes, sorry. I think I do want to go up to bed," I said, standing up and moving toward the staircase.

I stood at the bottom step and paused, thinking about Owen. I could feel Owen watching me, so I turned around. "Owen?"

"Yes."

"Do you plan to stay the night?"

"Well, yea, is that OK with you? I'll just stay down here on the couch, but if you'd rather I not stay I can call your mom or Eide. I just don't want you staying here alone."

"No, it's OK, you can stay. But you should take a bedroom upstairs; don't sleep on the couch. You won't sleep very well; I can attest to that."

182

I walked a few steps up the stairs and I stopped again and turned back again to look at Owen. "Owen?"

"Yep," Owen said, walking up to me and putting his arms around me. "Everything OK?"

"Thank you, this means a lot; all of this."

"Of course," Owen said, holding onto me, kissing me lightly down my cheek and into my neck.

"Owen," I said stepping out of his embrace.

"Yea," Owen said, smirking.

"Where's Arnold?"

"Oh, he's with Todd; I had him pick him up the other day. We'll get him after we go to the Sheriff's Office tomorrow. If that's OK."

"Yes, of course. Good night, Owen," I said, walking the rest of the way up the stairs. I could tell Owen was still standing there watching me.

"Good night, Karla."

I went into my room and changed clothes, meaning I just put on a different pair of sweatpants and another sweatshirt. Owen had never seen me this sloppy; and now he was staying at my house. I heard Owen come upstairs and go in the room next door. *This relationship has taken quite the turn, again,* I thought to myself, I can't think of any relationship I've been in with someone who would come into my house, check the locks on my windows and doors. I laid there in bed tossing and turning for a while. After tossing, turning and hollowed coughing, I decided to get up. I went downstairs for some water. I was standing at the kitchen sink staring out into the dark night. My brain was swirling, it's not like I could see anything out the window, but I stood there staring into oblivion when I heard Owen asking for me.

"Karla, are you OK?"

"I'm in the kitchen."

"Karla, are you OK?" Owen asked again as he came up behind me.

"Mostly," I said as Owen put is arms around my shoulders.

"I could hear you coughing and then you left your room. I thought something was wrong."

"No, I just couldn't sleep. Did I wake you?"

"I wasn't really sleeping, more like dozing. Come on," Owen said, taking my hand and leading me to the couch.

"What's up?" Owen asked when we sat down. He was holding my hand, looking at me. "Does it bother you that I'm here, cause if it does, we can change things. Your dad and I just feel that at least while that post is up somebody should be here with you."

"Everything bothers me, it's not just you. You just came in and took over; I haven't quite been able to fathom that."

"Well, get used to it, Karla. I like being with you, if you haven't noticed. I go crazy when you're out of town."

"I've thought about that, too."

"Whoa, oh, time-out," Owen said, holding up his hands in the time-out motion. "It's too soon to be thinking about work already, you just got out of the hospital like a few hours ago."

"Don't worry. I'm not going back to work yet; I wasn't even thinking that. I do need to check my email later and follow up with my boss and the client in Chattanooga. I've been thinking lately that I don't want to be assigned to the out-of-state clients; we have regional clients that need marketing assistance just as much."

"That the best thing I've heard, yet." Owen said, embracing me in his enthusiasm. "That's an awesome change and one I'd vote for, but you shouldn't make any big decisions until you're feeling better."

"I know."

"We'll figure everything out in due time, we don't need to worry about it now," Owen said, backing out of our embrace and kissing my forehead. I laid my head on his chest and we just sat in the dark.

Later in the night, I woke to the smell of fresh-brewed coffee and Owen was no longer sitting beside me. I got up and went to the kitchen. Owen was sitting at the table reading a magazine, drinking a cup of coffee.

"Hey, Owen. Have you gotten any sleep?"

"Um no, not really," Owen said, smiling up at me. "It's OK, I'm good; I took a shower and got into your coffee." "How'd you sleep—after you finally went to sleep?"

"My couch isn't really made for sleeping."

"Really, you've fallen asleep there several times recently; that proves otherwise," Owen said, chuckling.

184

"Well, maybe you've got a point."

"What time are we going to the Sheriff's Office?" I asked Owen, sitting down beside him.

"Beings that it's not even five a.m., I'd say it's a bit early. The deputy gave me a business card; I'll call him later and see what time works best, if he's even working today."

"I wonder if they've found anything?" I said, taking a drink of coffee. "Hmm, that's good—Owen you make good coffee."

"I don't know. The IT department was going to do some investigating."

"I'm not really sure what good that'll do."

"I wouldn't worry about it; I think he just wants to know that you're the homeowner."

"This is such a mess. I'm going to check my email and think about something else for a while."

"How about I make some breakfast, you can check your email later." Owen got up from the table and started pulling things from the fridge. I watched as Owen whipped up some eggs and grabbed some fruit that Eide had brought over. Owen shuffled around the kitchen like a five-star chef, better than I ever thought about cooking.

"This looks wonderful," I told Owen when he sat a plate down in front of me; there was an omelet and fresh fruit.

"Yea, I thought this sounded good; I haven't seen you eat much lately so I hope this helps."

"Thank you."

A few hours later, after Owen cleaned up the breakfast dishes and I took a shower, we left for the Sheriff's Office. In less than an hour's time, we had been to the Sheriff's Office and picked up Arnold.

"Well, that was a waste of time; this is so frustrating," I said to Owen as we walked in the house. "I can't believe they had nothing to tell us. I wonder if they even know you called them?"

"I know, when your dad and I talked to them that night we didn't have much faith in him, either. Don't get so worked up."

"I know but seriously, I just want that post taken down," I said, throwing my hands in the air. "I'm going to get it taken down

185

myself." As I stood there going on about the Sheriff's Office my chest started to burn. I started coughing and choking, my head was throbbing, and I couldn't see straight.

"Hey, calm down," Owen said, taking me by the arm. "You're not doing yourself any good. Come sit down and I'll get us something to drink."

I sat on the couch and watched Owen walk toward the kitchen; I laid back and put my feet up on the coffee table and closed my eyes. My head and chest still hurt but at least the coughing had subsided.

I was filling a glass of water for Karla when I could feel my phone vibrating. I grabbed my phone thinking it was someone from the Sheriff's Office or Karla's dad, but the caller ID showed it was my dad calling.

"Hey Dad, hang on a sec."

I took the glass of water to Karla; I was grateful to see that she had fallen asleep. *Funny, she thinks the couch isn't a good place to sleep but that's the only place she's been able to sleep.* I set the water on the end table and covered her up with the afghan from the back of the couch.

I hurried back to the kitchen and grabbed my phone off the counter and stepped out onto the patio with Arnold.

"Hey, Dad, sorry about that. How are you and Ma?"

"Oh, we're doing good. We just hadn't talked to you in a while and thought I'd call and check on you; but if now's not a good time, we can talk later."

"No, this is a good time, and I could use a good talk about now."

"Oh, everything OK, son?"

"I'm not sure, Dad."

"Trouble at work, Owen?" Dad asked.

"No, actually it's Karla—she's had a terrible week, so I've been trying to help her out."

I told Dad the whole story, including how now we're basically at a dead end and the cop didn't really tell us anything today. "Karla's just so frustrated, she doesn't know what to do and I don't even know what to do for her."

"Pray for her Owen, you can do that. Praying always helps, and I thought of something else while you were explaining this

186

situation. I'm not sure if Karla's up for it, but have you considered sending Karla out of town as if everything is normal. Sounds to me like someone knows her schedule. Then have someone else try and connect with whoever is responsible for the post; you know what I mean?"

"Yea, I think you might be right. If Karla's on board with it, we'll make sure she's out of town next week. Karla and I might come to the farm; would you ask Ma if that's alright?"

"I don't have to ask your mother. You and Karla, or even just Karla can come out anytime. We'd be glad to have you both. I have some plane parts I could use your advice on."

"I doubt I have any advice that you don't already know, Dad. Thanks for the talk, Dad, but I better go. I'll call you guys later and let you know more. Tell Ma hi."

"It was good talking to you, Owen. Tell Karla hi and we'll be praying for you both."

"Thanks, Dad, bye."

I went back to the living room; Karla was still sleeping. I sat down in the chair next to her and just watched the rise and fall of her chest as she slept. I could still hear the wheezing congestion in her chest—that must hurt like crazy; especially the other night when she came home. It must have taken everything she had to leave a client and project unattended, and I wasn't even there to pick her up.

"What are you doing?" Karla asked, looking over at me.

"I was watching you sleep."

"Oh goodness, what for?"

"Cause your beautiful."

"Please, you've never seen me like this before, not put together, anyways. You even saw me in a hospital gown, those things are the worst."

"I didn't think about you being in a hospital gown; I was worried about the reason you were there. Did you have a nice nap?"

"Hmm, so-so. You didn't just sit there and stare at me the whole time, did you?"

"No. As tempting as that sounds, I didn't. I was only sitting here staring at you a little bit and thinking about some things," I said chuckling. "My Dad called just as I was getting your water."

"I was only going to lay back and rest my eyes until you came back and then I was out."

"That's good, you need to sleep. Besides, I can still hear the congestion in your chest; I bet your chest still bothers you, too."

"It's fine. You said you were talking to your dad; how are they?"

"Oh, they're fine. Dad says hi, but we can talk about that more later. How about some lunch first?"

"Hmm, sure."

Owen went into the kitchen to get us some lunch. I decided to turn the TV on to see if I could find anything good. I flipped through several channels; flipping through the channels was about how my mind was. Flipping from one situation to another. Someone had my house posted on a home vacation site; my job kept darting me from one state to another and Owen was here waiting on me hand and foot checking doors and locks. Seemed like a case for Dr. Phil.

"Here's some lunch. Did you find something to watch?" Owen asked, setting a tray on the coffee table.

"No, I hardly ever sit and watch TV. I'm not even sure what cable I have."

"You've never sat and binge-watched something?"

"No, I might catch a movie once in a while; but I usually have portfolios to work on."

"I-I don't even know what to say to that, Karla," Owen stuttered, looking comically stunned. "Well, this weekend, we're not doing that. So, you better get comfortable watching TV, find a book to read or do a puzzle."

"A puzzle? Oh my, I haven't done a puzzle since I was probably like three."

"Yeah, I know, me either. I just thought maybe you had like a thousand-piece forest puzzle sitting around needing assembled. Let go with some Netflix," Owen said, picking up the remote.

"A forest puzzle, really," I said, shaking my head. "And, I don't have Netflix."

"I do," Owen said. "I've been watching this show, it's about a Wyoming sheriff."

We snuggled in together. Owen laid his arm out and I laid my head back on his shoulder. We both put our feet up on the coffee table. We sat in silence watching his show this afternoon. I could see the light fading from the day when I glanced out the window. I decided I needed to get up and at least stretch.

"You OK, Karla?" Owen asked as I attempted to get up.

"Yes, I don't think I've watched this much TV combined in the last ten years."

"Do you want to watch something else?"

"No, I'm going to the bathroom and then you had something you and your dad talked about?"

"Yea, I know, I've been thinking about that this afternoon. Do you want some supper first?"

"No," I said shaking my head. "I'm not that hungry. You can get something while I run down the hall."

"Nah, I'm good," Owen said.

I came back and Owen had a cup of coffee for each of us.

"Hey, thanks for the coffee," I said, picking up the cup and taking a drink before settling in on the couch beside Owen. He was looking at his phone. "Everything OK?" I asked Owen.

"Yea, I just have a text from Ty. I can text him later. I told Dad about what's happened this week and he thinks that you should leave, in the nicest sense of the word."

"Leave and do what? You just gave me grief about talking about work, let alone—"

"No, no!" Owen said, shaking his hands, interrupting me. "I don't mean for you to go work with a client. Dad thinks someone knows your schedule. So, if you planned to leave like normal; someone else could attempt to contact whoever put the post up. We'll visit with your family first before deciding; but I thought maybe I'd see if I can get some more time off work and then we could go down to the farm next week."

"It seems like we're just asking for trouble."

"We don't have to figure this all out tonight; you can think about it and if you're not comfortable with it just say the word and I won't even bring it up to your family."

"Can you even get another week off work, Owen? I mean, you've spent the week playing nursemaid and warden."

"HA-HA, nursemaid," Owen said, laughing.

"Ugh, I just want that stupid post taken down." I ran my hands through my hair and leaned back against the couch.

"I know. I do, too, Karla," Owen said, sitting up on the couch facing me, pulling me into a warm and comforting embrace.

189

"I'm going to take a shower and then I'm going to bed," I said, pulling out of his embrace and standing up. I started to walk away, and Owen stood up and hugged me before I started up the stairs.

"It will all work out, Karla; you don't have anything to worry about it."

"Yea, easy for you to say."

I stood there and watched Karla climb the stairs. I kept staring at the top of the staircase. I heard her come out of the shower and close the door to her room. I sat there on the couch and decided to turn on the Wyoming show again. I sat there thinking about Karla and her frustration; I wanted to come up with something to make all this go away for her, but I was at a loss. I decided a prayer for her to sleep well might be the best. "Dear Lord, sometimes the trials we have are greater than our strength. Please keep Karla in your faithful hands, Lord. Help her place her trials and concerns in your capable hands. Lord, help me to help her to the best of my abilities."

I turned my attention back to the show. I wasn't really that interested in the show, but I had a feeling Karla would be back down here before too long. I had yet to see her stay in her bed for more than a couple hours. It would be good to go to the farm, I thought, sitting there watching the show. I heard her bedroom door open. I sat there quietly waiting for Karla to descend the stairs. I watched as she made each step thoughtfully. Tired as she looked, I could tell she hadn't been to sleep. I waited until she had fully descended the staircase before saying anything, so I didn't make her jump and fall or something.

"Hey Karla," I said, getting up from the couch.

"Owen, I didn't realize you were still up."

"Yea, did you get some sleep?"

"No," Karla said thoughtfully, clearly something on her mind.

"How's your show?" Karla asked, referencing the show as she took a seat next to me. I held out my arm for her to lay against.

"I don't know, I haven't really been paying attention."

"I thought you were going to bed."

190

"I was, but greater thoughts prevailed," Owen said, chuckling. "I was thinking about taking you for a flight if we go to the farm. I think you kinda liked it when we went before."

"Are you kidding me? I loved that. Yes, I would love to do that," I said, smiling at Owen. "Do you think Ty will let you get his plane?"

"Yea, there'll be no problem. Ty and I are tight; we go way back."

"Did you guys go to school together?"

"Some, we mostly had church activities together. We started going to Sunday School and church together when we were about three or four. Ty and his mom lived behind the church for a while; during the sermons he almost always left, claiming that he needed to go to the bathroom. Well, the goof always went home to go to the bathroom and then he'd turn on cartoons instead of coming back to church."

"Oh no. Did his mom ever catch on to what he was doing?"

"Yea, she knew what he was doing. But she never forced anything on him, so she didn't go get him and bring him back. She did have him talk to the minister a couple times; eventually he started staying for the whole sermon."

"The minister must have said something to get through to him."

"I don't know about that; Ty's just always been his own guy and does his own thing in his own time. Do you want to lay down here on the couch, I can move over to the chair?"

"No, this is good laying here next to you."

"You should really get some sleep, Karla; you haven't slept much."

"I know, but I'm good like this. Keep telling me about you and Ty, I like it."

Owen motioned for me to move close into him to lay against him, I tucked my feet in behind myself and eventually covered up as Owen continued telling me stories of him and Ty.

"Ty used to come out to the farm and help my dad and brother and me with various things. He never was very good at it, but he always put a lot of heart into it. I don't know how many times he fell off a horse, but he always got right back on. Somedays we'd be moving cows and he'd end up covered in cow manure from his head to his toes."

"Oh goodness, poor kid, did he get hurt?"

"A bruised ego more than once, I'm sure. I think my ma washed his clothes just as much or more than his own mom. My dad has always tinkered with various plane parts and rebuilt different pieces for as long as I can remember. Eventually Ty and I hung around so much we started working on things with him. I suppose that's why Ty and I decided to get into flying."

"How did you go from working on plane parts in your dad's barn to Flight School?"

"When Ty and I graduated high school, we were looking into Flight Schools and this one was close by; and we thought *why not*. It was a small, local place, better suited for our needs. Soon after we graduated and got our pilots' licenses; we heard it was up for sale. Not really knowing what to do next, we bought it kind of on a whim and started seeing young kids just like ourselves come through; it felt good working with those kids."

"So how come you're not working with Ty, helping young kids anymore?"

"Well, I'm still a very silent partner. Ty handles everything but lately I've been drawn to other things. I heard about this program here at the Mountain Rescue Center and wanted to get involved. I started looking into it and then I came to visit the town and I wanted to move here even more."

Deep into the night Owen got up off the couch. "Come on, let's go."

"Where are we going, Owen? It's like four in the morning."

"Yea, I know. We're going to the kitchen. You didn't want any supper, and I'm hungry. You should eat something, so, we're going to make pancakes."

"I'm not even sure I have any pancake fixings."

"Don't worry about it; have a seat at the table and I'll take care of it."

Owen started pulling things from the cupboard and setting them on the counter. Owen started mixing the bowl of ingredients he'd assemble.

"How do you like your pancakes?"

"My pancakes?"

"Yea, you just want butter and syrup, or do you want some fruit or some peanut butter on them? I think I even saw some chocolate

192

chips in your pantry—we could have chocolate chip pancakes," Owen said, smiling.

"No, I'd just like them regular or original, maybe with some fruit."

"OK, one stack of buttermilk pancakes coming up," Owen said with a flair.

Owen started flipping pancakes like he was a short-order cook and soon handed me a plate of pancakes with butter and syrup and blueberries sprinkled on top.

"Nice, thank you," I said as Owen went back to the stove and cooked a few more. He came to join me at the table with his stack of pancakes.

"Owen, these are really good. I can't make pancakes at all; I've tried buying a mix and usually have a mess by the time I'm done."

"You don't need a mix," Owen said, shaking his head. "All you need is flour, baking powder, some eggs and buttermilk—Ma taught me."

"Well, these are delicious. You're a good cook, Owen."

"You're a good cook, too, Karla; we had lasagna here that was to die for. You brought chili and cinnamon rolls when I came in from work one day; those were awesome."

"Karla, do you need anything done today, laundry? Anything done around the house?" Owen asked as we finished the pancakes and he cleaned up the pancake mess. He refilled my coffee and sat down beside me.

"No, I'm good. You've already done too much as it is, Owen, you should take a nap."

"Maybe later, I still need to change your garage door locks and check the window locks in your bedroom. And if you're up for it your family is planning to come later this afternoon."

"Yes, I'm up for it, I'll text my parents later. I am going to check my email now and make sure everything is good with the way I left work since you kinda derailed me yesterday."

"OK, OK, I won't try to stop you. Just try and make it short. I'm going to go shower," Owen said, leaving the kitchen.

"Owen?"

"Yes, Karla?"

"Thanks for the pancakes, they were great," I said, getting up from the table.

Owen flashed me his million-dollar smile and said "umhmm" and continued his way.

Man, his smile could warm my heart.

I went to my office and logged into my email. Craig had emailed me several times; one of his emails mentioned that he was going to call me soon. Another one of Craig's messages said he sent Mindy, one of my associates, to continue with Mr. Jones' team. I hope she has better luck than I did; that was such a difficult group. Was it really the group, or was it just me? I think I was just tired and frustrated. I started to reply to Craig's email, but I really didn't know what to tell him. I just sat there looking through his emails. I had thoughts of talking to Craig about traveling so much, even before I got sick. Now there's this whole house situation. I almost felt like telling Craig thanks, but I quit. But I couldn't do that to my boss. I had more respect for him than that and besides, it wouldn't solve any of my problems. I decided on a quick note for now.

Hi Craig,

Yes, I've been sick and I'm on the mend. I'm going to take some additional time off. I have another situation that needs tending to. You can call me next week if you get a chance.

Thanks for sending Mindy to finish up with Mr. Jones' team; I hope it went well.

Thanks Again,

Karla

I was surprised that there wasn't a message from Mr. Jones. If Mindy went and smoothed things over in my absence, things should be good. I let it go and logged out. I went out to the living room to find Owen gathering up things he used while working on my windows yesterday. That fresh-washed, slicked-back dark head of hair; Owen looked so good, almost an air of mystery to him.

"Everything good with work?" Owen asked.

"Ugh, I guess. My boss sent about eight messages and one of them mentioned calling soon."

"I think he did, I saw your phone ringing sometime yesterday and the caller ID said Craig. I figured I'd let it go to voicemail."

"Oh well. I sent him an email and told him I was taking some additional time off work and he could call me next week."

"Really? Good," Owen said, somewhat surprised. "I was afraid you were going to come out here telling me you had to fly off to a client somewhere. You're still not 100 percent well—I can still hear it in your breathing, the congestion and coughing."

"No, I'm not going to work," I said, looking up at Owen, getting distracted again by his hair. "I get bored just sitting around the house, but oh well. Plus, we talked about going to your parents' farm."

"Have you thought about Dad's idea?"

"Yes, I have. I feel like we're inviting trouble, but on the other hand I wonder if we went ahead with this, we could just be done in short order. I don't think we can have the best of both worlds."

"Everything will be OK. Listen, why don't you go rest on the couch or turn the TV on. I'll go change out the garage door locks and then I'll come hang out with you when I'm done."

"OK, but you should think about a nap, too, Owen."

"Yes, ma'am," Owen said, saluting me jokingly.

I finished changing the door locks on Karla's garage and was walking towards the house. I decided to sit on the patio and call my boss.

"Hello, Aaron."

"Yea, Owen, how goes it?"

"Oh, alright. I guess. How are you?"

"Doing well."

"That's good. Look, the reason I'm calling—I told you about Karla, so things have taken a turn and her situation has changed."

"Uh oh, that doesn't sound good. How's she doing?"

"She's feeling somewhat better, but we have a bit of a situation with her house, and I'd actually like to take her to my parents' farm this week, so I won't be in the area."

"Of course, don't worry about anything. Just take care of things and we'll see you when we see you. If you need anything let us know."

"I will, thanks, Aaron. Appreciate it."

"That's alright, tell Karla to get well and we're thinking of her."

"Thanks, Aaron, bye."

"Bye, Owen."

I went into the living room and saw that Karla had fallen asleep on the couch. I stood there watching her for a moment and then went back to the kitchen to make some coffee. Huh, I thought, looking at Karla's coffee pot. I realized Karla and I have the same coffee makers. I picked mine up when I moved to town and just got this type because it was the one Mom and Dad always used. When I was trying to find this coffee maker, they had all these models that screamed about the one cup and put a pod in, what's wrong with the old-fashioned grounds? And seriously, who drinks just one cup of coffee? Lightweights. As I was waiting for the coffee to brew, I texted Darren to see about them coming over later. Darren replied they'd all be here. I took my cup of coffee and went back to the patio and dialed Ty; I never did return his text.

"Hey, Owe." Ty said, answering the phone. "I was beginning to think you forgot I existed."

"Not a chance, not a chance—how you been?"

"Oh, good, busy as usual. How about you?"

"Oh, alright, I guess. I'm thinking about heading down in a few days."

"Yea, you mean you can actually remember the way down here and actually make a visit to the folks?"

"Well, I might make it over to say hey to you, too."

"Wow, I feel honored to even be getting that out of you. You plannin' on bringing that pretty girl of yours?"

"Yea, well, that's sort of the reason for the trip. Karla's had a rough go here lately. She got sick on a work trip and came home."

"That's no good. How's she doing?"

"Oh, somewhat better, but that's not the end of it. When she got home, I met her here and we found people in her house, they said they rented it through a homeshare site. We found her house posted on the site for rent. Dad suggested she leave for a week and see if someone else can communicate with whoever has the listing."

"What? That's crazy, is she OK?" Ty asked

"She's really frustrated with this whole mess, that's for sure."

"I'm sorry, man," Ty said. "If you guys do end up coming down here; let me know and I'll mark you on the schedule for the plane."

"That'd be great, Ty. Thanks."

"Yep, no problem. So, who would do something like this? Seems unreal."

"No doubt, I haven't a clue. Dad thinks someone knows her schedule or knows when she'll be out of town."

"Really!" Ty exclaimed.

"Yea, I mean, it has some merit. How else would they know when to book it? I'll text you later," I told Ty after looking at my watch. "I need to let you go, her family's coming over shortly."

"OK, I hope things go good for you and Karla."

"Me too, thanks, Ty. Bye."

"See ya, Owe."

I stepped in the house, refilled my cup of coffee and poured a cup for Karla and went into the living room; she was still sleeping. I think this was the longest she'd slept since she got home from the hospital. I set her coffee on the end table and sat down on the couch in the small space beside where she was lying on her belly. I rubbed her back softly and brushed her curly brown hair away from her face.

"Hey Karla," I said, leaning down beside her cheek.

"Hmm."

"Your family's is going to be here shorty. I didn't know if you wanted to get up and freshen up or anything? I brought you a cup of coffee, too."

"Thanks for the coffee. I was pretty much awake; I thought I heard the back door open."

"Yea, sorry. I was out on the patio talking to Ty."

"Hmm, is he planning on us?" Karla said, rubbing her face.

"Probably," I said chuckling. "But that's just Ty. If you're going to get changed you should do so, cause your family's going to be here soon."

I went upstairs and changed clothes. I still wasn't turning heads at the moment; yoga pants and a sweatshirt was all I was going to muster. Meanwhile, Owen takes a shower, puts on the same jeans, and looks fantastic. I think Owen's planning to go to his parents' farm. I hadn't really told him I'd go yet, but he was trying so hard to help take care of this situation. I probably shouldn't think so much about it. The more I think back on things, people had been coming through here off and on all year, I just figured I was tired.

I came down the stairs as everyone was gathering in the foyer after Owen let them in. Well, all except Lane and Molly. *I wonder where they are.*

Mom came over and hugged me and asked how I was doing. "I'm doing good, Mom, much better."

Mom stood back and looked me over. "Well, you do look some better."

Levi and Eide also did their fussing.

"You guys, I'm fine."

"That's not what we heard," Levi said. "Mom said you could hardly breathe; you were coughing and making terrible sounds. It was just awful," Levi said theatrically, trying to mimic Mom.

"Hey, stop mocking me," Mom said. "She did sound awful; still does."

"She has sounded awful," Owen said as we sat down on the couch.

"How'd things go at the Sheriff's Office?" Dad asked.

"Ugh, huge bust. The deputy told us the IT guys were working on it and would get back to us. We drove over there and picked up Arnold and was back here in less than an hour; makes me want to scream. Owen and his dad seem to have come up with a plan, though."

"Are you sure about that?" Owen asked.

"Yea, we can at least talk about it."

"Hello, is anybody here?" Lane called out from the foyer.

"We're in here," Owen said.

"How come you're late? We've been waiting on you," Eide said bluntly as Lane and Molly stepped into the living room.

"Pizza," Lane said as he held up the boxes on display and then set them on the coffee table and opened the lids.

"I'll go get some plates and napkins," Molly offered.

"How's it going, Kar?" Lane asked, turning around from situating the pizza boxes on the coffee table.

"Oh, just great. I'm hacking and Owen's locking the place down like Fort Knox." I said, joking. Everyone laughing heartily at my crude joke.

"Wow," Owen said, looking at me chuckling. "I think that's the first joke I've heard out of you in like a month."

"I've got plates, napkins. So, let's dig in," Molly said. "I stole some bottled water from your fridge, too, Karla."

"Oh, no worries. Eide probably put it there; thank you guys for that, by the way," I said, looking at Eide and Levi.

"Yea, sure, no problem. Enough chitchat, though," Eide said, holding Levi's hand.

"We all looked up at Eide questioningly. "What's up with you? Lane asked. "You seem a bit cranked up."

"Levi and I want to talk to you before we get back to Karla's situation; not that this isn't important, honey," Eide said, looking at me. "But this is, too."

"Oh god, what'd you do, Levi?" Lane joked.

"Pipe down, Lane," Eide scolded Lane as she motioned for Levi to stand with her.

"Now listen up. Levi and I hope you all had a great time in Mexico. Cause it turns out Levi and I had just a little more fun than the rest of you. Come September we're going to have a little Grainer join the clan." There were gasps, ah's, rounds of cheer and congratulations to Eide and Levi.

"I guess you did do something, bro. Congrats, brother," Lane said, slapping Levi's shoulder.

"So, Karla, sorry to preempt your situation. I just thought we could all use some good, happy news."

"Are you kidding me? This is the best thing all week—all month, for that matter. I'm so happy for you guys."

"I think that's that the most I've seen you smile in quite a while," Owen said, smiling back at me. "Hey, wait a minute, Eide. Is this what you were going to talk to Karla about the other night when she was at the hospital, and you said it wasn't important. I knew something was up, I told Karla more than once you wanted something."

"HAHA, guilty as charged," Eide said. "It was more important to take care of the imminent situation, and besides, this is better that you all find out together."

"Well, good, I'm glad it worked out this way," Owen said.

"Yes, I agree."

"So, Owen, what's this idea you got that Karla mentioned earlier?" Dad asked.

"It was my dad's idea; he seems to think someone knows Karla's schedule. So, he suggested she take a trip and someone else attempt to contact whoever's behind all this."

"Sounds like a pretty good idea," Lane said. "We gonna send Kar off on some luxury vacation?" Lane asked, looking at me, chuckling.

"Ask Captain Owen. He's in charge."

"I talked to her about going to my parents' farm next week, if she's up to it. That's as far as I've gotten."

"I can take care of the rest," Lane said.

"How ya figure?" Dad asked, grabbing another slice of pizza.

"Set up a new email address, go to this site and request to stay. I was looking at the site earlier and it says something about, 'Yea we know we're booked but send us an email and we'll notify you in the event of a cancellation. Give me a break. They only say that cause Owen's dad is right, they know when Kar's home and not home."

"Who knows your schedule?" Levi asked.

"Not very many people that I'm aware of. Craig, my boss. A few others at work that send out the proposals," I said, coughing. "Owen, he's been my cab driver! Dad, and sometimes the rest of you. If I get a chance to tell you."

"Anybody else you can think of?" Dad asked.

"Well, I think you should try this plan," Lane said, interrupting Dad. "I can get an email address in about five minutes."

"What do you think, Karla?" Owen asked. "I said we wouldn't go through with it if you weren't comfortable."

"I don't know. Like I told you earlier, I feel like it's inviting trouble. What if they don't catch Lane's message and they rent to someone else and then what?" I was starting to cough again. This cough had calmed down some, but it still reared up at the worst times.

"Hey, it's OK," Owen said, rubbing my back. "We don't have to decide right now."

"Hey, listen to this," Lane said. "I was just reading the reviews that people have left; this is wild."

"Yea, you're telling me. I've been coming home, thinking I was crazy."

"One person said it was 'great, quiet location.'"

"Another said, 'perfect-sized house, close to skiing and shopping.'"

"'Great location, easy transaction, we had a nice vacation. Hope to be back.'"

"Lane, this isn't helping," I told Lane, getting more perturbed all the time.

"Oh, listen to this one: 'My fiancé and I had a nice stay. We did forget a bottle of nice champagne in the fridge; hope someone enjoyed it.'"

"Oh wow—well, guess that explains that one," Eide said. "I actually threw it out when I was cleaning the other day."

"Lane!" I hollered, standing up off the couch.

"What?" Lane asked, looking up from his phone, confused.

"Send an email," I said, irritated. "I don't know how many times I've come home, and something wouldn't be right—the fishy smell in the kitchen, the dirty bathroom, the light in the bedroom. And then there's the whole situation with the security alarms while we were in Mexico, I just always chalked them up to being some sort of systems error."

"You mentioned things in passing but I didn't know it was this bad," Dad said.

"I didn't think they were this bad," I said through a coughing fit. "Like I said, I just wrote them off...oh god," I said, coughing again as I grabbed my head and stood up from the couch.

"What is it, Karla? You, OK?" Owen said, standing beside me. "You've got to calm down."

"That night the bedroom light was on—I think I told you I thought I heard the front door open and close late at night and then again early the next morning," I said, coughing and nearly in tears. "When I went to shut the light off it was already off. I think someone was in the house that night." Everyone just looked at me stunned for a moment. "I can't believe I was so stupid to overlook these things."

"Hey, you're not stupid, sis, don't be so hard on yourself," Levi said. "We could all be in this place; we get tired and busy and start overlooking things."

"It's alright," Owen said, putting his arm around my shoulder. "We'll take care of this."

"Lane, did you get the email set up?" Dad asked.

"Yea, I have a new email address and I sent them an email that said I'd like to see about staying soon for some fly fishing in the area."

"Oh, nice touch, hon," Molly said.

"Alright, good deal," Dad said. "Let us know if anything comes about that. For now, I think I'm ready to head home, it tires a man out learning he's going to be a grandfather at such a young age. You guys, really, a baby already," Dad said, shaking his head. "You just got married."

"Sure are, gramps. You're going to be the perfect grandpa," Eide said.

"Yea, we'll see about that, what do you say, Laur, you ready to go? Is everyone going to be at church tomorrow?" Dad asked.

Between resounded laughter over Dad's joke about being a grandfather and agreeing that we'd all be at church in the morning, everyone else said they too were going to leave.

By the time everyone got out another round of congratulations to Levi and Eide, it was another twenty minutes before everyone had left. It was almost nine that night. Owen and I returned to the couch after they left and sat down.

"Wow," Owen said. "Are you OK, you kinda turned into full-on firecracker there with Lane for a while. Are you feeling alright?"

"Yes, I am. It's just those reviews—they really made me mad. And when Lane said someone left a bottle of champagne, it just flipped a switch in me."

"I know, you jumped off the couch like it was on fire," Owen said. "So, you're good with Lane emailing whoever's behind all this?"

"We could be inviting trouble, but it's just a house, Owen. You and I will be gone, that's all that matters. Let someone come, I think people have been coming in and out all year long."

"This sounds more like the Karla I know, standing up to a challenge, ready to fight," Owen said.

"When were you thinking of going to your parents' farm?"

"That's up to you, Karla, whenever you feel up to it. I talked to my boss today; he said I could take whatever time I needed."

"I'm up to it."

Owen and I stayed on the couch, neither one of us seem to have any intention of getting up. The conversation moved from one topic to another. It was nearly dawn and we were still there talking. Owen prayed to God for strength and encouragement in his light. He also asked God to fill me with healing strength. Owen asked God to enfold us in his care and remind us of his constant love and healing power. Owen was a man of great wisdom.

"I should go make us some breakfast," Owen said, sounding sleepy. Neither of us tried to move—I don't think either of us were really that hungry anyways. The pizza boxes were still out from last night. Owen took my hand, and I leaned my head against his chest.

"You're pretty wonderful, Owen," I said just as sleepily as Owen.

"Mmm, K," Owen whispered.

Owen and I must have fallen into a very deep sleep, lying there in each other's arms. I woke up later to the doorbell ringing. I was warm and comfortable lying there in Owen's arms. Owen was trying to move slightly, but he saw that I was trying to move as well.

"Sorry," Owen said. "I didn't mean to wake you."

"You didn't wake me, the doorbell rang."

"It did?" Owen asked as the doorbell rang again and I heard Dad call out.

"Owen, it's almost one. We missed church," I said, looking at my watch as Mom and Dad walked into the living room.

"Hey guys," Owen said, sitting up at the edge of the couch, rubbing his eyes.

"Hi Mom, Dad."

"Everything OK? We missed you both at church," Mom asked, looking concerned.

"Yes. We were up all night and fell asleep early this morning."

"Oh, OK," Mom said. "I was just concerned; we were all concerned, actually."

"Yes, everything really is OK. Come have a seat?"

"No, that's OK," Dad said. "We just wanted to check on you guys."

"Actually," Owen said, "would you mind sticking around for a little while? I need to run a few errands if you guys don't mind?"

"Sure, no problem," Dad said. "Take your time, Owen."

"Guys, Owen can leave. I'll be fine."

"Yeah, we know, kiddo. Sit back down, we're going to have a discussion," Dad said, waving to Owen as he went to the door. "We'll see you later, Owen."

"I won't be gone long," Owen said, laughing as he headed out the door with Arnold.

"So, how's it going Kiddo?" Dad asked.

"I'm fine, Dad, really," I said, sitting on the couch.

"No, I mean you and Owen," Dad said, chuckling. "He's been here since you got out of the hospital."

"Dad!"

"Spill it," Dad said, still laughing at himself.

"I hadn't really thought about it, but Owen hasn't been home, has he?"

"No, he hasn't," Dad said, shaking his head. "He was called out immediately after he dropped you off at the airport. He was out in the field the entire time you were gone."

"I think he went home for a short time at night while you were in the hospital, but that's it," Mom said. "The rest of the time he's been with you."

"I know. One night I was lying in bed for a while; I had been coughing, tossing and turning. I finally got up to get some water. I thought Owen was sleeping in a room down the hall, but as I stood at the kitchen sink, he came downstairs looking for me, nearly scared the daylights out of me. We ended up moving to the couch and talking; and then I feel asleep later, but I don't think he ever did. The next night was about a repeat, except when I got up and came downstairs, he was still here watching TV. We talked until about four a.m. when he decided we needed to go make pancakes."

"Oh gosh, the pancakes," Mom said, looking at Dad. "Your Dad made me pancakes thirty-eight years ago, in the middle of the night and we were married a few months later."

"I did?" Dad asked, looking confused.

"Yes, you did," Mom said. "One of my favorite memories with you."

"Really, pancakes?" Dad asked, still looking confused. "I never made you pancakes; I don't cook."

"You do to cook," Mom said. "And you made pancakes that night."

"Well, don't worry, guys; I think Owen was just hungry."

"You guys need to get some sleep," Dad said. "From the sounds of it neither of you has had much of it lately."

"No, I guess we haven't, now that I think of it. I've had a lot on my mind."

"We'll get all this sorted out and everything will calm down," Dad said.

"Well, that's only part of it. I'm thinking about changing my work schedule, I haven't been super excited about it for a while. I told Owen I was considering telling my boss I want the regional accounts back."

"I think that's a good idea," Mom said.

"Yes, I agree," Dad said. "We see less of you now than when you lived in Denver. Actually, I'm surprised you haven't opened your own firm, yet."

"I hadn't thought of that. That's an even better idea; then I can take on the clients where and when I want," I said, smiling back at him thoughtfully.

"Don't make any decisions just yet, Karla," Dad said. "You've got a lot going on here and you just got out of the hospital. You've got time to figure everything out."

"Hey guys, I'm back," Owen called out as he came through the front door. "Sorry to have kept you waiting."

"That's no problem," Mom said. "We were having a nice chat."

"Did you have a good outing?" I asked Owen.

"It was, I got a few things to take to Ma and Dad's."

"When are you guys leaving?" Dad asked.

"Hmm, Karla?" Owen asked, looking at me.

"Up to you. I got nothing doing. Nothing but time on my hands, you don't even let me help you fix a meal."

"Right and you're not going to. You worked yourself silly and got a hospital stay out of the deal. I'm going to keep you on the DL for a long as possible," Owen said, laughing. "Here, I bought you a book you can read," Owen said, handing me a book called *Angels Walking* by Karen Kingsbury.

"This looks good," I said, looking at the front and back cover.

"We talked about tomorrow sometime," Owen said, looking at me.

"OK, well, you guys get some sleep first," Dad said. "We're going to head out; take care and we'll see you when we get back."

"Thanks, guys," I said, hugging them both.

"Just have a good week," Mom said as they walked to the foyer.

"Thanks for everything, Owen," Dad said.

"No problem," Owen said. "See you later, bye, guys."

"Thanks for the book," I told Owen as we headed back to the couch.

"You're welcome, I've seen Ma read some like those. I hope you like it. Did you have a good visit with your folks?"

"It was nice, a little interesting. You know my dad."

"I wondered when I left," Owen said, chuckling. "Are you good with leaving tomorrow?"

"Yes, I'm looking forward to it."

"I am, too," Owen said, sitting next to me, putting his arm around my shoulders, guiding me to lay my head on his chest.

Chapter 15

Early the next morning, it was still dark out when I looked out the window. Owen looked over at me and asked if he could help me with anything or I needed any laundry washed. We had dozed on the couch off and on yesterday, but for the most part we had talked. We discussed everything under the sun—or the moon in our case—from money to politics and religions.

"I'm good, I could go pack, since I'm obviously not sleeping. Maybe if I left you alone for a little while you'd get some sleep."

"I've been awake for a while," Owen said. "If you don't have laundry, I was thinking of getting us some breakfast and then hitting the road. Would you be up for that?"

"Yea, that's fine."

"Do you want some help packing?" Owen asked. "I can help before I get us some breakfast."

"No thanks, I've got it. At this point I've earned a master's degree in packing."

"I won't argue with ya there," Owen said, getting up as I headed upstairs. About an hour later, Owen had our luggage packed and we pulled out of my driveway. I laid my head back on the seat and stared out into the dark road.

Later that morning, I woke up to the sun shining in my face. I had been asleep but didn't really know how long.

"Hey sleepyhead, have a good nap?" Owen asked.

"Yea, actually I did," I said, stretching. "How long was I asleep?"

"Hmm, quite a while; you pretty much fell asleep as soon as we hit the county line."

"I'm sorry."

"Don't be sorry, you're beautiful when you sleep and don't worry about the snoring. I don't mind, and I don't think Arnold does, either."

"Please, I don't snore."

"Uh, yeah you do. It a cute little sounding snore," Owen said laughing.

"I think you're full of it, Owen."

I pulled into the yard by Ma and Dad's house. They stepped out of the house onto the porch, they must have heard me pull up.

"Hi Ma, Dad."

"How you two doing?" Dad asked as he came up to the pickup. "We didn't expect you this early. Good grief, Owen, you look terrible; when's the last time you slept?" Dad asked as he came around to my side of the pickup.

"Nice to see you too, Dad."

"Hi Karla, how are you?" Mom asked.

"Hi Rosie, nice to see you. How are you?"

"Here, Rose, grab a bag or two and we'll help the kids get inside," Dad said.

"Oh, that's alright, Dad, I can get them."

"Oh, yes, I can get my bags," Karla said.

"You must have left really early today. You never get here this early."

"Yea, we were up. So, we just decided to take off."

"Can I get you guys something to drink?" Mom asked.

We all sat down at the table and Ma poured us a cup of coffee, then sat down at the table to join us.

"How are you feeling, Karla? Owen said you were in the hospital and then all this trouble with your house."

"I'm doing much better, Rosie. Owen here has been waiting on me hand and foot since I got out of the hospital. He's been very good to me, almost annoyingly good."

"That's good. Let him be annoying," Mom said, smiling.

"Dad, how's that panel coming?"

"Oh, it's coming along," Dad said. "Actually, doesn't look too bad. We should go look at it."

"Yea, that'd be good. Is that alright with you if we go out to the barn, Karla?"

"Yep, I'm good. I'm sure your mom and I can find something to get in trouble with."

"Ah, no, not really what I had in mind."

"We'll be fine, Owen," Mom said, chuckling.

"We'll be back in a while, Rosie dear," Dad said as we went out the door.

"So, how you really doing?" Dad asked as we stepped into the barn.

"I'm doing fine. Karla, on the other hand, she still coughs, and I can hear the congestion in her chest even though she says she's feeling better. I can't imagine it feels very good; she's frustrated about things, and she doesn't sleep much."

"And so, in turn, you haven't slept much," Dad said.

"Nah, I'm fine, Dad."

"Owen, it's written all across your face, you can go blow smoke somewhere else."

"Don't worry about me. So, how's this panel coming along?"

"Hard not to," Dad said. "As far as the panel, I still have quite a bit of machining to knock out."

"I can help with that some this week."

"Ah, we'll see about that."

That night after everyone went to bed, I sat on the couch. Dad and I had worked in the barn for a while today. He had done quite a bit of work on the panel. I had all but forgotten about him working on it until Karla and I were on the way down here.

"Owen, what are you still doing up?"

I heard something down the hall and thought Karla was getting up, this has been about the length of time she's stayed in bed this week.

"Owen?" Mom whispered.

"Oh Ma, sorry, did I wake you?"

"No, I got up to go to the bathroom and heard the TV. What are you still doing up? You need your rest."

"Just sitting here, thinking, mostly."

"Are you OK?" Mom asked, sitting on the couch beside me.

"Oh, yea, I'm fine. Karla hasn't been sleeping well and usually gets up shortly after going to bed, so I've waited for her and then sit and talk with her."

"You should go to bed. She'll let us know if she needs something."

"I don't know. When she got home from work that day, she called me, and I couldn't even pick her up from the airport and then she just wanted to go in and go to bed. And then all this with her house, I can't even figure that out."

"Owen, you are doing something, you're supporting her," Mom said.

"It doesn't seem like it's enough, Ma."

"Trust me, Owen, it's everything to her. Now go to bed."

"I don't know, Ma."

"She's sleeping, Owen, and you should be, too. Go look in on her and then go to bed, yourself."

I looked in at Karla, Ma was right, she was sleeping so I went down the hall and went to bed. I laid in bed hoping I wouldn't miss Karla if she got up.

Two mornings later, I was sitting at the table drinking coffee with Dad when Karla came walking into the kitchen. I couldn't believe it; I was pretty sure she had slept for two nights in a row now and was sounding better all the time.

"Good morning, guys."

"Good morning, how'd you sleep? Would you like some coffee?"

"I can get it," Karla said, brushing past me on her way to the cupboard.

"Morning, Karla, how are you'?" Dad asked.

"I'm good, how are you, Joe?"

"How'd you sleep?" I asked her again as she sat down at the table joining Dad and me.

"Great," she said, looking at the book I bought her before we left home.

"I see you've been reading."

"Yes, I have, it's a very good book. I'm not used to just sitting around reading."

"Good, and yes, you should just be sitting around reading. Do you want some breakfast? Dad and I were talking about some. I can put something together."

"Um, sure; do you want some help?"

"You should have Rosie take you to her bookstore," Dad said, referencing the book Karla was reading.

"Yea, she mentioned she has some that I should read after this one, they're part of a series."

"How's scrambled eggs for you two?" I asked, bringing two plates over to the table.

"Thanks, Owen. Looks good," Dad said.

"Yes, thank you Owen," Karla said.

I grabbed my plate and joined them at the table. "You think you might be up for a flight today?" I asked Karla.

"Somebody should ask you the same thing, Owen," Dad said.

"I'd love to go with you, are you sure you want to fly?" Karla asked. "We don't have to go today; we can go another time."

"No, it's all good. I'd like to take you. I sent Ty a text and told him we'd probably be around later this morning."

"You guys be careful," Dad said. "I'm headed to town—you want anything?"

"Good morning, everyone," Mom said as she came into the kitchen.

"Good morning, Ma, there's some eggs on the stove if you want 'em."

"Ah thanks, son! What are you all doing?"

"Not much, Rosie dear," Dad said. "Just sitting here with our coffee. Owen made eggs and we were talking about the day; the kids are going flying."

"Oh nice, you guys will enjoy that. I had a son that used to take me for a plane ride occasionally... hmm, wonder whatever became of him?" Mom said, chuckling at her musings.

"Why don't you come with us, Rosie?" Karla said.

"Ya, Ma, that's a great idea. Come along. You too, Dad. We can stop and get what you need from town on the way back."

After Ma finished her breakfast, we all went over to the Flight School and took off flying over the mesas that morning. I could see Karla relaxing for the first time. I think she really was feeling better, and she had a smile plastered on her face through the whole flight.

That evening we returned from flying and had a quiet supper and were sitting in the living room. Karla was leaned up against me reading her book. She abruptly got up and said she was going for a walk.

I looked at her for a minute and wondered if she should, but I let her be. "Do you want any company?"

"Um yes, actually, that'd be great."

"It really wasn't the walk I was after." Karla said after we got outside. "I was glad you offered to come with me. Have you heard anything from Lane?"

"No," I said as I opened the tailgate of the pickup and motioned for her to have a seat. "They all told us they'd let us know if something came up—you shouldn't worry about it, Karla. Why don't you call Lane and just see?" I said, handing her my phone.

"Thanks, Owen."

"Hey Owen, how goes it?" Lane said, answering.

"Hi Lane, it's Karla and Owen—you're on speakerphone."

"Hey Kar, how are you doing'?"

"I'm good, I was just thinking about all this—have you heard anything?"

"No, Kar. I'm sorry, I haven't received any emails."

"Oh," Karla said, sounding deflated.

"Hey, it's OK," I said, putting my arm around her. "I told you nothing to worry about."

"Yea, Kar. There's nothing to worry about," Lane said. "We've all been checking on your house; you just try and relax."

"I'll take that," I said, squeezing her in a half-embrace.

"OK, thanks, Lane. Bye."

"No problem, guys, call anytime," Lane said before Karla ended the call and handed me my phone back.

"Are you OK now?"

"Yea, I guess. How about that walk now?"

"Sure," I said, taking her hand as we stepped off the tailgate and headed towards the barn.

"Karla, you're braver and stronger than you think; we got this. It's going to take time, but it will be taken care of and then someday we're going to look back and say that's all that was, laughing in its wake." I turned and faced Karla, wrapping my arms around her in a gentle embrace. I slid my chin against hers and brushed my lips against hers and held them there, exploring.

"Would you like to take another flight tomorrow, just the two of us?" Owen said, looking up.

"What did you have in mind, Owen?" she asked, smiling brightly back at me.

"There's the smile we all know and love—now either that was some kiss, or I've just embarked on a really fantastic idea."

"Hmm, perhaps a little of both."

"Good to hear, how about we take a mid-afternoon flight and we'll come back after supper?"

"Hmm, sounds intriguing, I'm in."

"It is. For now, as nice as it's been strolling out here under the moonlight with you, we should probably go in before you get too cold," I said, brushing a kiss across her cheek.

"Owen."

"What? The smile gets me every time."

I faced Karla again and met her again in a heart-melting, soul-stirring kiss. As we stood back, staring in each other's eyes, Karla thanked me, breathlessly.

"Thank you for what?" I asked Karla, repeating her statement.

"Everything. Mostly you, being you."

"Well, if you haven't realized, Karla, you might mean a little something to me. But hey, a discussion for another time." I slipped my arm around the small of her back, holding her tightly.

The next morning, I was in the kitchen having coffee with Ma and Dad and realized I'd left my phone in my room and decided to go back to get it. I found I had a missed call and message from Darren asking me to call him when I got this. I texted him back and told him Karla wasn't up yet. We'd call when she did get up.

Darren just wrote back "10-4."

I headed down the hall to go back to the kitchen. When I walked by Karla's room, I was pretty sure I could hear her in her room, so I backed up and stopped outside the door and listened for a sec. Just as I was about to knock; the door opened.

"Oh, good morning, Karla."

"Owen were you just loitering outside my door?" she asked, hugging me.

"Yes, no. Well, sort of. I needed to talk to you and was headed back to the kitchen, but I thought I heard you and was about to knock when you opened the door."

"What did you want to talk about?"

"I got a message from your dad; he wants us to call him. I can call him if you want to go have coffee?"

"I wonder what's going on," she said, looking at me concerned. "We just talked to Lane last night."

"Yea, I don't know," I said, shaking my head.

Karla grabbed her phone, and we went to the kitchen. She called her dad and put the phone on speaker. I explained to my parents that Darren asked us to call as the phone was dialing.

"Morning kiddo, how are you?" Darren asked, answering the phone.

"I'm fine, Dad. Owen and I are sitting here with his parents. Owen said you wanted us to call—what's up? We talked to Lane last night and he said nobody's contacted him."

"I suppose that's still true; I haven't talked to him today. The reason I'm calling is to see if you've talked to Deputy Montez."

"No, why?"

"Well, I don't know. He was by the office yesterday and I wasn't here. He left his card with Ruby and said he would return today. Ruby just told me this morning when I got to the office; I thought maybe he tried to call you."

"We haven't gotten a call, Darren."

"Maybe we should come home," Karla said, looking at me with that worried look of hers.

"No," I said shaking my head. "Likely we wouldn't make it before the deputy returns to talk to your dad and he can tell us what he came to talk to him about. And then we can decide about returning home then. If we need to, we can use Ty's plane and make it there in less than an hour. Besides, we have plans for this afternoon, remember."

"Owen's right. I'll call you after Deputy Montez leaves," Dad said.

"Thanks, Darren. Talk soon."

"Yea, thanks, Dad, bye," Karla said as she disconnected the call.

"This just gets more messed up all the time—why is he contacting my dad?"

"The deputy probably went to your house and didn't find you home," Dad said.

"Dad's right, he knew you traveled a lot. He probably figures you just went back to work."

"Hmm, maybe."

"Alright, who's up for some breakfast?" Mom asked as she refilled our coffee cups.

"Sure thing, Ma," I said, looking at Karla.

"Rosie, would you like some help?" Karla asked, still looking concerned. I hope I can take her mind off things this afternoon.

"Um, sure. Do you want to set the table?"

I got up and started to get things out of the fridge and soon Karla and I fell in a jovial nature helping Ma get breakfast ready.

We sat down to enjoy breakfast of bacon and waffles. "Ma, you always make the best waffles."

"Well, Owen, they're no different than the pancakes I make."

"Well, you make both of them better; I can never get the batter the right consistency."

"I don't know about that," Karla said. "I liked them when you made them for me the other night."

"You made her pancakes, Owen?" Mom asked, pointing her fork at me.

"Yea, we'd both been up all night and hadn't had any supper."

"Hmm, Joe, did you catch that? Owen made her pancakes."

"I heard, Rosie," Dad said in his noncommittal, relaxed tone.

"Thanks for the pancakes, Rosie dear. I'm going to the barn, now. You care to tag along, Owen?"

"Yea, I'll come for out a while, but Karla and I are going to leave around noon; we have plans today," I said, looking at Karla.

"I'll be ready," Karla said.

"So, did you buy that ring yet?" Dad asked as we got into the barn.

"Um, no, not yet." I said, shaking my head.

"What are you waiting for, Owen? You plannin' on perfecting your pancake recipe? Your mother made me pancakes oh so many moons ago and I moved in with her that night."

"You did not, Dad," I said, laughing.

215

"Well, maybe not that night; but darn close."

"Loves not built on pancakes."

"No, but when a couple cooks and shares time in the kitchen together, they learn and grow together. Life isn't based around a McDonald's sack rushing down the highway; it's built around the table as a family unit. So, when you gonna buy that ring?" Dad asked again.

"I'd give more than anything to propose to Karla, right now, any time, and spend the rest of my life with her. But I'm not sure that right now is such a good time; it's not as though I'm going anywhere. I've stayed with her practically every minute since she left the hospital, which brings up a whole other issue, but I just wanted her safe. After we leave here, if that post is still up, I don't know what to do. I don't want her to stay at her house by herself."

"You need to find some balance and pray about this situation, Owen. And as much as I am an advocate of not wanting you boys to live with someone before marriage, I think this is a bit of a different situation. You and Karla will have to discuss this before moving forward; she might have a different opinion now that she's feeling better. Owen, take my advice: don't wait too long for the ring. Life's too important; and you've got one heck of a gal in there," Dad said, pointing to the house.

"I know, thanks, Dad."

I went up to the house later to get ready to leave with Karla for the afternoon. I noticed she was sitting at the kitchen table with a different book. When I stepped into the porch, taking my coat off, I just stopped and smiled for a moment, thinking back on the discussion Dad and I had that morning. I knew Dad was right and I didn't plan to wait too long, I thought as I continued into the kitchen.

"What's that look for?" Karla asked as I stopped behind her and put my arms around her.

"What look?" I asked.

"I saw you over there; lost in thought."

"I was just taking in the beauty. Are you ready to go? I told Ty we'd be there in about a half hour."

"I'm ready, I'll be waiting here for you."

We pulled into the Flight School and Ty came hightailing it out of the hangar. "You've been here for days, and this is the first I've seen of you, what's that all about?" Ty said, ranting.

"Nice to see you, too," I said, laughing. "We were out here yesterday and got a plane; you were nowhere to be found."

"Ya, I know," Ty said. "I was out with a class when you got here, when you came back, I must have been at the bank," Ty said skeptically.

"Uh huh, sure, is that what you're calling it these days, 'the bank'?" I said, smiling. "You remember Karla?" I asked Ty.

"Yes. Hi, Karla. How's it going? Besides your keeping' Owe under wraps."

"Hi, Ty, and it's more like Owen keeping me under wraps."

"Owe, you sly dog, you."

"All right, all right, time for a pre-flight check. You don't talk about the bank—maybe you'll introduce me sometime?"

"Well, you never know," Ty said. "We may have to discuss a balance sheet."

Once Ty and I completed the pre-flight checks, I got Karla to board the plane with me; she always stands back, watching us from a distance. We boarded the plane, Ty and I had a few more checks and were cleared for takeoff; I taxied out of the airfield behind the Flight School. I radioed the control tower and told them we were headed for the Grand Canyon.

"Owen, did you just tell them we were headed for the Grand Canyon?"

"Sure did. Is that alright?"

"Perfect," she said, leaning back in her seat and taking in the view below.

We made our way over to the Grand Canyon; I made a big loop. Looking at the Grand Canyon we took in each of the views of the north and south rims. I started changing altitude and moving through the corridors of the Grand Canyon, only an option for smaller planes. Then I started climbing over the Marble Canyon area and made a pass across Horseshoe Bend, which I think might have been Karla's favorite by the look on her face. I made another pass across the rims as we headed to Sedona and prepared to land.

I picked out a place for supper in Sedona overlooking the red rocks. The temperature reading outside this afternoon for Sedona read seventy-six degrees, which should make for a beautiful afternoon. I radioed in for landing in Sedona and was cleared for landing at the airport. I taxied in and shut down.

"Oh wow, Owen. There are no words to describe this. Those were some stunning views," she said, taking my hand. "What's next?"

"I have supper reservations with another great view—or so that's what their website crows about." We grabbed a taxi, and I told the driver the name of the restaurant.

The driver dropped us off at the restaurant about twenty minutes later and we went inside. I told the hostess we had reservations and we were shown to the outdoor seating.

"This has been wonderful, thank you," Karla said.

"It has been a great day, I'm glad you like it. This restaurant is fabulous and sitting out here is so nice."

The waiter came and took our drink order; we both declined the wine list and just went with water. I was flying and the two didn't mix.

We were asked about appetizers and Karla declined; I declined as well. I noticed they had swordfish on the menu. That sounded good, so I ordered that, and Karla ordered the salmon. The waiter stepped away and Karla and I resumed the discussion of our flight over the Grand Canyon.

"You really know how to put together an adventure. The weekend in San Francisco, our moonlight walks in Cancun. I'm not going to know how to act when it's time to go back to work."

"I'll be here, I'm not going anywhere, Karla. We have plenty of adventures together," I said, extending my hand out to Karla from across the table. She set her hand in mine.

"This sure beats the fish we had at the Fish House in San Francisco," Karla said.

"I know, I don't know what they thought they were doing to that fish, but they totally annihilated it. You have to work hard to make it that bad."

"Mine's really good, how's yours?"

"Oh, it's great, do you want to try it?" Owen asked.

"Actually, yea, can I?"

"Sure, grab yourself some."

We finished our meal and were still raving about how good it was when the waiter came and asked if we wanted to see the dessert menu.

Karla and I both declined. The waiter left the ticket with me, and I paid.

"Are you ready to go?" I asked Karla as I stood up from the table and held my hand out for her. We walked out of the restaurant and the air was warm and breezy.

We grabbed a taxi, and I told the driver to take us to the airport. We were cleared for takeoff; I taxied off the airfield runway. We hadn't heard from Darren to tell why the deputy had come to visit with him. I was curious about it, and I knew it had to be weighing heavily on Karla's mind.

The next morning, Karla was the only one in the kitchen when I came in to get coffee. "Morning," I said as I came up beside her and nuzzled the side of her neck, kissing her. "How are you? How did you sleep?"

"Good, I've slept great lately."

"I'm glad, Karla," I said, rubbing her shoulders as I stood behind her chair, looking at the book she was reading. "So why are you up so early this morning?"

"Did you talk to my dad yesterday?"

"No, I didn't, Karla, I thought about that when we were flying back last night. Don't worry it, he'll call soon."

"Good morning, you two," Mom said as she came into the kitchen.

"Good morning, Ma, sorry we missed you and Dad last night."

"What about Dad?" Dad asked as he came into the kitchen shortly behind Ma.

"I was just saying I'm sorry we missed you guys' last night."

"Did you two have a good trip?" Mom asked.

"We did, Rosie, Owen has excellent ideas."

After we finished up with breakfast Dad and I went out to the barn and worked on the plane panel. Ma and Karla came in later, looking around and inspecting our work.

"We're going to town for some shopping, lunch and who knows whatever other kind of trouble we can stir up, right, Karla?" Mom announced excitedly.

"Right, Rosie, we'll see you guys later."

"There're sandwich fixings in the fridge," Mom said as she turned to leave.

"How do you like that business?" Dad said. "We get stuck with sandwiches, and they go into town."

"I'm pretty sure you told Karla to have Ma take her to the bookstore, Dad."

"Oh, right," Dad said, smirking.

"I can get us some lunch, Dad, or we can go to town on our own for lunch."

"Hmm, we might just have to see about that, Owen," Dad said, pondering as we went back to machining the panel. We worked on the panel for several hours. Dad stopped and propped his side up and looked over at me.

"I think we'll go to town, now."

I secured my end. Just as we were coming through the barn door, Ty came driving in.

"Hey, what are you two characters doing?" Ty asked.

"Impeccable timing as always, Ty," Dad said. "You must have sensed we were going after lunch."

"Well, it is your normal lunch time, Joe. Can't fault a guy."

"Come on, Ty, you're driving. We'll even let you buy," Dad said, laughing and patting Ty on the shoulder.

"Ah well, I think I'm getting called away," Ty said joking.

"Get in, Ty," I said. "You're driving."

Ty pulled up to the Burger Barn when we got to town. "Man, Ty, I haven't been here for a long time." "I know, Owe; I figured you were due," Ty said getting out of his Jeep.

As we walked up to the door my phone started ringing and I figured Karla was calling. I pressed the connect button. "Hello."

"Hey, Owen, you guys busy?"

"Darren, hi. No, we were just headed in to eat lunch."

"Oh, is Karla with you?"

"No, she and my mom are out shopping and having lunch today; I'm not really sure where. I can call her and go meet up with her and we can call you back."

"No, that's OK, I was just going to tell you guys the deputy came back this morning. He's a strange one."

"Everything about this is strange, Darren. What did he tell you?"

"Well, it's a bit confusing. The deputy came into reception asking to speak to the owner or manager of the business, so Ruby called me to step out to the lobby."

"The deputy explained that he was investigating a break-in situation at Karla's house. I said yea, I know. Karla's my daughter. He almost acted like he didn't believe I was her dad or the fact that I was there that day."

"So, what did he tell you, Darren?"

"He said his IT department did some investigating and one of the IP addresses used to make the post is linked to my internet account."

"Where did he get an idea like that. This has to be some sort of mistake. But you said one of the IP addresses; what about the others?"

"Yea, I asked him about that, but he couldn't divulge that information," Darren said, sounding irritated.

"Does he think you're a suspect or something, Darren?"

"Well, I don't think so, he didn't arrest me. He just informed me of the investigation and said we'd be in touch."

"We need to find out about the other IP addresses; this one's a mistake. I'll talk to Karla, and we'll call you later. She may push to come home, now."

"Let me know." *This situation just gets more troublesome all the time*, I thought, walking into the Burger Barn to joined Dad and Ty.

"Is everything OK?" Dad asked. "I ordered us all some burgers and fries."

"I don't know. I was just talking to Karla's dad; the deputy on this case did some investigating with the post on her house. They got more than one IP address hits and one of them is linked to the internet account at Darren's development company."

"What?" Ty asked.

"Yea," I think it's a mistake. I want to know about the other IP address or addresses, whose internet accounts they're linked to. Maybe there's some correlation."

"Maybe somebody stealing her dad's internet." Ty noted.

"Maybe," Dad said. "I've been thinking about a few things; who would have access to her house keys, security alarm and obviously a schedule of her comings and goings? I hate to say it but maybe it's someone who works for Darren."

"That's a good point, Dad. I need to go talk to Karla about this." As I stood up to leave our burgers and fries arrived.

"Sit down, Owen, let's eat and talk about this. I have an idea."

"No offense, but your last idea isn't working out so well."

"I know, I'm sorry about that. Eat up, were going to go call Darren before you track down Karla."

"I just talked to Darren; I figure Karla's probably going to want to go home after this."

"That may be, but the three of us are going to call Darren back and ask him some questions about his business."

We finished our lunch and I texted Darren and told him I was going to call him back in about a half hour, Dad had some questions for him.

Darren replied. "Yea, that'd be fine." Dad, Ty, and I went in the barn when we got back to the farm. *So much for having a quiet lunch with the ole' man*, I thought as I dialed Darren and put him on speakerphone.

"Hey, Darren. I've got my dad, Joe and good buddy, Ty, here."

"Hello, what can I do for you?"

"At first, I was thinking it was a mistake. They say the IP address is linked to your internet account, but Dad brings up some good points," I said, motioning to Dad.

"Hi Darren, Joe Kaster here. I was thinking about Karla's situation. I still feel like someone knows Karla's schedule. I think more and more that one of your employees is responsible, especially since the deputy identified one of the IP addresses. Does anyone in your company know anything that's happened to Karla the last couple weeks—they probably know better than to proceed with any bookings or communications. Who in your company knows about what's happened to Karla? Who would have access to her house keys, security alarm code, her schedule?"

"Hmm, that's an interesting point, Joe. I think everybody here probably knows about what's happened. Her house keys and security alarm code are in my desk drawer."

"Who has access to your desk drawer?" I asked Darren.

"Well, I don't exactly keep my desk or my office under lock and key. I've never had a problem."

"What about her schedule?" Dad asked. "Can we account for that?

"Do any of your employees live near Karla and could account for her activity?"

"No, I'm not sure where most of my employees live. When Karla moved into that house, she immediately started traveling out of state. I told her she should let me know when she was going to be gone. She said she'd just add her trips to my calendar."

"What calendar, Darren?" I asked.

"My work calendar, the only one I have."

"Geezus, Darren. You just armed someone to do this," I said, rubbing my face with the palm of my hand. "Who in your company would do something like this?"

"I-I-I don't know," Darren said, stammering. "This is not something I'd suspect of anyone that works here."

"Well get to thinking, Darren. Karla needs to know and move on to more important things in life," I said, disconnecting the call. *Wow*, I thought. *How could you be so careless, Darren?* I was just as ready as Karla was to put this all behind us, but now I think it just blew up. We all sat there nearly stunned at what had just happened.

"I need to get going," Ty said, standing up from his stool. "Good luck with all this, Owe. It was good seeing you," Ty said, shaking my hand and slapping my back.

Dad and I stood up from our stools and followed Ty out to his Jeep.

"Yea, you too, thanks man."

"We'll talk soon," Ty said, shaking my hand.

"Why don't you plan on making a trip north soon?"

"Yea, maybe soon," Ty said, looking in his rearview mirror.

As Dad and I were saying goodbye to Ty; Ma and Karla came driving up the road.

"We'll see ya, guys," Ty said.

Dad and I walked over to Ma's car, after she'd parked. I proceeded to the passenger side where Karla was riding and opened her door. "Hey, how was the trip to town?"

"It was nice," Karla said looking at me inquisitively.

"Good, what can I carry in for you?"

"Ah, wait, Owen. What are you not telling me? I can see it in your face."

"Ya, we need to talk, I was just going to wait until we got inside."

Ma looked at us, concerned. "Come in the house," she said. "I'll start a pot of coffee."

"Are there things in the car that need brought in?" Dad asked.

"Yea," Rosie said, "there's a few bags of groceries and a couple other items; we can grab them as we go."

Dad and I grabbed the bags from the backseat and went inside.

"How come you didn't call me?" Karla asked, sounding irritated.

"Ah that's my fault," Dad said. "Have a seat and Owen and I will explain everything here straightaway."

"Alright, I'm inside, what's up, then?" Karla said shortly.

"Your dad called, and my dad convinced me to wait. We came back here and called your dad back. Remember how the deputy wanted to investigate the website with the post?" I asked Karla.

"Yea, I guess," Karla said.

"The deputy told Darren his IT department linked the IP address to his company internet account."

"Well, that's a mistake," Karla said.

"That's what I thought. But your dad said this was just one of the IP addresses the deputy discussed, and the deputy refused to divulge additional information. My Dad has some ideas you should hear about; he makes a lot of sense and poses some good questions."

"How would they have access to your house keys, security alarm code and obviously your schedule?" Dad asked Karla. "That's why considering an inside connection to your dad's company is worth looking at. I asked your dad about these things and found out quite a bit, Karla."

"No," Karla said, crying. "This is all a mistake—that IP address has nothing to do with my dad's company." Karla got up from the table and looked me and dad over. "My dad has good people

224

working for him. Some of them are like family. I'm going for a walk," Karla said shaking her head.

"Do you want—"

"No, Owen, I don't want any company," Karla said, cutting me off as she walked out the door into the cool afternoon air.

"I'll go with her," Ma said, walking out the door behind her. I walked over to the kitchen window and looked out into the yard and could see Ma talking to Karla. Before too long, Ma was walking back towards the house.

"She said she's fine," Ma said, coming into the kitchen. "She's going to call her friend."

"Yea, Eide. They haven't talked in a few days. It would probably do her good to talk to Eide, except not outside," I said, looking out the window again.

"Owen, don't just stare at her out the window, come sit down. She'll come in when she's ready."

"But it's cool out there, and she's still recovering from an illness."

"Do you know anybody that works at her dad's company?" Dad asked.

"Just one, Garratt, longtime family friend, went to college with her brothers. He even went to Mexico with us."

"Do you know anything about him?" Dad asked.

"Not really, he's been to some family dinners. He's always hung out with Lane and Levi, but recently they've been saying they've had a hard time getting ahold of him. They were all surprised he came to the wedding in Mexico."

I came outside, getting more and more chilled as I stood by Owen's pickup. Why couldn't bad things happen in warmer weather? A walk would have been great. But for the moment I just needed some air. I dialed my phone to call Eide.

"Karla, honey, how are you?"

"Oh Eide, good grief. This is all crap."

"What's crap—did Lane get a response?"

"This whole mess with my house; there's some information going around about IP addresses and Owen and his dad have decided that someone at Dad's office is behind this."

"What? What are you talking about?"

225

"One of the IP addresses linked to the internet account used to create the post for my house supposedly came from Dad's office."

"That's bizarre, why would they say that? Do Levi or Lane know this?"

"I don't know."

"Hold on," Eide said. I could hear her hollering for Levi.

"I'm going to conference Lane and Molly in," Eide said.

"We're here, what's up?" Molly said.

"Do either of you guys know about a deputy coming to talk to Darren about IP addresses today?"

"Oh yea, Dad told us about that. If you ask me somebody's got some serious explaining to do," Levi said.

"Am I the last to know anything?" I could feel tears bubbling up in my tear ducts; this was going from bad to worse.

"Owen and his dad think it's one of Darren's employees," Eide said.

"What do you mean?" Lane asked.

"Well for one, why haven't you gotten a response to your inquiry?" Eide asked Lane.

"So, that don't mean anything," Lane said.

"Joe and Owen have decided that since Dad has the keys to my house and security code in his desk—"

"And Karla you've been adding your trip information to Darren's calendar," Eide said interrupting me. "You know who's been doing this?" Eide said thoughtfully

"Doing what?"

"Renting your house out. That little weasel, Garratt. I'd been having dreams about you being chased and thought it looked like Garratt. You notice how he's slowly been backing away and not being involved in things," Eide said heatedly. "He barely showed up for our wedding."

"Eide, wait a minute," Levi said. "Dreams don't mean anything."

"Eide, what dreams are you talking about?" I asked. *What dreams is she talking about?* I thought.

"My dreams mean something; I've had dreams about you, I tried to tell you I was worried about you."

"You tell me that all the time; Garratt's like family and you know it," I said, yelling back at Eide while tears continued to build up and then came out in a rush down my face.

226

"Owen?" Molly called out.

"Owen's not here, he's in the house with his parents." Now I was just mad at Eide, she should know better.

"Why's Owen not there?" Molly asked.

"Because I told him not to follow me."

"Hey Kar, are you alright?" Lane asked.

"Yes," I said, sniffling and sobbing. "I just don't think Garratt did all this this. It's not Garratt, you guys, don't put this target on his back. I gotta go, Owen's headed this way." I disconnected on my end; no doubt they all stayed on the line talking. I sat there on the tailgate of Owen's pickup watching him walk towards me. I tried to wipe the tears from my eyes.

"Karla, are you alright?" Owen asked, looking concerned and brushing tears off my face.

"Yes, never mind. You didn't have to come after me."

"Yea, I did. I'd been watching you from the kitchen window and then I got a mysterious text that said, *Karla needs to talk, a shoulder to cry on, maybe a hug.*"

"Let me guess, one of two people? Eide or Molly."

"Molly, so how about all three. I take it your call didn't go so well?" Owen asked, sitting on the tailgate next to me.

"I called to talk to Eide, but she got Levi on the phone, and conferenced Lane and Molly in. I told them what our dads talked about and before we were done Eide's spouting off that she thinks Garratt's done all this."

"Garratt?" Owen asked, questioning what I'd said.

"Yea, you know Garratt, the one my brothers have hung around with practically our whole lives; the one who went to Mexico with us he stood up for Levi alongside Lane? I don't see him doing something like this."

"Well, she might be right, Karla. I'm sorry to have everyone against you, but I'm looking from the outside in, and I don't know Garratt as well as you do. I've only been around him a few times, and thinking back, considering what we know now, I tend to agree. Think about the wedding; the security alarm messages you kept getting. We all sat at the dance when you got a call, and you called the Sheriff's Office. Garratt disappeared pretty quicky and the next

227

morning he took a flight home. Now at the time, no one suspected a thing. But now, don't you think it was a little odd?"

"Let's just go for a walk," I said, changing the subject. I liked walking out here. I knew what Owen was saying about Garratt had merit. I did think it was odd that he disappeared so quickly.

Owen took my hand as we stepped off the tailgate of the pickup and walked down past the barn. There was a big beautiful translucent moon coming up over the hayfield and we walked along the dirt road leading to the empty corral panels where Joe once had a few horses. You could feel spring coming on, you could see it in the trees, there was beauty all around us.

"Owen, how come your dad doesn't have any horses anymore?"

"He says he's too old to keep up with them. Max and I don't come around much anymore to help with them." "Dad sold off most of the herd last fall and the rest just after the first of the year. He'd rather repair plane parts; and I think Ty keeps him pretty busy."

"Are you guys about finished with the panel you've been working on?"

"Oh, we're gaining ground; do you want to see it?"

"Yes, can I?"

"Of course."

We turned back and headed into the barn. "You really like working with your dad, don't you?"

"Well, it's more than working. We've had several important discussions out here. Dads dispensed a lot of advice over the years from that stool; even some very recently that I have yet to act on."

"Like today?"

"I'm not so sure he was passing out advice today, just questioning theories." Owen said, taking my hands and looking deep into my eyes. Owen moved to embrace me, wrapping his arms around my back, laying my head into his chest, rubbing his strong hands along my spine.

"That feels so good."

"Yea, you like that?"

"Yes, you can do that anytime."

The next morning Rosie and I made some breakfast while Owen and his dad loaded Owen's pickup. I told Owen last night we needed to go home; it was time I visited with the sheriff. We all gathered around the table and started eating after Joe blessed our meal and asked for God's hand in the challenges we've been presented.

"Rosie, thank you so much for everything this week," I said as we were cleaning up the kitchen after breakfast. "I'm sorry we're heading out early."

"It's OK. Owen talked to us this morning, we even talked about coming to visit. Owen has really been pushing for that. So, I think Joe and I will take a trip soon and visit you guys. I just hope you got a chance to relax while you were here; Owen really wanted that for you. Do you know that first night you were here; I got up a couple hours after we went to bed, and Owen was still up? He thought you might be up before too long and wouldn't be able to sleep, he was going to sit up with you. I was pretty sure you were asleep; I chased his butt to bed."

"I might be at fault for that, Rosie. I didn't sleep well those first few nights after getting out of the hospital, Owen sat up talking with me. We talked about everything from pancakes to Ty and Owen's Flight School."

"Are you ready to go?" Owen asked as he stepped into the kitchen. "Arnold's sitting in the backseat perched like a statue; I almost felt like I should buckle him up."

"Oh gosh, that dog, always something with him," Rosie said, chuckling.

"Did you tell her about the howling?" I asked Owen.

"Oh no, I didn't. OK, so one afternoon I got called out, Karla and I were up in the mountains having lunch. After we got to the hangar, I told Karla to take my pickup and we'd connect later. Right before I go in, I remembered Arnold and asked Karla if she could go let him out. Well, long story short he spent the night with her and then it was the next night before we met up again and then she had to fly out Sunday and was gone all week. Well, that whole week, anytime the phone or doorbell rang ol' Arnold would howl a blue streak. Then Friday night when she got back, she came over. She rang the doorbell, he howled something fierce until I opened the door and then later when the rest of her family got there, he was like eh, no big deal."

"Now, that's pretty good," Rosie said, laughing. "He missed you."

"Yea, tell me about it," Owen said. "We better head out."

"You kids be careful," Joe said as he and Rosie followed us outside.

"We will, Dad, thanks for everything. Let me know how things go with that panel. And don't forget you said you'd come for up for a visit."

"We will, Karla and I talked about it this morning. We'll be up," Rosie said. "Love you two."

We really hadn't said much since leaving. I had been thinking about what we were going to find when I got home. Owen must have been thinking along the same lines; he had the music turned up and I had been watching the side of the road go by as Owen traveled down the winding roads near his parents' farm.

Owen turned the music down and looked at me. "Karla?"

"Yes?"

"I want to run something by you, at least something for you to consider. I don't want you to go to your own home, at least not for a while."

"What do you mean, Owen?"

"Well, number one, whoever made this post, Garratt or whoever, hasn't been identified and we don't even know if that's the only site it's posted on."

"I never thought about it being on more than one site; there is more than one site that it could be posted to."

"And another thing; you've slept much better since we left your house."

"I can't run from my life, Owen."

"I'm not asking you to run from your life. I just want you to be safe."

"You're one to talk, you put yourself in danger every time you go to work. I don't know what to do, I've even thought about quitting my job."

"Well, I told you before, I'd vote for changing your schedule, mostly for selfish reasons. What have you been thinking about?"

"That afternoon when you ran out before we left to go to your parents', and you got my parents to babysit me."

"Ha, ya," Owen said, chuckling.

"I told them I've considered telling my boss that I wanted the regional clients back. Mom and Dad said they thought it was a good idea, but Dad said he was surprised that I hadn't started my own firm yet and then I could choose my own clients and more importantly where they were located. It got me thinking, I'm considering starting an online platform for marketing analysis."

"I think that's a great idea, Karla, you should go for it. So, where's home base going to be?"

"I don't know, find a new home I guess and sell the one currently welcoming unexpected visitors."

"That's what I'm getting at, Karla; I don't want you home alone at least for a while. Here, would you answer my phone?" Owen said as he handed me his ringing phone.

"Oh, it's my dad," I said, putting him on speaker.

"Hi Dad."

"Hey kiddo, where's Owen?"

"He's driving, we're on our way home. He's listening, I have you on speaker."

"Why don't you find a place to pull over, Owen. I have quite a bit to talk about."

"OK," Owen said. "There's an exit coming up."

"How long have you guys been on the road?"

"About two hours," I said as Owen took the off-ramp and parked in a truck stop parking lot.

"OK, Dad, Owen's parked. What's up?"

"Did you talk to Eide yesterday?"

"Yea, I called her, why?"

"Well, she was here at the office when we opened this morning."

"What for?"

"She came in ranting as soon as Ruby unlocked the front door, demanding to see Garratt."

"Yes, she went off about that yesterday, but honestly, I don't think he did it. I mean its Garratt."

"Well, Eide was rambling about where Garratt was and this whole house business. She finally had Ruby scared enough, Ruby called the sheriff on her. Before a deputy arrived, Garratt came into work and Eide started firing off at him and eventually pummeled him."

"She pummeled him? She can't do that, she's pregnant."

"Yea, well she did and I gotta say I thought Garratt could have taken it better. He laid on the floor long enough, Eide finally sat on his chest until he admitted to making the post about your house."

"Oh no," I said, rubbing my face. "This just keeps getting worse," I groaned. "What happened to them?"

"Garratt was arrested, I called Levi down here to pick Eide up and we told the deputies about your case and why Eide was rambling on.

Eventually the deputy investigating your case was called and he confirmed that Garratt was a suspect because of the other IP address. I didn't want to believe it was Garratt either," Dad said. "Eide said she was convinced all night that it was Garratt, she told Levi she was going to track Garratt down today and get to the bottom of this. Levi didn't think she'd attack him; he figured she'd just call and chew him out."

"Eide kept pushing that it was him; but I didn't think she was right, is she alright?"

"I think so. Your mother said something about pregnancy hormones on overdrive, but Levi was going to take her to the doctor to get her checked out just to be on the safe side."

"Well good, I'll call her later. I need to apologize to her. What's going to happen to Garratt now?"

"I don't know, kiddo; maybe the deputies will fill you in. They don't like sharing information with me since I'm not the homeowner."

"I'm going to let you go, Dad. Owen and I will call you later, after we talk to the deputy, and we decide what we're doing."

"OK, take care, kiddo, you too, Owen."

After I disconnected the call, Owen and I just sat there in silence for a while. Finally, Owen asked me if I was OK.

"I don't know; I can't believe Eide pummeled him or sat on his chest."

"That part's kinda funny," Owen said, holding my hand and rubbing it. "I always said Eide was crazy. Let's go get a cup of coffee. We can discuss this new job idea of yours and where you're going to stay when you get home." "Most of my concerns are still valid; just because we know who now doesn't change my other concerns."

Owen and I sat down in the truck stop restaurant and ordered coffees. "You really have slept lots better since you haven't been home."

"I know, you know, your mom knows," I said, chuckling. "Who else knows about my sleeping habits?"

"What?" Owen asked, chuckling.

"Nothing, Owen," I said, shaking my head. "Thanks for being there for me."

Chapter 16

Three months later

"Hi Owen, how was work?" I hollered out from my temporary home office when I heard him come in the house talking to Arnold.

"This is the same place I left you when I went to work. Please tell me you at least got up for food and drink?" Owen asked, coming into my office, putting his hands around my shoulders.

"I did and I even let Arnold out to go to the bathroom a time or two, despite what you were questioning him about," I said, looking at him skeptically.

"What are you working on, today?"

"I was looking at rental properties; I really need to find my own place. We can't keep this up; it's been three months. I need to get back to my own life."

"I'll help you look in a couple weeks, we can discuss it later, though. Tonight, I have something else to discuss with you. I was thinking today, and I talked to Ma and Dad on the way home from work so, you really can't say no," Owen said, looking at me hesitantly. "I was thinking that with the Fourth of July weekend coming and somebody's birthday, we should make a big weekend of it. Your parents, my parents, Levi, Eide, Lane, Molly, Max, Elaine and the kids and I'll see if Ty and 'the bank' can make it. My parents haven't met any of your family and vice versa. What do you think?"

"This is a great idea, I love it. You should call Max and Ty tonight, so they don't make other plans. I'll send everyone else a text right now."

"Oh good, does this mean you're going to stop working on all this other stuff?"

"Um, yes. For today," I said, jokingly slapping Owen. "Besides, I told you I wasn't working; I was looking for a rental and you distracted me, once again."

Owen spent the whole week planning and getting ready for this, I think he's planning to go all-out on the fireworks, and I think we have enough food to serve a platoon, I thought, finishing up and saving my files as I heard Owen answer the doorbell and greet his family that afternoon. *He's been so excited for this, getting everyone together.*

Ty came into the living room holding hands with a very petite, red-haired young woman. "Owen, I'd like to introduce you to Rachel Weist. Rach, this Owe, the good buddy I've told you about."

"Oh sure, you tell her about me, but all I get is I'm at the 'bank,'" I said jokingly.

"Of course, you get the 'bank.' Rach is a loan officer at the bank where our accounts for the Flight School are held."

"Oh, nice one, Ty. You always were bad with numbers, it's good you're finally getting some help with that," I said, shaking my head. "It's nice to meet you, Rachel," I said, shaking her hand.

"How about we all go out to the patio, and I'll get us some drinks before we have supper. Hi Ma," I said, walking up beside her hugging her as we walked out to the patio.

"Hi son, thanks for having us."

"Absolutely, glad you could make it, it's going to be a great weekend. I need to check the smoker; I'll be right back." I heard Ma ask Karla how she was. Karla told her she was good, really good. "There's lots to tell, Rosie, but we have all weekend; I'll get you up to speed." I was glad to hear Karla sound so happy.

The next morning, the kitchen was buzzing, the ladies were working on getting some breakfast. Max, Dad, Ty, and I took our coffee out to the patio to watch the kids play; seems a certain uncle bought and assembled a totally awesome massive fort system in the backyard. Talk about massive, the thing took almost all last weekend to assemble it; but it was worth every minute; those kids have been running excitedly practically every moment since they discovered it last night. Max had to drag them off it to put them to bed last night.

"So, how'd that plane panel work out once dad got it finished up? We never really discussed it," I asked Ty.

"Oh, it's perfect. Your dad never disappoints; you should come down later on. I'm planning on taking a tailpiece to your dad to look at; looks to be an interesting item to fix."

"What happened there?"

"One of the students tore it apart when we were preparing for take-off the other day."

"Oops, did somebody fail the class?"

"No, I think he was just having a rough day. He's a good student, showing great potential."

"Well, good. I don't know how soon I'll be down, but I'm sure Dad can take care of a rebuild for you."

"Ah, there's something else I want to talk to you about, Owen."

"Oh, what's that, Ty?"

"The Flight School."

"What about the Flight School, Ty? Is everything OK?"

"Yes, everything's great, business is great; that's why I bring this up."

"Alright Ty, out with it."

"I want you back. I know my timing isn't great; but you always said you'd be there for me, and I need you back."

"Ty, you think your timing isn't great, I think your timing is terrible," I said, running my hand through my hair, sighing. "Let me talk to Karla, I'll help you figure something out. Really now, Ty."

"Alright Karla, tell us what's been going on. Owen calls, but he always just says everything's fine. He usually asks Joe what he's working on, he asks how we are and that's about the extent of his calls."

236

"Nothing much has changed. I'm still living here. I keep telling him I need to find my own place. I told Owen just last week I needed to get back to some semblance of a normal life."

"I'm not worried about that," Rosie said.

"Well, other than the fact that we know who—Joe pretty much had it figured out that it was somebody in my dad's company."

"Yea, that's what Joe and Owen were discussing when you went outside."

"I'm sorry, what are you guys talking about?" Rachel asked.

"I'm sorry, I just figured you knew all about this. A family friend that worked in my dad's company had my house posted on a vacation home rental site, doing short-term rentals when I wasn't home, which was almost weekly. Back in April, I came home early cause I was sick. Owen and I found people's belongings all over my house, Owen called the cops. When I got out of the hospital, Owen took me to Rosie and Joe's, while my brother tried to be a decoy.

Joe, Owen, and Ty were figuring it out; but my best friend did, too, and she decided to confront him. He was arrested and released, and we haven't heard or seen him since."

"Wait, how come he was released?" Elaine asked, looking concerned.

"He made bail, I guess. These rental situations have become a huge deal across several cities in the U.S., some resulting in multi-million-dollar lawsuits. Some people are even illegally renting out abandoned city buildings. It's quite the deal, I'm grateful nothing worse happened."

"He rented out your home while you were gone for work. That's awful," Rachel said.

"Yes, or weekend trips, he had my schedule from my dad's calendar, and obtained a copy of the keys and the security alarm code from dad's office. Owen and I practically built our relationship on pickup and drop-offs at the airport; it's a wonder Owen ever came back to pick me up," I said chuckling. "So, Garratt had plenty of opportunities."

"I remember hearing something about this," Rosie said. "Owen would sometimes call on the way back from dropping you off at the airport."

"Do you still travel as much?" Elaine asked.

"No, thank goodness. I was getting frustrated with all the traveling before this homeshare rental stuff came to a head. My dad sort of planted a seed and when Owen and I traveled home that day. I told him what I was thinking and about a week or so later, I quit my job. I still offer marketing for clients, only now I do it online. I can have video meetings instead of face-to-face meetings with the clients at their offices. But this way I can utilize web-based channels to spread the company's message about their brand, products, or services to its potential customers through email, social media, display advertising, and search engines."

"Nice," Rachel said. "Before I leave, I'd like some of your cards. I might know of something; if you're open to some more clients."

"Absolutely. That'd be great."

"Anyway, Owen's been worried that Garratt made additional posts on other sites, so he's convinced me to stay here; even though Owen changed the locks at my house.

"Oh, Karla. I wouldn't worry about it, Owen's just concerned for you," Rosie said.

"I know, I'm grateful for everything Owen's done, including this weekend. He decided on it, then went full steam ahead. I'm thinking there's enough fireworks in the garage to light up the sky for hours tomorrow night and I'm not sure, but the kids may get bored with that many sparklers."

"Oh, I don't know, I think a sparkler or two might be kinda nice," Rosie said, smirking.

"I know but there's tons and their giant—can your kids even handle that large of ones, Elaine?"

"Oh yea, they'll be fine. We'll help them," Elaine said. "Owen's just excited."

After we finished breakfast, Dad, Ty, Max, and I took a trip over to the Mountain Rescue Center. I know Dad and Ty were looking forward to it. Dad was looking at the pictures on the wall of the various training sessions we've done.

"Wow Owen, you guys do some incredible work here, I had no idea."

"Thanks, Dad. We do training scenarios at least once a week and then provide a platform for community education about outdoor safety, quite often. The rest of the time we keep the planes, helicopters and equipment in great shape and pray to God we don't have to use them."

"Hey, Kaster. What are you doing here today, I thought you took this weekend off?"

"Hey, Aaron. I did take the weekend off; I brought some of my family over. This is my dad, Joe."

"Dad, this is my boss, Aaron."

"Aaron, nice to meet you. I was just looking your pictures over; you guys do incredible work."

"Yes, we do. I have a great group of team members," Aaron said, smiling at me. "Well, you guys enjoy looking around; we'll see you next week, Owen. It was nice meeting you, Joe."

"See ya, Aaron. Come on, Dad, I'll show you the plane I fly."

That evening we sat around the fire pit out at the patio. Karla came over and sat next to me. "So, did you guys have a nice trip this afternoon?"

"We did, sometimes I think Dad's never seen a plane before. Every time he sees another one it brings a whole new joy to him. How was your day?"

"Oh, it was great. I enjoyed visiting with your mom, Elaine, and Rachel. I think Rachel's going to be a good fit for Ty, someone to corral him, and she's probably going to be one of my new clients."

"That's great, you do know where's she's located? What time's your family coming tomorrow?"

"I told them around five, but I'm sure they'll be early."

"OK, that'll be good. I think everyone is going their separate ways in the morning. Dad wants to take Ma up to our spot in the mountains."

"Oh, very nice, Joe. Rosie will love that for sure."

"There's a parade and train ride down in the village Max and Elaine are taking the kids to, and Ty and Rachel are going hiking. So, it's just you and me in the morning; you're stuck with me once again."

"I think I'll manage. You're not so bad to hang out with."

"Is there something you want to go do? Maybe a little birthday celebrating?"

"What are you two doing with your own sideshow going on over here?" Max came venturing in.

"We were just talking about tomorrow. Somebody over here's having a birthday tomorrow," I said, pointing a finger over Karla's head.

"Right, tomorrow," Max said. "Busy day, well happy early birthday, Karla."

"I was just asking Karla if she wanted to go do something in the morning."

"I don't know," Karla said. "I hadn't thought about it."

"Well, you think on it."

At little before five a.m. my alarm went off on the morning of the fourth; although I don't really think I needed an alarm. I was awake and ready to get up.

I quickly got dressed and crept over to Karla's room, lightly knocking on the door; I doubt with that light of a tap, she heard it. She's slept much better in the last few months. We hadn't had any all-night chat sessions. *Maybe a few late-night ones*, I thought, amusing myself at our time together. I walked over to the side of her bed; and leaned across and brushed her long, curly, brown hair out of her face.

"Hey sleepyhead, happy birthday. You need to get up now." She looked at me skeptically with only one eye opened.

"Why are you wanting me to get up?" Karla groaned back at me.

"I thought we were going to do something this morning," I said, kissing her again.

"I don't remember giving you an answer—and why are you so chipper, Owen, it's early."

"Yes, it's early. It's a little after five a.m."

"Then why do we have to be up this early?"

"You'll see, let's just get going, I'll go get us some coffee and meet you in the kitchen."

I found Ma and Dad sitting at the table drinking coffee when I got to the kitchen.

"Good morning, Owen. How ya doing?" Dad asked.

"Great, Dad. How are you guys? How's the coffee situation? I told Karla I'd get us some to take along."

"She doesn't have any idea, does she?" Mom asked.

"No, I think she's half-asleep."

"You take this coffee, and we'll make some more to bring along."

"No, no," I said shaking my head. "Just get some at the donut shop. They sell it by the boxful; it's all ordered." "All you have to do is pick it up; it's under my name."

"Really, in a box?" Dad asked, looking at me skeptically. "Never heard of coffee served in a box."

"Yea don't worry about it. You'll see, it's all good." Karla came in the kitchen, nicely dressed in denim capris, a t-shirt with stars on the front and carrying a jacket. Perfect for a morning like this. I grabbed us a blanket earlier and stuck it in the pickup, just in case.

"Good morning, Joe, Rosie. How are you guys? You're up early, are you coming with us?"

"Mornin', Karla," Dad said.

"Good morning, honey," Ma said half-hugging Karla. "No, we're not coming with you and Owen this morning. You'll have plenty of us later."

"Are you ready?" I asked Karla, handing her a cup of coffee.

"I guess, mystery man," Karla said, chuckling. "Nice seeing you two this morning," she told Ma and Dad as we went out the door.

"Where we goin', Owen?" Karla asked as we stepped out in the starry, cool, brisk morning air.

"Not too far. You didn't tell me last night if you wanted to do something this morning. So, I took matters into my own hands."

"Well, I didn't think I had to decide before five a.m."

I drove out of town and headed up the mountain, and before too long, Karla realized where we were headed.

"I thought your folks were coming up here?"

"They are, later. But I thought we'd come see the sunrise this morning."

"Well, that's great but you're a little early for a sunrise."

241

"I know," I said putting the pickup into park.

I grabbed the blanket out of the backseat and made a comfy spot on the tailgate of the pickup to overlook the water down below, the moon and stars reflecting off the water. "Come sit with me, Karla?"

"I'm coming, I just love it here."

"I know you do, that's why I brought you here," I said, putting my arm around her shoulder. "See, it's not so bad getting up this early."

"No, it's beautiful, the moonlight shining down reflecting on the water."

I stood beside Karla, reflecting, thanking God for bringing this amazing woman into my life.

"It's beautiful, isn't it Owen?"

"Yes, it is Karla; come sit with me up here.

"Karla, I've been wrestling with something for quite some time."

"What?"

"I've wanted to talk to you about this for months now, but the timing hasn't been right. So, I finally decided to just make it the right time. I talked to my dad last winter and your dad more recently. I've been planning for this moment ever since."

"Owen, are you saying what I think you're saying?"

"Karla, shh," I said, kissing her, and then I stepped down off the tailgate, leaning down on one bended knee.

"Owen?"

"Karla, you're my whole world, my everything. I want us to be us, forever, and do this life, our life and everything in between. Not just the crazy bumps in the roads, but the good things in life. A marriage, babies, whatever God brings our way. Karla, will you marry me?" I asked, pulling the ring out of the box, presenting it to Karla. I had bought this ring months ago, an oval-cut moissanite halo engagement ring with leaves on the band.

"Yes, Owen, with all my heart. I will marry you," Karla said, holding her hand out for me to slip the ring onto. Then she grabbed my face and kissed me. Between the kissing and excitement, which hey, I'm not complaining, I turned my head briefly, yelling at the top of my lungs, "She said yes! She said yes!"

As I was yelling, kissing, and holding Karla, both of our families came out of the trees, surrounding us with shining giant sparklers. It was truly an awesome sight, one I never dreamed would be this awesome.

"Owen, I can't believe I balked at getting up so early. This is beautiful, exciting, and wonderful. You're wonderful."

Ty came over and handed each of us a set of sparklers to join in the affair. "Here ya go, congrats by the way, and happy birthday, Karla," Ty said, winking at us as he backed into our family circle surrounding us, holding massive sparklers.

After everyone offered their congratulations, Dad told everyone there were more donuts and coffee in his pickup. Everyone migrated toward the food. Karla and I went back to the tailgate of my pickup, we sat down looking at each other, holding onto the moment. I thanked God again for blessings he's bestowed upon me.

"This is a great something to do this morning, Owen.," Karla said, breaking into my thoughts. "I'm glad I didn't tell you anything differently."

"I would have wormed it into this."

We moved over to the donut party for a short time, but everyone seemed to be packing up to leave. Karla and I said our thanks again and stole some donuts and more coffee. We told everyone we'd see them later back at the house for an evening celebration. Dad said he might need a nap before then. Karla and I returned to the back of my pickup to watch the sunrise with our coffee and donuts.

"So, was this all part of your plan this morning, too?" Karla asked, referring to the coffee and donuts.

"Heck yea, we can't get engaged without coffee. Half the time we've dated has been over a cup of coffee. I had Dad and Ma go pick them up; Dad still can't figure out the coffee in a box thing."

"How'd you pull all this off? It's pretty awesome, by the way."

"Well, you said a while ago you celebrate your birthday with fireworks, so I enlisted the help of our parents. I'm just surprised everyone was able to keep it under wraps.

"I started planning in May. I talked to your dad; went and bought the ring. My dad's been after me since like February to ask you."

"Hmm, smart man you have for a dad."

"I know, right. So, do you have any thoughts on a wedding?"

"Your dad's barn in September," Karla blurted out and then immediately slapped her hand across her mouth.

"I'm sure that could probably be worked out," I said, laughing, taking her hand off her mouth, kissing her softly. "I think that's a great idea."

"Come on, let's go ask your dad."

"Stay here, we don't have to ask him," I said, kissing the side of her cheek.

"There's something else, I want to talk to you about. Ty asked me for some help; he just brought it up yesterday. I haven't given it much thought; but I wanted you to know about it so we can discuss it together."

"What's that, Owen?"

"Well, you know Ty and I are partners in the Flight School?"

"Yea."

"Ty told me last night he wants me back; he needs more help. He knows his timing is terrible, considering I was planning to propose; but I figure he wanted to talk about it in person."

"Owen, I think we should definitely do this, no question. Unless you want to keep up your work with the Mountain Rescue Center. But as far as I'm concerned; I'm all for it."

"Well, I'm not sure about the Rescue Center, but what about your family?"

"Hmm, they'll be fine. I'll just make you fly me up to visit," I said, laughing.

"Are you sure about this, Karla? I think we should pray on it before we completely decide."

That evening everyone gathered around Owen's patio for food and fireworks in his backyard. It had been an exciting day, starting before dawn when Owen arranged to have everyone be there when he proposed to me at sunrise this morning. It was awesome and

244

beautiful to be surrounded by all those sparklers. I knew he had an awful lot of fireworks in the garage. I couldn't have imagined anything better. "All right girl, we want to see your ring," Eide and Molly said as I was putting the last of the table settings together.

"Oh honey, now that's a rock," Eide said. "Wedding details?"

"That's a joke, right, Eide? You made everyone wait a week before you told us your plans."

"I'm going to bring the brisket out, are you ready?" Owen asked when he walked by to get it.

"Yes, all good."

Owen brought the meat back and cut it up, then he told everyone to gather round, it was time to eat.

"Ah, well hold up there a minute, Owen," Lane said, holding Molly's hand. "Molly and I have something we'd like to talk about for a minute, if that's OK."

"Ah, come on, Lane, we're hungry," Levi said. "Hurry up and congratulate Owen and Karla so we can eat already."

"Well, yes, that's part of what I was going to say. Congratulations, Owen and Kar, and happy birthday Kar," Lane said, taking Molly's hand. "We're very happy for you both and were not exactly trying to preempt your day here, Owen. Which by the way you could have picked a different hour of the day." Lane said, laughing. "In any case, way to go with that proposal, Owe. There's another reason I'm up here yammering on." Lane was waving his hand almost like he was nervous about speaking to us.

"Molly and I have something to share with you all."

"Whoa, whoa, hold the phone," Eide said. "Did you guys elope?"

"Boy, Eids, them hormones are really kicking in now," Molly said, shaking head. "No, we didn't elope."

"What I was trying to say before I was so rudely interrupted, Eide, Molly and I are engaged; I asked her a couple months ago."

"You what, you've kept this under wraps for two months?" I asked Lane.

"Yea," Lane said. "We debated about telling you today but figured you guys would be making your own wedding plans and we didn't want to overlap."

"Unless you want to," Molly said. "Because that'd be OK."

"No, that's OK, we have our own plan," I told Molly.

245

"Wait a minute," Mom said. "Lane, you've always said you guys were eloping?"

"I know, Lane's always said they were going to elope; that's why I asked," Eide said.

"Yea," Lane said, smirking. "I lost that one, Molly wants a Christmas Eve wedding at the church."

"Oh my, that'll be beautiful," Mom said, holding her hand to her face in awe. "You may think you've lost, Lane, but that's going to be such a beautiful wedding, I can't wait." Molly smiled and shook her head in agreement.

"Ah, that will be nice, congratulations," I told Lane and Molly.

"Well, what about you two?" Mom said, looking at Owen and me after all the excitement of Lane and Molly's announcement calmed down.

"Before I had a chance to answer, Owen nonchalantly announced, "We're eloping," as he grabbed a couple chips from the bowl on the table and stuffed them in his mouth.

Later that night, showers of blues, reds, and silvers crackled in the sky as Ty lit off the fireworks Owen bought. Owen stood behind me with his arms wrapped around me, swaying back and forth to the music playing.

"Owen, we're gonna have to tell them were not eloping, especially my mom."

"Yea, I know," Owen said, laughing. "That was funny. I wanted to see the look on your mom's face when she heard we were eloping."

"I know, I thought she was going to crack."

"Actually, I already told her when we were sitting down to eat. I told her there's a barn wedding on the horizon for the future Mrs. Karla Kaster and I think she kinda liked the idea. I got a little smile and saw a glisten to her eyes."

We continued standing there watching the fireworks emit in the warm night sky. I thought what a wonderful day it'd been, one of the best birthdays I've had, surrounded by our families and now I had Owen's arms wrapped around me. Just as he's always been since Eide embarrassingly threw him into my life. "That has a nice ring to it, don't you think? The future Mrs. Karla Kaster. I love you!" Owen said, whispering in my ear.

246

Made in the USA
Middletown, DE
22 May 2022

66053460R00149